Walker smiled that gorgeous grin and Maddie's knees felt weak

They weakened more as his eyes traveled over her.

"Do you know how good you look?"

"I just put on warm clothes."

"They're certainly warming me up."

She thumbed toward the fireplace. "It's the fire."

"Not unless it has blue, blue eyes, a curvy body and blond hair."

They stared at each other for a long moment. Almost in slow motion his hand circled her neck and pulled her forward. His lips touched hers tentatively at first and then the warmth of the room, the warmth of each other engulfed them.

Dear Reader,

When I was asked to write what Harlequin novels mean to me, I was happy to do so. Back in the sixties I was diagnosed with rheumatoid arthritis and had a hard time dealing with the drastic changes in my life. A friend gave me a box of Harlequin books. I was hooked. Whatever I was going through, I could open a Harlequin novel and lose myself in happy ever after. It didn't take away the pain, but the books made me feel better, made me believe in love and happiness.

After reading so many books, my family encouraged me to write one. I thought they were crazy. But the more I thought about it the more I liked the idea of giving someone else that special gift of feeling better just by reading the written word. It was a dream. No way could it come true for a country girl from Smetana, Texas. But with hard work and perseverance my dream became a reality. I'm working on my twenty-fifth book, and it is the greatest feeling in the world. Thank you, Harlequin, and happy 60th anniversary from all of us who dare to dream.

With love and thanks,

Linda Warren

P.S. It makes my day to hear from readers. You can e-mail me at Lw1508@aol.com or write me at P.O. Box 5182, Bryan, TX 77805 or visit my Web site at www.lindawarren.net or www.myspace.com/authorlindawarren. Your letters will be answered.

Madison's Children
Linda Warren

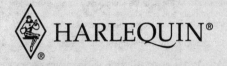

TORONTO • NEW YORK • LONDON
AMSTERDAM • PARIS • SYDNEY • HAMBURG
STOCKHOLM • ATHENS • TOKYO • MILAN • MADRID
PRAGUE • WARSAW • BUDAPEST • AUCKLAND

Recycling programs
for this product may
not exist in your area.

ISBN-13: 978-0-373-78337-3

MADISON'S CHILDREN

Copyright © 2009 by Linda Warren.

All rights reserved. Except for use in any review, the reproduction or
utilization of this work in whole or in part in any form by any electronic,
mechanical or other means, now known or hereafter invented, including
xerography, photocopying and recording, or in any information storage
or retrieval system, is forbidden without the written permission of the
publisher, Harlequin Enterprises Limited, 225 Duncan Mill Road,
Don Mills, Ontario, Canada M3B 3K9.

This is a work of fiction. Names, characters, places and incidents are
either the product of the author's imagination or are used fictitiously,
and any resemblance to actual persons, living or dead, business
establishments, events or locales is entirely coincidental.

This edition published by arrangement with Harlequin Books S.A.

® and TM are trademarks of the publisher. Trademarks indicated with
® are registered in the United States Patent and Trademark Office, the
Canadian Trade Marks Office and in other countries.

www.eHarlequin.com

Printed in U.S.A.

ABOUT THE AUTHOR

Award-winning, bestselling author Linda Warren has written twenty-four books for Harlequin Superromance and Harlequin American Romance. She grew up in the farming and ranching community of Smetana, Texas, the only girl in a family of boys. She loves to write about Texas, and from time to time scenes and characters from her childhood show up in her books. Linda lives in College Station, Texas, not far from her birthplace, with her husband, Billy, and a menagerie of wild animals, from Canada geese to bobcats. Visit her Web site at www.lindawarren.net.

Books by Linda Warren

HARLEQUIN SUPERROMANCE

1167—A BABY BY CHRISTMAS
1221— THE RIGHT WOMAN
1250—FORGOTTEN SON
1314—ALL ROADS LEAD
    TO TEXAS
1354—SON OF TEXAS
1375—THE BAD SON
1440—ADOPTED SON
1470—TEXAS BLUFF
1499—ALWAYS A MOTHER
1574—CAITLYN'S PRIZE *

HARLEQUIN AMERICAN ROMANCE

1042—THE CHRISTMAS CRADLE
1089—CHRISTMAS, TEXAS STYLE
    "Merry Texmas"
1102—THE COWBOY'S RETURN
1151—ONCE A COWBOY
1226—TEXAS HEIR
1249—THE SHERIFF OF
    HORSESHOE, TEXAS

*The Belles of Texas

A special thanks to Kim Lenz for going above and beyond in sharing her hometown of Milano, Texas.

And Melinda Siegert for explaining a nervous stomach.

And Susan Robertson for bringing me up to speed on all things little boys. And to Luke for answering pesky questions.

And Lara Chapman for kindly offering information on Giddings, Texas.

And Naomi Giroux, RN, for graciously sharing her knowledge of ovarian cancer.

Also, The American Cancer Society for their invaluable information.

All errors are strictly mine.

DEDICATION

I dedicate this book to the wonderful editors at Harlequin Books who have influenced my work and my life. With the sale of my first book in 1999, I had the good fortune to work with Paula Eykelhof, Executive Editor, who guided me through the new-author nervous jitters with patience, kindness and skill. She is, to me, the very best example of an editor.

And Kathleen Scheibling, Senior Editor, Harlequin American Romance. My good luck held when Kathleen was appointed my editor. She follows in Paula's footsteps with her talent, insight and understanding. She's an exceptional editor, and makes my writing life a joy.

Also, Wanda Ottewell, Senior Editor, Harlequin Superromance. I was nervous when I first met Wanda, but her warmth and friendliness put me at ease. A true Harlequin editor.

Thank you, ladies, and happy anniversary!

CHAPTER ONE

SOMETHING ABOUT BEING the good sister made Madison Belle want to be bad.

Very bad.

She laughed at the thought, the sound snatched away by the late November breeze. Hunching low, she kneed her horse, Sadie, on, faster and faster as they flew over hills and valleys, slicing effortlessly through the wind. They cantered into the barn, the chill nipping at her bare nape above her Carhartt jacket. But it felt great. She was alive and enjoying every minute.

As she jerked Sadie's reins to stop, the horse reared her head, prancing, wanting to keep running. Maddie patted her neck. "Whoa, gal, we're home."

Maddie's heart pounded from the exhilarating ride, and she took a moment to catch her breath. The barn was quiet, and the scent of alfalfa, leather and dust tickled her nose. Swinging her right leg over the back of Sadie, she dismounted. Her knees almost buckled and she had to grab the saddle. Darn!

Her sister Cait didn't tell her that staying in the saddle most of the day made your butt numb and exhausted your muscles. She wasn't that much of a city girl, was she?

Begrudgingly, she admitted she was. She'd been raised in Philadelphia by her mother. Summers and holidays she'd spent with her father, Dane Belle, on the High Five ranch in Texas. Dane had three daughters, all by separate wives.

Caitlyn, the oldest, had always lived on the ranch because her mother had passed away when Cait was born. Skylar, the youngest, was raised by her mother in Kentucky. Every year the sisters looked forward to their summers together.

Madison was the predictable middle child. Her sisters knew what she was going to do before she did it. Easy, compassionate Maddie—the consummate Goody Two-shoes. Even if she wanted to be different, Maddie knew she'd never change.

She undid the saddle cinch, took hold of the saddle and threw it over a sawhorse. The muscles tightened in her arms and she smiled. Oh, yeah. She was getting stronger. When Caitlyn had called her sisters home to face a financial crisis, Maddie had been skin and bones. Now she was healthy again, or she prayed she was.

After the crisis had been settled, she'd planned to return to Philadelphia. But she'd found peace here at High Five and her grandmother needed her.

Caitlyn had married the man of her dreams and moved to the neighboring Southern Cross ranch. They needed someone to run High Five. Maddie didn't know a lot about ranching, but she was happy to stay and take over the reins.

Removing her worn felt hat, she placed it on the saddle horn and tucked stray blond hairs behind her ears. After the chemo, she'd lost all her hair. It was growing back now even thicker than before. It was long enough to pull back into a ponytail, although her hair had a way of working loose by the end of the day.

Three years and she was cancer-free, but to save her life the surgeon had taken everything that mattered to her—the ability to have a child.

The ache around her heart pulsed for a moment. She allowed herself to feel the pain, and then she let it go. It was an exercise she'd practiced many times.

Rubbing her horse's face, she said, "Ready for some feed, ol' gal?" The horse nuzzled her with a neigh, and Maddie relaxed in the comfort of something warm and real.

Cooper, the foreman, said the horse wasn't worth much, but with her speckled gray coat, black mane and tail, Sadie looked beautiful to Maddie. Soon she learned that with a little coaxing Sadie could fly like the wind. Finding the good in Sadie was something she never let Cooper forget. She firmly believed there was good in everyone—no matter how flawed.

She led Sadie into the corral and removed her bridle. Cooper had put out sweet feed earlier. Sadie trotted to the trough, knowing exactly where it was.

With a sigh, Maddie turned back to the barn, looking forward to soaking in a hot bath. Her muscles screamed for it. So did her aching feet. Her arches were still getting used to living in cowboy boots.

As she secured the bridle on a hook, she heard a noise. It sounded like a sneeze. Looking around, she didn't see anyone. The open-concept barn had a dirt floor; horse stalls were on the left with stacks of hay on the end, saddles and tack on the right with a supply room. A hay loft with more bales was above—a place where she and her sisters had played many times. The big double doors opened on one end to the corral and the other to the ranch.

It must be the old tomcat that lived in the loft, making the barn his home. Then she spotted the feet barely visible under a horse stall door—two sets of sneakers, one trimmed in pink. They certainly didn't belong to ol' Tom.

What…?

Mystified, she walked over and opened the door. There stood two wide-eyed young girls. One was blonde and about ten, and she had a small boy at least three or four cradled on her hip. His face was buried in her neck. The other girl had dark hair and was older, maybe fifteen or sixteen, and she was very pregnant. They all wore jeans and heavy Windbreakers. Maddie was at a loss for words for a full thirty seconds. This certainly wasn't predictable.

She cleared her throat. "What are you doing hiding in the stall?"

"We're not hiding," the younger girl replied in a defensive tone, "we're waiting for someone."

"Who?"

"Brian Harper," the older girl said.

Maddie frowned. "There's no one here by that name."

"He works for Ms. Belle."

"You mean Caitlyn?"

The girl nodded.

"Caitlyn doesn't live here anymore. She married Judd Calhoun and lives on the Southern Cross."

The girl's face fell. "She still owns this ranch, doesn't she?"

"Yes. She's part-owner with our sister, Skylar, and me."

The girl made a sucking lemon type face. "Who are you?"

Maddie didn't feel she had to keep answering questions, but the worry in the girl's eyes swayed her. "I'm Madison Belle." Her glance swept over the trio. "What are your names?"

"I'm Ginny," the girl responded readily. "And this is Haley and Georgie."

The boy raised his head. "I'm Georgie."

"Shh, Georgie." Haley cradled the boy closer against her. Even with the winter clothes, Maddie could see the girl was very thin, and she didn't seem to have the strength to keep holding the boy.

"I wanna go home," Georgie wailed.

"Shh." Haley stroked his back.

Maddie watched this with a sense of trepidation. Something was very wrong, and she decided to get to the bottom of what the kids were doing here. They surely had parents, and those parents had to be worried.

"Why do you want to see Brian Harper?"

Ginny rested her hands over her swollen stomach in a protective gesture. "He said if I ever needed anything, he'd help me."

"And we need money to buy bus tickets to Lubbock," Haley added. "My mom lives there and we have to see her."

"Mama," Georgie mumbled.

Maddie listened carefully, but none of it made any sense to her. "So basically you're running away. I assume you have family in High Cotton."

"That's none of your business," Haley spat in a defensive tone.

Maddie lifted an eyebrow. "You made it my business by hiding in my barn."

Before the kids could form a reply, the pounding of hooves caught their attention. Cooper Yates and Rufus Johns rode in and dismounted. The cow dogs, Boots, Booger and Bo, followed. Rufus began to unsaddle and feed the horses, seeming oblivious to the kids. But that was Rufus. He spoke very little and minded his own business.

They were the only two cowboys on the ranch and both were ex-cons. Caitlyn trusted them with her life and Maddie now knew why. They were as honest and reliable as the day was long.

Rufus was in his seventies and had worked on High Five all his life. His wife, Etta, was the cook and housekeeper. In his younger days, he'd gotten into a fight in a bar, trying to protect a woman from her abusive boyfriend. Rufus was a big man and one blow from his fist sent the man flying into a table. He hit his head and died instantly. Rufus spent three years in a Huntsville prison for involuntary manslaughter. He came home to Etta and High Five and never again strayed from the straight and narrow.

"Stay here," Maddie said to the kids, and walked over to Cooper. He removed his hat and slapped it against his leg to remove the dust.

Cooper was a cowboy to the core. There wasn't anything he didn't know about ranching, cattle and horses. His passion was horses, and he had worked at several thoroughbred horse farms. The one in Weatherford, Texas, had been his downfall.

Several expensive horses had died from the feed being mixed incorrectly with pesticides to kill weevils. The owner pointed the finger at Cooper. In anger, Coop had gotten into a fight with the man, who'd filed charges. Coop had been convicted for assault and killing the horses.

He spent six months in prison before the truth came to light. The owner had mixed the feed incorrectly to collect the insurance money. Cooper was released, but people now looked at him differently. He was an ex-con and people didn't trust him, but Caitlyn and Dane Belle had. At Cait's urging, their father had given Coop a job when no one else would.

Maddie nodded at Cooper's bay gelding. "I told you Sadie could beat that bag of bones." She and Coop had become good friends, and each day after work they'd race back to the barn. Coop usually won, but today she'd outsmarted him. She'd gotten a head start.

He slid his hat onto his head in an easy movement. "You cheated, and that old gray mare can't outrun Boots." The dog lay at his feet. At the mention of his name, his ears lifted.

"I beg to differ since I was here first and that old gray mare is in the corral eating sweet feed."

Coop grinned, and he didn't do that often. His past weighed heavily on him and he was a bit of a loner. Over six feet tall, Coop had sandy-blond hair and green eyes. The townspeople said he was bad to the bone, but Maddie knew he had a heart of gold.

Coop eyed their visitors. "What's going on?"

"They're looking for Brian Harper. Do you remember him?"

"Yep. Dane hired him back in the spring, but he left to work in the oil fields."

"Do you know where?"

"No. Cait might." Coop glanced at Ginny. "God, she's pregnant. How old is she?"

"I don't know, but I'm guessing Brian Harper is the father."

"That kid had a head full of dreams of making big money. If she wants him to take responsibility, I can tell you that's not gonna happen."

"He's not the responsible type?"

"Nope. Far from it. He's out for himself and that's it."

Maddie hated to hear that. The girl was too young to have a baby. Something inside Maddie twisted at life and its cruelties.

"You might try calling Walker," Coop said.

"Why?"

"Those are his kids."

"What?" That shocked her. Walker was the constable and the only law in High Cotton, Texas. She'd met him at a party at Southern Cross. He'd made an offhand comment about her looking as young as his daughter. What he'd really meant was that she looked like a child. No woman wants to hear those words from a handsome man. It still rankled.

"Are all of them his kids?"

"No. Just the two small ones."

She thought about that for a second and what Haley had said about her mother. "Where is Walker's wife?"

Coop shrugged. "All I know are rumors."

"Tell me, anyway. I have to figure out what to do with these children."

"They say she left him for another man."

"What about the kids?"

"She left them, too."

What kind of woman would do that? A child was a gift—the most special gift. Anger simmered inside her. How could a woman disrespect that gift and walk away from the love and care her babies needed?

Coop pointed to her face. "You're getting those little lines around your eyes when you're angry."

"I do not get little lines." She stuck her nose in the air and desperately wanted to look in a mirror.

"If you say so." He glanced at the kids huddled together. "Good luck." He ambled out of the barn, leading his horse, the dogs trotting behind him.

She faced the kids, trying to think of a solution. "Let's go to the house for milk and cookies and I'll call Caitlyn."

"We don't want your cookies," Haley said, and Maddie realized the girl was angry, probably from everything that was happening in her young life. And she had to wonder if the mother even knew that Haley was planning a surprise visit.

"I want a cookie." Georgie raised his head.

"Then you shall have a cookie." Maddie held out her arms. "Want to come with me?"

"No, he…"

Haley's words trailed off as Georgie went to Maddie. His weight in her arms caused her throat to close up. He was adorable with caramel-colored eyes and brown hair. She melted from the contact. Turning, she headed for the house. The girls had no choice but to follow.

THEY WALKED INTO A WARM, big kitchen, and Etta swung from the stove, a spoon in her hand. A spry, thin woman, she was in direct contrast to her big husband. Her eyes opened wide when she saw the children.

She zeroed in on Ginny. "Lordy, Lordy, Ginny Grubbs, you're pregnant."

"Yes, ma'am." Ginny removed her Windbreaker and slid into a chair at the table, as if to hide her stomach.

Etta had a lot more to say, but Gran entered the room. Dorthea Belle was a delicate, ethereal creature who seemed to float instead of walk. Her hair was completely white and curled into a bun at her nape. She gave the appearance of being fragile, but Maddie knew her grandmother's inner strength.

Maddie kissed her cheek. "Hi, Gran. We have company."

"I see." Gran's eyes swept over the boy in her arms. And Maddie knew she was thinking what Maddie had pushed to the back of her mind. She would never have a child of her own.

To block those thoughts, she removed Georgie's jacket and placed him in a chair. "Etta, we need milk and cookies, please."

"Coming right up."

"I have to call Cait. I'll be right back." She leaned over and whispered to Gran, "Watch them, please."

Gran winked and Maddie hurried to her office. Judd answered on the second ring.

"Hi, Judd. Is Cait there?"

"She's right here." There were muffled voices and whispers. Then silence. Maddie waited. What were they doing? Now, that was a real stupid question.

Finally, her newly married sister came on the line, sounding out of breath. "Hey, Maddie. What's up?"

"Do you two ever stop?"

"No." Cait giggled. Her sister was happy. Maddie wondered if she would ever be that happy.

"Enjoy, sister dear."

"Oh, I am." There was another muffled silence. Then Cait asked, "Is this important?"

"I found three kids in the barn. Cooper says two of them are Walker's kids. The other is Ginny Grubbs and she's pregnant. She's looking for Brian Harper. Do you know where he is?"

"Good heavens, I haven't seen him since the spring. I have no idea where he is." She now had Cait's full attention. "How did they get there?"

"I don't know."

"Call Walker immediately. He must be worried out of his mind about his kids."

"Do you have his number?" While she waited, she tapped her fingers against the desk, thinking. After making the remark at the party, Walker had asked her to dance. She'd refused. Skylar had danced with him instead, saying something silly, like they only let Maddie out of the attic on special occasions. The tapping grew louder. Her childish behavior was now a little embarrassing. The man probably thought she was insane, just as Sky had insinuated. She'd never acted like that before in her life.

Cait rattled off the number and Maddie quickly jotted it down. "Have a fun evening," she said before hanging up. She paused over the phone for a moment and then punched out the number.

"WHAT DO YOU MEAN YOU DON'T know where they are?" Walker stared at his aunt in disbelief. She wasn't the most reliable babysitter, but she was all he had. He and his aunt had inherited the general store in High Cotton, and they lived next door to each other in homes their ancestors had built.

His aunt had never married and was set in her ways. She wasn't fond of children, either. He was going to have to make other arrangements because this was unacceptable.

"Did Haley get off the bus?"

"Of course." Nell Walker rang up a sale and handed Dewey Ray his change. "She took Georgie to the back room to do her homework. When I went to check on them, they were gone. That's why I called you. They're your responsibility—not mine."

The bell jingled over the door and Frank Jessup came into the store. "Hey, Walker."

Walker nodded. He was too worried to say much of anything else.

"Did that part come in I ordered, Nell?"

"It sure did," his aunt replied. "I'll get it."

"See you later, Frank." Walker charged outside before he lost his temper. God, he was doing a lousy job of caring for his kids. Haley hated High Cotton and skipped school regularly. She didn't fit in with the other kids. Instead she hung out with the Grubbs girl, who was so much older. That was unacceptable, too.

Talking to his daughter was a waste of his breath, though. She had so much anger in her that at times he thought she was going to explode from the sheer magnitude of it. And his son cried constantly for his mother. If he ever saw his ex-wife again he might just strangle the life out of her. Leaving him was one thing, but leaving her kids was something entirely different.

He drew a long, tired breath. High Cotton was small, with barely five hundred people. Someone had to have seen them. First, he'd check with Earl Grubbs to see if they were there. Since the kids made fun of Ginny and her pregnancy, Haley had somehow become her champion. Two outcasts facing the world.

As he reached for his cell, it rang. "Yes," he answered.

"Is this Walker?" a very feminine voice asked. A voice he recognized. *Madison Belle.* His nerves tightened.

"Yes, what is it, Ms. Belle?"

There was complete silence.

"Ms. Belle?"

"I just wanted to let you know that your children are here at High Five."

"What!"

"Haley, Georgie and a girl named Ginny."

"How did they get there?"

"I'm guessing they walked. You really need to keep a closer eye on your children."

He gripped the phone so tight it almost came apart in his hand. "I'll be right there. Do not let them leave."

Running for his car, he cursed under his breath. Madison Belle had taken an instant dislike to him, and now he had to face the woman and see his failings as a father in her blue eyes.

He'd rather take a bullet.

CHAPTER TWO

MADDIE HUNG UP THE PHONE and made her way to the kitchen. On the way she thought about Walker. He was an enigma for sure. She didn't even know his first name and she'd never heard anyone mention it, either. He was just Walker to everyone.

She'd met him four times; at the party, at High Five, at the convenience store, and at Cait and Judd's wedding. Funny how she remembered every encounter. He always said hello, but little else, and she couldn't blame him. *Avoid crazy lady,* she could almost hear him thinking.

He seemed very stern, very disciplined—a by-the-book type of man. Cait had said he'd been in the marines and later had joined a search-and-rescue team in Houston. He'd only returned to High Cotton because of his children. Cait hadn't said anything about the mother, but she must be a fine piece of work.

Her sister Skylar thought Walker was a hunk. Maddie rolled that around in her head for a moment. He was tall and impressive, with broad shoulders, caramel-colored eyes like Georgie's, brown hair that curled into his collar, lean, sculptured features, and a body that rivaled Arnold Schwarzenegger's.

Her taste ran more to indoor guys in tailored suits and J. Crew shirts, who didn't wear cowboy boots, Stetsons or risk their lives in the line of duty.

That described Victor, the man she'd been dating in Philadelphia. Tall and thin, Victor never got his hands dirty. As a doctor, he was very meticulous and fastidious in everything he did, even away from the hospital. He was fifteen years older than Madison and at times he made her feel like one of his children, which irritated her. But he was a compassionate, caring man and that's what had attracted her.

Wasn't it?

Victor wasn't a muscled, gun-toting-hero type like Walker. The constable was all muscle and raw power.

He was too…too manly.

She almost laughed out loud at the description. Could a man be too manly?

As she entered the kitchen, Gran was telling the kids about Solomon, their pet bull. Maddie and Cait had raised him from a baby when his mother had died. Solomon was now quite large, and it wasn't uncommon for him to be at the back door waiting for her in the mornings. He wanted feed and he didn't like waiting.

She never knew how he got over the board fence until she saw him jump it one morning. Solomon's father had had the same bad trait, and it had led to his demise. Maddie wanted to break Solomon of the habit. So far she hadn't had any luck.

"Can I see him?" Georgie asked. His upper lip sported a milk mustache and his cheeks were smeared with chocolate from the chocolate chip cookies. He was so cute. How could his mother leave him?

"No, Georgie," Haley told him. "We're going to find Mama."

"Oh." Georgie stuffed more of the cookie into his mouth.

Ginny saw her standing in the doorway. "Did you get Ms. Belle?"

"Yes," she replied, walking farther into the room. "She hasn't seen Brian since he left High Five for the oil fields and she doesn't have an idea where he might be."

"Oh." Ginny hung her head and Maddie's heart broke for her. It was time for a heart-to-heart and she didn't want Georgie to hear them.

"Gran, would you take Georgie to the veranda? Solomon might make an appearance."

"Oh, boy." Georgie bounced up and down in his chair.

Gran took his hand, which was covered in chocolate, and quickly reached for a napkin to wipe his hands and mouth.

After that, Georgie wiggled one arm into his jacket, but seemed unable to get the other one inside the sleeve. Maddie came to his rescue and zipped the Windbreaker.

"Come on, little one," Gran said, leading him to the door. The screen banged behind them.

Maddie took his seat. "Ginny, I'm not trying to pry, but is Brian the father of your baby?"

"Yes, ma'am." She still hung her head.

"And you think he'll take responsibility for the child?"

"Oh, no, ma'am." Ginny raised her head, her voice sincere. "It's not like that. I mean, Brian dropped me after...well, you know. I just want the money to get us to Lubbock and Haley's mom. I'm planning to keep my baby."

The dream of a young girl who hadn't a clue about life. Maddie wondered how she'd manage.

She looked at Haley, who was playing with her glass. "Haley, does your mother know you're planning a visit?"

Her caramel eyes turned dark. "That's none of your business."

"Watch your mouth," Etta said before Maddie could form a response.

Maddie shot Etta a silencing glance and said, "She doesn't, does she."

Haley clamped her lips together and no response was offered. Maddie had her answer.

She stood. "Haley, you're a minor, and I had no choice but to call your father."

"You bitch." The words were fired at her with such venom that it took her aback for a second.

Etta tapped Haley's head with her wooden spoon.

"Any more words like that, young lady, and I'll wash your mouth out with soap."

Haley rubbed her head and glared at Etta.

Maddie took a breath and sent another silent message to Etta to cool it. She'd felt the sting of that spoon many times as a kid and knew that Etta meant well, but Haley wasn't in their family and not theirs to discipline.

She focused on the fury in Haley's eyes. "I'm doing what's best for both of you."

"Dad will take Ginny home and her dad hits her all the time. He'll make her lose the baby and the baby is all she has." Haley's words were delivered with all the fervor of a brokenhearted little girl.

Ginny touched her arm. "It's okay, Haley. We don't have any money so we have to go home."

"It's not fair." Haley crossed her arms over her chest.

"Your father will do what's best for you," Maddie tried to reassure her.

"He doesn't even want Georgie or me, and he bums us off on Aunt Nell all the time."

"Haley…"

"You don't know my father. You have money, so just give us some so we can go to Lubbock."

All kinds of questions tumbled like broken glass through her mind. Was Walker taking the pain of a failed marriage out on his children? Haley seemed to hate him. What had Walker done to warrant that? Did he not want custody of his kids? Maddie now had misgivings about calling him, but if anything was amiss, Cait would have said so.

"I want to help you. I really do, but—"

There was a knock at the front door.

"Please don't make us go home," Haley begged, tears glistening in her eyes.

Maddie's heart dropped like a rock, and she felt like the bad guy. But she had no choice. "Stay here while I talk to your father." As she hurried to answer the door, she wondered how she'd gotten caught in the middle of this. Her predictable world just got blown to hell.

Before she could fully open the door, Walker said, "Where are my kids?"

His attitude got to her. He made to pass her, but she held out her arm. "Just a minute. I want to talk to you."

"Ms. Belle, I don't have time for—"

She stepped out on the veranda and closed the door behind her. Shivering, she wished she'd grabbed her jacket. "Make time."

He frowned at her, and she could see the resemblance to Haley. She sat in one of the old rockers on the porch and looked up at him, then wished she hadn't. All that male testosterone was just a little too close. Her breath caught in her throat.

For the first time, she took a really good look at this strong, rigid man. What she saw was a frightened father. Tiny worry lines crinkled around his eyes. His mouth was slashed into a stubborn line. His well-built body seemed restless. He was dressed only in jeans and a shirt—he had no jacket even though the temperature was in the forties. He must be thick-skinned, too.

His eyes told a different story, though. What he could hide with toughness and bravado, his eyes couldn't. He was hurting, but she knew he would never admit it.

He was the type of man who never showed weakness. That was clear from his strong stance. She also knew he was at a loss at how to handle his own children, but he would never harm them. She understood all of that from the desperate look in his eyes.

She wrapped her arms around her waist. "Do you know what your daughter has planned?"

"No." He pushed back his Stetson. "My daughter has an aversion to talking to me."

"Why is that?" She stared directly at him, and the heat from his stare washed over her. Suddenly she wasn't cold any longer. Her body felt hot, sticky, and the rocker creaked as she moved uncomfortably.

"Ms. Belle, I appreciate you taking care of my kids, but this is really none of your business." The words were calm and direct, not angry like she'd expected.

Even though he was intimidating, she didn't fold like a used wallet ready to be tucked away out of sight. She lifted her chin. "Your daughter made it my business by hiding in my barn."

"What?" He was genuinely puzzled. "Why would they do that?"

"They were looking for Brian Harper. Evidently he told Ginny he would give her money if she needed it."

"Why would they need money?" he asked slowly.

She had to tell him the truth, and she didn't pause in doing so. "For bus tickets to Lubbock to find Haley's mom."

"Shit." He swung away, his body taut as he gazed at the barn and corrals. "Haley doesn't know where her mother is."

"Why does she think Lubbock?"

He swung back to her, his jaw clenched. "Trisha's sister lives there, so I assume Haley thinks her mother is there, too."

"And she's not?"

"Where are my kids?" The questions were clearly over, but Maddie wasn't finished.

She stood and took a step backward. Standing close to his male heat made her breathless, but she had a point to get across and she was determined to do it. "Before I came to live at High Five, I was a counselor in a hospital. I dealt with a lot of children. Usually when a child runs away and doesn't want to go home, there's some sort of abuse in the home." She paused to gather her courage. "Haley doesn't want to go home, so naturally I heard warning bells. But talking to you I know that isn't the problem."

He tensed. "Very big of you."

She ignored the sarcasm. "Ginny doesn't want to go

home, either, and in her case I'm inclined to believe she's being abused."

"Her father's a drunk and gets his kicks by beating his wife and kids."

"Can't you do something?"

Walker was all out of patience, and Madison Belle was treading on his very last nerve. But there was something in her blue eyes that stopped him from giving her a full dose of his anger. *She cared.* She had to have been born under the sign of the Good Ship Lollipop, fairy tales and happily ever after. *Good* was probably her middle name, and she believed in it to the hilt. He avoided women like her because they usually had their head in the clouds with reality nowhere in sight.

He'd seen the worst in people, and when push came to shove, the worst always won over the good. But Goody Two-shoes Madison would never believe that.

He dragged his thoughts back to her. From the first moment he'd seen her, at a party at Southern Cross, he'd thought she was the most beautiful woman he'd ever laid eyes on. At the time, he'd said some off-the-wall remark that had irritated her. As he'd looked into her shining eyes that day, his good sense had taken a hike. That was a first for him.

Her sisters, Caitlyn and Skylar, were beautiful, too, but he had no trouble talking to them. Something about Madison tied him up in knots. He didn't like the feeling. He was in control—always. Over the years he had mastered it, but somehow she had broken through all his defenses with just one look. He didn't like that, either. So he avoided Madison Belle.

Now she was in his face, demanding answers and wanting the good to shine through in this situation. He'd dealt with Earl Grubbs before, and the man didn't have an up-close-and-personal relationship with good. How did he explain that to her, though?

"I'll do what I can" was all he could say. But he was going to make sure Earl got the message this time.

"That's it?" She arched an eyebrow that spoke volumes.

Against his will, his eyes swept over her. Her soft curves were emphasized in the tight jeans and western shirt. Her blond hair had come loose from its ponytail and hung enchantingly around an angel face perfect in every way—smooth, gorgeous skin, pouty lips with a sexy curve and an expression of wholesomeness minimized by pure, come-hither blue eyes. Exactly what every man would want in his Christmas stocking.

He put brakes on his thoughts and took a long breath. "Ms. Belle, I appreciate your concern, but now I'm taking my kids home." He opened the door and went inside with her on his heels like a pit bull.

Hearing voices, he headed in that direction. Haley and Ginny sat at the table eating cookies. Etta Johns was watching them.

Haley looked up and saw him. "Daddy," she said in a guilty voice.

"Let's go. Where's Georgie?" He tried to keep his

voice calm, but it came out as stern, probably a side effect caused by Ms. Belle.

Haley rose to her feet, her movements nervous. Her eyes were like his, but her hair was blond like her mother's. Her jeans and knit top hung on her thin body. His daughter had a nervous stomach, and he didn't know how to make her eat without getting sick. The divorce had hit Haley hard, and he wanted to make her world happy again. Maybe with a little of Madison Belle's good.

He didn't know how to accomplish that, since his daughter seemed to hate him and blame him for Trisha leaving. His gut twisted a little more each time he looked into her anguished face.

"He's outside with Miss Dorie."

"I'll get him," Madison said. In a minute she was back with Georgie in her arms, Miss Dorie behind her.

Madison was talking softly to him and Georgie was smiling. Walker was mesmerized by the picture of Madison's face close to Georgie's. She seemed so natural with a child in her arms.

"Daddy," Georgie shouted when he spotted him. He wiggled free from Madison and ran to him. Lifting his son into his arms, he held him tight. His daughter might hate him, but Georgie didn't. He was grateful for that small miracle.

"Daddy, I saw a bull," Georgie said, his eyes bright. "A big bull." He stretched out his arms as far as they would go.

"You did?"

Georgie nodded. "I 'cared of him."

"He won't hurt you," Madison assured him.

"Is he talking about Solomon?" he asked Madison.

"Yes." She smiled, and his heart kicked against his ribs with the force of a wild bronco. "He's getting so big."

Walker had been there the day Caitlyn had brought Solomon home. Back then, Cait and Judd were at odds. High Five and the Southern Cross ranches were adjoined, and Cait's bull was always jumping the fence to get to Judd's registered cows. Eventually, one of Judd's cows gave birth and died shortly after. When Cait saw the calf, she realized it was from her bull and took it home. Walker felt sure there would be a fight over the calf, but Judd had allowed Cait to keep it. That's when he knew Judd had finally forgiven Caitlyn.

The last time he saw the calf, Madison was cooing at it as if it were a child. Somehow he knew she'd make a pet of him.

He forced his eyes away from the light in hers. "Let's go," he said, and glanced at Ginny. "I'll take you home, too. I want to talk to your father."

"You can't take her there." Haley scrunched up her face in anger. "He hits her."

"I'll take care of it."

"No, you won't. You just want to get rid of us." Everything in him screamed at his daughter's attitude, but he was powerless to change it. God knows he'd tried.

"Don't talk back," he said, "and thank Ms. Belle for any inconvenience."

"Thank you," Haley mumbled, grabbing her jacket and running toward the front door.

He slowly followed with Georgie and Ginny. Outside they came to an abrupt stop. A young black Brahma bull stood on the stone sidewalk. Haley seemed frozen.

Madison ran around them and grabbed the bull's halter. "Solomon." She stroked his face. "You're scaring our guests." The bull rubbed his face against her and a deep guttural sound left his throat.

The thought crossed Walker's mind that if she stroked him like that, he might make that sound, too.

"It's okay," she called. "He won't hurt you."

Haley and Ginny made a wide circle around him. Walker stepped close to Madison. "You know, a bull is not a pet. He's male—all day, every day, and potentially dangerous."

Her eyes locked with his. "Yes. I know what you mean."

He had a feeling she wasn't talking about the bull.

CHAPTER THREE

WALKER TURNED ONTO THE DIRT road that led to the Grubbs's trailer house. No one spoke. He glanced toward the backseat and saw Georgie was asleep. Haley leaned in close to him, always there, always protective of her baby brother. But her face was a mask of pain.

How was he going to reconcile with his daughter?

"Mr. Walker." Ginny turned to him in the front seat. "You can let me out here. I'll walk the rest of the way. I'll tell my dad I missed the bus."

"Sorry, Ginny. I need to talk to Earl."

"Why, Daddy?" Haley asked in her usual angry tone. "It's only going to cause trouble."

"Mr. Walker…"

"Trust me, girls."

"Yeah, right." He heard Haley mutter under her breath.

He ran a hand over the steering wheel, feeling lower than sludge. Neither girl had any faith in his abilities to defuse a potentially dangerous situation. He'd have to show them. This time Earl was getting the full brunt of his anger.

Pulling into the lane that led to the Grubbs's place, he made to get out and open the aluminum gate covered with chicken wire.

"I'll get it, Mr. Walker," Ginny said, and hopped out.

Earl raised goats, pigs and chickens. They were all over the cluttered yard. Ginny shooed chickens and goats away so she could open the gate.

He drove through, and Ginny quickly got back in the car. The old trailer was straight ahead. Not a blade of grass grew in the dirt yard. The aluminum siding was rusted in spots, and the screens were missing. A makeshift porch attached to the front looked ready to collapse. In stained overalls and a discolored flannel shirt, Earl lounged in a chair propped against the trailer. He was raising a jug to his lips. Walker knew it was homemade wine. And *good* was nowhere in sight.

Earl could be a decent-enough guy when he was sober, but those occasions were very rare. He had an aversion to getting a job, and he blamed God, the government, neighbors and anyone who came within his vision for his poverty.

Walker glanced at Haley. "Stay in the car with your brother."

"Like I want to get out" was her clipped response.

Walker opened his door and the stench from the pigpen filled his nostrils. It took a moment to catch his breath. How did people live like this? He shooed chickens away and was careful not to step in goat crap.

Two hunting dogs barked and pulled at their chains at the end of the trailer.

"What you done now, gal?" Earl asked when he saw Ginny, his words slurred. He took another swig from the jug. "If you're in trouble again, I'm gonna beat your sorry ass."

Ginny stood next to him, and he could see her trembling. She was frightened to death. Fueled by anger, Walker started up the steps, the decaying boards protesting under his weight.

"My daughter and Ginny missed the bus, so I brought Ginny home." It was a lie, but it would suffice for now.

"She got legs, she can walk. There ain't nothing wrong with her but stupidity."

"Go inside," Walker said to Ginny.

"You don't tell my daughter what to do," Earl spit out.

Walker nodded to the girl, and she opened the screen door. A thin woman holding a small girl stood there. Four other children of various ages were behind her. He noticed the woman's bruised face before she quickly pulled Ginny inside.

"You better have supper ready on time," Earl shouted at his wife. "And stop mollycoddling those brats."

Walker had had enough. He jerked the jug out of Earl's hand and flung it into the yard. It hit a chicken and she flapped away squawking.

"What…the hell…?"

Walker kicked the chair forward with his foot. Earl spit and sputtered, but being drunk, his reflexes were slow. Taking Earl's face in his hand, he yanked it up so he could look into his bloodshot eyes.

"Listen up, Earl."

"You…y-ou b-bastard."

Walker squeezed tighter and Earl's straggly beard scratched his fingers. "You're not paying attention, Earl. Now, listen. If you lay one hand on Ginny, I'm coming back with both fists loaded, and I'm going to show you what a beating feels like. You got that?"

"Y-ou…y-ou…" Earl sputtered.

Walker squeezed even tighter. "And lay off the wine."

Earl's eyes almost bugged out of his head and Walker released him. Rubbing his face, Earl said, "You can't tell me what to do on my own p-property."

"I have a badge that says I can," Walker replied. "And you better listen to me. I'm coming back tomorrow and the day after that and the day after that. If Ginny, your wife or any of your kids have bruises, I'm arresting you and throwing your ass in jail. I'll make sure you get convicted, and Earl, those inmates in Huntsville don't care for child abusers. They'll have a good old time with you."

Earl's bugged-out eyes opened wider. "Y-you can't…"

Walker straightened. "This is a warning. Next time I won't be so nice."

"I can't go…go to jail. I got kids to feed."

Walker looked at this man who had reached the very bottom. "Think about it, Earl. All you have to do is stop drinking and take care of your family instead of using them as punching bags."

"You think you're high and mighty—"

Walker pointed a finger at him. "Get your act together. I'll be returning in a couple of hours to make sure you heed my warning." Saying that, he swung off the porch and headed for his car.

And clean air.

THE RIDE HOME WAS AGAIN in silence. Georgie woke up as he pulled into their driveway. The house was a block away from Walker's General Store. He had no interest in running the store, but Nell had. So they worked out a compromise. They split the profits fifty-fifty and she drew a salary.

Walker had also inherited his father's house and land. Nell lived in his grandfather's house, which was next door. When he'd first brought the kids to High Cotton, Nell had helped him, but he could see now it had been a mistake. Her life was the store, and there wasn't room for anything else. He would have to find other babysitting arrangements when he had to go on a call.

He lifted Georgie out of his car seat, and they went inside the white clapboard two-story house with the wraparound porch detailed with black gingerbread trim. The Walkers before him had taken very good care of the house, so it was in good shape. When he'd returned, he'd had central air and heat installed for the kids.

Since he was an only child, he'd often wondered what he was going to do with the house, land and store in High Cotton. He had no desire to live here. He'd been away too long. But life had a way of mocking his plans. At the ripe old age of thirty-six, this was the only place he wanted to raise his kids now.

He set Georgie on his feet in the big kitchen. "It's about suppertime, what—"

Haley made a run for the downstairs bathroom and he could hear her throwing up. Dammit! He didn't know how to help her. She'd started having problems when she was about six. The doctor thought she might have irritable bowel syndrome, but she didn't. More tests were run and the diagnosis was a nervous stomach. She needed a stress-free environment and a healthy diet void of spicy and high-acidity foods. No matter what he and Trisha had tried, nothing completely cured Haley's problem.

The divorce had triggered a major upset, and Walker could see his daughter wasting away before his eyes.

"Haley sick," Georgie said, twisting his hands.

"Yeah." Walker tousled his son's hair. "She'll be okay." She had to be. "Daddy will be right back. Do you want to watch a movie?"

"Uh-huh."

"How about *Shrek?*" he asked, making his way into the living room.

"No. *Finding Nemo,*" Georgie shouted from behind him.

Walker found the movie and slipped it into the DVD player and pushed buttons on the remote. Georgie grabbed his Curious George off the sofa and settled in front of the TV. Walker hurried to the bathroom.

Turning the knob, he saw that the door was unlocked. He tapped so as not to invade her privacy.

A muffled "Go away" came through the door.

"Haley, sweetheart, it's Daddy."

"Go away."

He couldn't do that. "I'm coming in." He opened the door and glanced around. The bathroom was large and had an antique bathtub with claw feet. Everything in the room was antique from the pedestal sink to the pull-chain toilet. Haley was sitting by the toilet, her back to the wall, her forehead on her drawn-up knees.

Ignoring the horrible smell, he sank down by her. Honestly, he didn't know what else to do.

"Are you okay?" He stared at his boots, searching for the right words.

"Just leave me alone," she muttered against her knees.

"I'm your dad and I'm not leaving you alone—ever."

"Oh, yeah." She raised her head and his heart took a jolt at her pale face. "You leave us with Aunt Nell all the time."

"I have a job, and I'm not leaving you alone here at the house." They'd had this conversation before. It was the only thing Haley had opened up about.

"Why not?" Her watery eyes suddenly cleared. "I'm ten years old and I can take care of Georgie. If something goes wrong, we live in the middle of High Cotton and I could get help in no time."

"So you think you're responsible enough."

"As much as Aunt Nell."

He mulled this over and wanted to meet her halfway. "I'll think about it."

She placed her head on her knees again.

Several seconds went by. "We need to talk about today."

She didn't respond.

"I don't know where your mother is."

Her head shot up, her eyes filled with something he couldn't describe. It was almost like fear. Was his daughter afraid of him?

"You do, too."

"Haley, I don't."

"You're lying."

"I have no reason to lie." He tried not to raise his voice. "You're old enough to know your mother left of her own free will. I have sole custody of you and Georgie."

"You made her leave." The fire was back in her eyes. "You were gone all the time helping other people and you should have been home helping us."

"Your mother and I had problems for a long time, and yes, a lot of it was because of my job. I can't change that now, but I can be here for you and

Georgie." He paused and prayed for a break in her implacable armor. "Please give me a chance."

"I want to see Mama," she sobbed against her knees. "I have to see my mama."

He tried to put his arm around her, but she jerked away. Oh, God, his heart stopped beating and he hurt for her. He felt her pain deep inside him—a place that was created the day he became a father.

The mass in his throat clogged his vocal cords. "Your mother…"

She lifted her head, tears streaming down her face. "I know she left us, and you know where she is. You just won't tell me. I…I…" Sobs racked her thin body, and this time he pulled her into his arms and held her, searching for those magical words that would help them both. But they were elusive, and he hated that he was so bad at being a parent.

"Please, Haley. Give me a chance." His words were hoarse, and he had to swallow a couple of times to get them out.

Before she could say anything, Georgie came running in and wiggled into his lap. "Oh, it stinks in here." He looked up at Walker. "I'm hungry." The odor didn't seem to bother his appetite.

"Suppertime," Walker said, and tried to act normal. "Haley, would you like chicken noodle soup and a grilled cheese sandwich? You usually can hold that down."

"I guess." She straightened and moved as far away from him as she could. That hurt a little more.

"I want peanut butter and jelly." Georgie gave his menu choice. "Grape jelly. I don't like any other kind." Walker had made the mistake of using strawberry one time and Georgie had never forgotten it.

"I know, son." Walker stood with the boy in his arms. "And we can have ice cream afterward."

"Yay!" Georgie clapped his hands. Haley was silent. She was silent all through dinner. She was silent as they washed the dishes. Instead of watching TV, she took a bath and went to bed.

Soon he tucked Georgie in, but Walker couldn't sleep. His mind was in overdrive. His children's well-being was at the front of his mind—always. All he could do was be here for them and maybe Haley wouldn't try to run away again.

Not only was he worried about his kids, but Ginny was on his mind, too. If anything happened to her, he would never forgive himself, not to mention that he'd have no hope of his daughter ever forgiving him.

An hour later, he still wasn't asleep. He got up, dressed and went into Georgie's room and gathered him into his arms. He carried him to Haley and tucked him in beside her.

"Daddy," she mumbled sleepily.

"I'm going to check on the Grubbs family. Take care of Georgie." He handed her the portable phone. "Call my cell if there's a problem." She wanted responsibility, so he was going to give it to her—for a while.

"Oh." Her voice sounded excited.

In less than thirty minutes he was back. Earl was passed out on the sofa. Verna, his wife, said everything was fine. Ginny seconded that and Walker felt a lot better.

He fell into bed exhausted, but the worry over his kids was always there. What was he going to do? He needed help.

Blue eyes edged their way into his subconscious. His eyes popped open. *Madison Belle.* It was hard to explain his reaction to her. When he was a senior in high school, he and his dad had gone on a fishing trip to the Gulf Coast. They'd rented a cabin on a secluded cove outside Rockport, Texas. The cabin was shaded with gnarled, bent oaks, tempered and tried by the Gulf winds. The water in the cove held him mesmerized. It was the purest blue he'd ever seen, as if it had been untouched by nature and its wrath. He thought he'd never see that color again.

Until he looked into Madison's eyes.

She had that same purity. That same quality of not being tainted by the ups and downs of life. It had to be an illusion. No woman could be as pure or as good as Madison appeared.

For a cynical man like himself, he knew it was an illusion. His motto was to avoid the woman in case she could look into his soul and see all his sins.

MADISON SLEPT VERY LITTLE. She couldn't stop thinking and worrying about Walker's kids. And Ginny.

She was so young to be pregnant. Her family situation seemed dire, and she wondered how the girl would cope?

A baby.

Maddie would give everything she had for a child. It seemed so unfair, but she'd come to grips with her situation long ago. Every time she thought about it, though, she felt that empty place inside her that would never be filled.

She had a ready-made family waiting for her in Philadelphia. All she had to do was accept Victor's marriage proposal. Victor's wife had died five years ago, leaving an eleven- and a fourteen-year-old who needed a mother in their lives. But Victor was a friend, a very dear friend. She didn't have passionate feelings for him. Hadn't even gone to bed with him. She'd told him how she felt, and he'd said those emotions would come later. She didn't believe that.

Soon she'd have to go home and face Victor and her future. But for now her life was here on High Five. Maybe she was in denial. Maybe she was hiding. Or maybe she believed in miracles and love.

She went to sleep with that thought.

The next morning she dressed in jeans, a pearl-snap shirt and boots, her customary garb. Oh, yes, she was a cowgirl now and she was getting damn good at it.

She hurried to Gran's room as she did every morning. Gran was up and winding her white hair into its usual knot at her nape.

"Good morning, my baby." Gran smiled at her.

Maddie sat on the stool beside her in front of the mirror. Gran called her three granddaughters "baby." At thirty-one, Maddie was past being a baby, but it was useless to mention that to Gran.

"Caitlyn's coming to pick me up. I'm going to Southern Cross for a visit," Gran told her, patting her hair.

Maddie lifted an eyebrow. "So the honeymooners are having company?"

Gran slipped on her comfortable shoes. "I'm not company. I'm the grandmother. Besides, we were all at Southern Cross for Thanksgiving."

"Everyone but Sky." Maddie worried about her baby sister and wished Sky would just come home.

"Sky has a mind of her own."

"Mmm." Maddie linked her arm through the older woman's. "Let's go down for breakfast."

"Yes, my baby. It's the first day of December and we have to start thinking about the upcoming holiday."

Maddie would rather not. But soon she'd have to tell her mother that once again she wouldn't be in Philly for Christmas.

The scent of homemade biscuits met them in the hallway. "Oh, my, isn't that wonderful?"

"Makes my mouth water," Gran replied.

Etta pulled a pan of biscuits out of the oven as they entered the kitchen. "Good morning, lazy bugs."

Maddie glanced at the clock. It was barely seven,

but she saw the dirty plates on the table. Cooper and Rufus had already eaten and gone.

Grabbing a biscuit, she juggled it to the table. It was hot, hot, hot. She opened it on a napkin and dribbled honey over it. Picking it up, she headed for the door. She had to catch up with Cooper and Rufus.

She took a bite of the biscuit and stopped in the doorway. First, she had something else to do.

"I need to make a phone call," she said to Gran and Etta.

On the way to her study, she finished off the biscuit. Damn, she'd forgotten her coffee. Where was her brain? In Worryville.

She licked her fingers and punched out the number Cait had given her yesterday. Walker's number. He answered on the first ring.

"This is Madison Belle," she said quickly.

"Ms. Belle." His deep, strong voice came through loud and clear. "Is there a problem?"

She curled her sticky fingers around the receiver. "No. I was just wondering how the kids are?"

"Mine are fine. Haley's getting ready for school and Georgie's eating breakfast. Anything else?"

Yes. Lose the attitude.

"And Ginny?" she asked without even pausing.

The silence on the other end was loaded with four-letter words, and they weren't nice.

She waited, licking her fingers.

After a moment he replied, "Ginny is fine, too. I had

a talk with her father about what was going to happen to him if he hits her again. I checked on her last night and the family was fine."

"That was so sweet of you."

"I'm not sweet, Ms. Belle," he shot back in a voice tighter than a rusted padlock.

"But your gesture was," she reminded him just because it annoyed him so much.

"Anything else, Ms. Belle?" The way he said *Ms. Belle* was beginning to irritate the crap out of her.

"You might try working some of that 'sweet' into your attitude." The words were out before she could stop them. Not that she tried very hard.

"And you might try minding your own business."

"Ginny needs someone to help her, and I'm beginning to think that Haley might, too." After saying that, she slammed down the phone.

She reached up to see if steam was gushing out of her ears. She was so angry. How could he be so…so ungrateful? And stern. And rigid. And infuriating.

Blood pumped through her veins with renewed fervor. She hadn't felt this angry in a very long time. She took a long breath and blew it out her mouth. Mr. Attitude hadn't heard the last of her.

CHAPTER FOUR

MADDIE HURRIED TO THE BARN to catch up with Coop and Ru. A little exercise was what she needed to untangle all the anger inside her. After all, Walker was the children's father and she was sticking her nose into his business. But she cared. Children were her weakness. In this situation, though, she needed to tread carefully. Or not. Annoying Walker might become the highlight of her day.

In the doorway to the barn, she stopped short. Cooper was shoving bullets into a rifle, and Rufus held another one in his hand. Her heart skipped a beat.

"What's going on?"

Coop turned to her. "Ru got a call from Mr. Peevy. Wild dogs killed two of his baby calves last night. We have to be prepared."

"Prepared?"

Coop handed her the rifle, and she just stared at it. "Put it in the scabbard of your saddle."

She shook her head. "Oh, no. I don't do the gun thing, and since you're on probation, you shouldn't, either."

His face darkened. "I promised Cait to help you run High Five, and I'm not going to let a pack of feral dogs slaughter our calf crop."

She could see the anger in his eyes, which was very rare. Ever since he had the fight with the man who had framed him, Coop kept his anger on a tight leash. Although Coop was cleared of all wrongdoing in the killing of the horses, he was on probation for the assault. The man refused to drop the charges. Maddie understood Coop's anger. Anyone would have lashed out at being used as a scapegoat in an insurance scam, but she didn't want him to get into any more trouble.

Gently, she touched his arm. "I know High Five means a lot to you, but you have to be careful."

He took a deep breath. "I'll be very careful. Out here no one knows."

"Let's keep it that way."

"Okay." He raised the gun in front of her again. "Learn to use it. You have to be able to protect your animals."

Against every objection in her head, she took it. The gun felt heavy and deadly in her hands. Her first instinct was to throw it on the ground and say *no way*. But High Five was still struggling and they couldn't afford to lose a calf crop. The last hurricane had ripped through the ranch and had caused tremendous damages. They were still rebuilding. She had to step up and do her job, like she'd told Cait she could.

But a gun?

This is where the city girl and the country girl collided. Who was Madison Belle?

"There are six bullets in the magazine," Coop was saying. "It's already loaded." He pointed to a spot on the gun. "There's the safety. Always keep it on. If you have to shoot, push it to off and line up your prey with this guide on top. Then pull the trigger." He tapped a forefinger against the guide.

"I'm not sure I can do that," she admitted.

"Would you like to practice?"

"No, thanks." Firing the gun wasn't on this city/country girl's agenda. "Hopefully I won't ever have to use it."

"Mr. Peevy's place is about five miles away. The dogs could travel in another direction, but like I said we have to be prepared."

She placed the gun by her saddle, not able to hold it one minute longer. "How do they become feral dogs?"

"People haul dogs they don't want out to the country and leave them. The dogs begin to scrounge for food. They meet up with coyotes or wolves and mate. Suddenly there's a pack of them, all hungry and killing everything they can to survive."

"How awful."

"Yeah, animal activists have tried to change things to no avail. Sometimes you just can't stop people. Animal shelters are full and now charge if you bring in a dog. People who don't want a dog are not going to pay. It's a vicious cycle and ranchers pay the price."

"Miss Dorie used to take in every stray dog that showed up at High Five," Rufus said, shoving his gun into his saddle scabbard, "but since Mr. Bart died she lost interest in a lot of things. If one shows up, I take it to the shelter so they can find it a home."

"Good for you, Ru," Maddie replied.

"And Booger's a stray we kept. He's part Australian blue heeler and learned to work cattle. He's a natural. Wish we could keep 'em all, but we can't."

"If everyone did that, there wouldn't be a problem."

"But we have a problem now," Coop said. "Ru and I were talking, and we think it might be best to round up all the cows fixing to calf and keep them in the pen next to the corral. Except the hurricane took down the fence, so we have to repair it first."

"Go for supplies and we'll get busy." That was an easy decision to make.

Coop hesitated.

"What?"

"Cait always went for supplies. Ms. Nell doesn't want me in her store."

"Well, that's insane." Maddie couldn't believe Cait tolerated such behavior. "Make a list and I'll pick up everything." And she'd have a talk with Ms. Nell, too. Since she was sticking her nose in other people's business, she might make it a trend.

THIRTY MINUTES LATER she walked through the double worn doors of Walker's General Store. A bell jingled over her head, and it reminded her of the summers she'd spent at High Five as a kid. This was a favorite spot of the Belle sisters—candywise the store had everything.

She breathed in the scent of apples, spices and cedar, a hint of the upcoming holidays. The store was the same as it had been when she was a child: faded hardwood floors, a rustic wood ceiling from which sundries hung, and shelves of gallon jars filled with every candy a child could want.

The aisles were cluttered with everything imaginable, from buckets and fishing poles to barrels of apples, pears and oranges. Homemade quilts hung on a wall. A couple of Christmas trees were propped in a corner. A feed and hardware department was at the back. Every now and then the scent of oats wafted through the tantalizing aroma of the holidays.

Maddie walked over to the counter where Nell Walker stood waiting on a customer. Cigarettes took pride of place in the glass case beneath. A gallon jar of jawbreakers sat on the counter among chewing tobacco, gum and tempting candy bars. She always went for the jawbreakers—they were her favorite. She resisted the urge to stick her hand in the jar.

Instead, she studied Ms. Walker. She had aged since Maddie had last seen her. Her gray hair was cut short like a man's and the lines of her stern face were set into a permanent frown. A tall, big-boned woman, Nell Walker exuded a persona of toughness and rigidity, the same as her nephew.

The customer left and Nell swung her gaze to Maddie. "May I help you, Ms. Belle?"

She noticed that Nell's eyes were a cold gray like a winter's day. As she pulled the list from her pocket, she thought that Nell looked very unhappy.

"I'd like to pick up some supplies." She placed the list in front of Nell.

Nell looked it over and then shouted, "Luther."

A man in his sixties ambled from the back.

"Is your truck out front?" Nell asked Maddie while glancing at the list and scribbling it into a record book.

"Yes."

"Give Luther your keys and he'll load your supplies."

"Oh, okay." She'd never done this before so she wasn't sure how it worked. Digging in her purse, she found her keys and handed them over.

As Luther took the list and walked out the door, Nell said, "I'll put everything on your bill. Anything else I can help you with?"

Maddie swung her purse strap over her shoulder. "Yes, there is."

Nell raised frosty eyes to Maddie's, and for a moment, a tiny moment, her resolve weakened. She stepped closer to the counter. "A lot of days I'm busy and don't have time to come in for supplies, so I'll be sending Cooper Yates, my foreman, in for them. I hope that's not a problem."

"I don't want him in my store." The words were delivered like an errant baseball smacking someone against the head. Unexpected and painful.

Nervously, her hand tightened on her purse strap, but no way would she bend. Coop deserved better than this kind of treatment. "Fine. If that's the way you feel, I'll just take High Five's business into Giddings, and I'm sure Caitlyn will agree to do the same for Southern Cross."

A telltale shade of pink crawled up the woman's face. Losing two ranches' business would hurt the store. Evidently hitting her in the pocketbook was talking her language.

"I don't want ex-cons in here. It's bad for business, but—"

"Is there a problem?" Walker strolled from the back, Georgie on his heels. Georgie smiled and she smiled back for a second.

Then she glanced at Walker, tall and imposing in a white shirt, snug jeans and boots. His Stetson was pulled low and hid his eyes, but just the sight of him made her heart go pitter-patter.

She took a breath. "Yes, there is. Ms. Walker refuses to allow Cooper to pick up supplies." She stood her ground when she wanted to take a step backward. The man was just so…so intimidating, frustrating and… handsome. There, she'd admitted it. He was too handsome for her peace of mind. And that sincere note in his voice was sidetracking her.

"Is this true?" Walker asked his aunt.

"We can't have ex-cons in here. Business will drop."

"Caitlyn and I will certainly take our business elsewhere if the status quo doesn't change."

"It will change, won't it, Nell?"

Nell puffed out her chest. "I was just about to tell Ms. Belle that."

Walker swung his gaze to her. "Good, then there's not a problem."

Her insides did a crazy flip-flop. What was wrong with her? Earlier she was annoyed at his attitude, but now she was acting like a ridiculous teenager. Before she could gather her wits, Georgie stuck his hand into the jar for a jawbreaker. Nell quickly slapped his hand with a resounding swat. Georgie let out a wail.

Walker gathered the boy into his arms, his eyes turning as cold as Nell's. "You will not hit my child."

"He eats too many sweets and he'll choke on those things."

Maddie walked over to a jar on the shelf and used the scoop to fill a bag with jelly beans. "Put this on my bill," she said to Nell, and handed them to Georgie. She waited for Walker to say he could pay for his own kid's candy, but he didn't say a word, just looked at her. "It's okay, isn't it?" she asked, to hide her nervousness under that gaze.

"Yes."

"See?" she said to Georgie. "These are smaller and chewy. They're good."

Georgie wiped away a tear and poked his hand into

the bag. He popped two into his mouth and nodded with a grin.

The door jingled and Luther came in and handed Maddie her keys. "All loaded and ready to go."

"Thank you." She looked at Nell. "I trust we won't have any more problems."

"No, ma'am."

"Bye," she said to Walker and Georgie, and headed for her truck.

Walker watched her leave with a funny feeling in his gut. God, he was falling for her caring attitude. *No.* It was just a natural reaction to her kindness to Georgie. He had enough problems without even thinking of Ms. Belle and her pure, pure blue eyes.

He had parked out back. His office was next door so it was always easy to leave Georgie with Nell. After resigning from his search-and-rescue unit in Houston, he hadn't planned on going back to work. But Mr. Pratt, the constable, had passed away, and the commissioner's court, by way of Judd, begged him to take the job.

There were two years left on Mr. Pratt's term and Walker thought he could handle that. Then he would decide if he wanted to run for the office or not. He was already a state-licensed law enforcement officer so he'd agreed. After in-service training, he was appointed the constable of High Cotton and the surrounding precinct.

As an associate member of the Texas Department of Public Safety, his job was to keep the peace, enforce traffic regulations, go on patrol, undertake investigations and arrest lawbreakers. Since he didn't have a jail, he coordinated his activities with the sheriff of the county.

At the time he'd taken on the job, he thought he would need something to keep him busy. But now he wished he'd thought it over a little more. He was needed at home.

Juggling his kids was getting harder. He never knew Nell was using physical discipline. That he wouldn't tolerate.

He'd gotten a call that the Grayson brothers were fighting again. He'd planned to leave Georgie for just a little while with Nell. Now he'd changed his mind. He'd take Georgie with him. He didn't have any other choice. His part-time deputy constable, Lonnie, was in Brenham visiting his parents.

The Graysons weren't dangerous, just idiots fighting over a fence that was ten inches over the line. He had to talk to them about every six months to defuse the situation.

He walked closer to his aunt. "You might try losing that holier-than-thou attitude, because if the Belles and the Calhouns take their business elsewhere, Walker's General Store will be in trouble."

"I handled it, didn't I?" She tucked a receipt into the register and slammed it closed.

"Yes, in a disagreeable fashion."

"Now…"

"No." He held up a hand. "This discussion is over.

When Cooper Yates comes into the store, you will treat him cordially."

"People don't know their place."

He gritted his teeth and let that pass. "And you will never slap my kids again—ever."

"They need discipline."

"Ever, Nell. Are we clear on that?"

She raised her chin. "Yes."

"Okay, Georgie." He jostled the boy, who had a mouth full of jelly beans. "Let's go see what the Graysons are doing?"

"Aren't you leaving him here?" Nell called.

"No," he said over his shoulder, "not ever again."

As he strolled toward his car, he thought about Ms. Belle. No one stood up to Nell. Most people in town would rather diffuse a bomb than cross her, yet Ms. Belle had no qualms about speaking her mind. About Cooper.

Although he was appalled at Nell's tactics, he had to wonder if there was something going on between Ms. Belle and Cooper. When the crisis at High Five had been settled, she was supposed to return to Philadelphia. But she'd stayed. Why?

And what did he care?

MADDIE WALKED TO HER TRUCK and saw that the barbed wire, steel posts and bag of steel-post ties were loaded. As she was about to get in, she saw a young girl crossing the street to the store. It was Ginny. The school was just across the highway, but school wasn't out. It was too early.

Ginny sat on the bench in front of the store, huddled in her Windbreaker, which didn't reach across her protruding stomach. Her face was pale.

Maddie walked over to her. "Are you okay?"

Ginny looked up. "Oh, hi, Ms. Belle."

"Why aren't you in school?"

"I felt sick and the nurse said I could go home. My dad delivers eggs here and I'm waiting on him."

"Maybe you should see a doctor?"

"No. I'm okay—just pregnant."

"Still…"

"We can't afford it, okay?" The words were angry, defiant. Ginny rested her head against the wall. "God, I wish Brian had been at High Five and then I could be out of this awful place."

Maddie eased onto the bench beside her, thinking the girl might need someone to talk to. "Haley doesn't know where her mother is, so you could have been stranded, too."

"That would be better than this dump of a town."

"Ginny…"

The girl sat up straight. "Please don't give me a lecture. I've heard enough from the school counselor and the teachers."

"They have a point. You're so young." Maddie had a good idea of what the counselor and teachers had told her.

"And stupid, like my dad is always telling me." Ginny chewed on a fingernail that had been gnawed to the quick. Her greasy hair was pulled back into a limp ponytail. Food stains speckled her jeans, even the Windbreaker, and her sneakers were a dirty tan. The girl needed a bath. Maddie wondered at her home life.

Suddenly Ginny turned to her. "Ms. Belle, please help me. A social worker came to our house and my dad told her I was giving the baby away. He says he can't afford to feed another kid. I want to keep my baby."

"Ginny…"

"I have an aunt who lives in Temple, and she said I could stay with her. She'd let me keep my baby and she'd help, too. I just need money to get there. Please, Ms. Belle, help me."

Maddie could feel herself weakening under that desperate tone, but she had to be careful. So many times she let her emotions rule her head. She had to remind herself that Ginny had a family.

"Why doesn't she come and get you?"

"She's had knee surgery and she's not driving yet. I can help her, too."

"What about your mother?" Maddie kept holding back, trying not to let her emotions get involved.

"My dad hates my aunt. She's my mother's sister and my mother can't even visit her. My mom won't go against my dad."

This was all sounding very odd to Maddie. "How did you hear from her?"

"I called her from school to tell her what my dad was planning. I need to see a doctor and she told me to come, but not to tell my father."

"You haven't seen a doctor?" This one thing stuck in Maddie's mind.

"No, ma'am. We can't afford it."

"But there are free clinics—if not here, then in Giddings."

Ginny shook her head. "My dad wouldn't let me go. He said if I was so stupid to get pregnant then I could have the baby at home just like my mom had all of us."

Good heavens, this was terrible. The girl needed to see a doctor.

"Do you know when the baby is due?"

"No, ma'am."

Maddie took a deep breath and looked off to the vehicles traveling on the country road, some stopping at the gas station/convenience store across the highway, others at the local café and the rest continuing on to their homes and ranches. A cool breeze wafted Ginny's unwashed scent to her.

Everything in her told her not to get involved with a girl she didn't know, but she couldn't ignore the fact that Ginny needed medical attention and more.

Oh, she hoped she didn't regret this. "What's your aunt's name?"

"Thelma Jenkins."

"Do you have her phone number?"

"Why?"

Maddie bit her lip. "I'll give you the money to get to Temple, but I want to talk to your aunt first."

Ginny smiled and her whole demeanor changed. "Oh, Ms. Belle, thank you." Ginny glanced at the pay phone beside them. "I'll call her now if…if you'll loan me two quarters."

Maddie cursed herself for not bringing her cell, but she'd been in such a hurry to catch Cooper and Rufus that she'd left it behind. Opening her purse, she dug for change and handed it to Ginny. The girl jumped up to make the call.

The traffic was deafening, and Maddie couldn't make out what Ginny was saying. Ginny held out the phone to Maddie and she spoke to Thelma Jenkins.

The lady assured her she would do everything to help Ginny. Hanging up, Maddie felt much better.

"I'll give you the money for bus fare, but you have to tell your parents where you're going."

"Sure. They won't care."

Maddie couldn't imagine a parent not caring.

"And I'd like your aunt's number and address."

Maddie pulled a pad from her purse and handed Ginny a pen. After Ginny scribbled the name and number, Maddie tucked it into her purse. She then reached for her wallet and counted out fifty dollars.

"That should be enough for the fare and a little extra."

"Oh, thank you, Ms. Belle. You're so nice."

"And please check in at the school and let them know you'll be gone for a while."

"I will."

Maddie motioned toward Ginny's stomach. "Take care of that baby."

"I plan to." Ginny hugged her briefly, and Maddie got into her truck and drove away, hoping she was doing the right thing. If Ginny wanted to keep her baby, she should be allowed to. Every woman had that right.

As she neared High Five, she met Walker going in the opposite direction. She would call him tonight and let him know about Ginny. That was the least she could do. After all, he was worried about Haley and her involvement with Ginny. She'd probably get a lot of attitude and a sermon about minding her own business.

She'd call, anyway. He had been nice today, and maybe they had reached a new understanding.

Maybe.

CHAPTER FIVE

By the time Maddie's day ended, she was exhausted. They managed to finish the fence around the pen, and her arms ached from stretching barbed wire, but it was done. She was proud she had the strength to keep up with Cooper. As she fell into bed, she relished that feeling.

Before sleep claimed her, she remembered she hadn't called Walker. Thoughts of him caused her to move restlessly beneath the covers. What was it about the man that triggered every feminine response in her? Maybe it was because he was so different from the men in her city life. Or maybe it had been so long since she'd been with a man that her feminine sensory receptors were out of whack. Or whatever. She was too tired to think anymore.

She should call him, but it was late and she might wake Georgie. The morning would be a better time.

At five Maddie was up and not so raring to go. She felt as if she'd just closed her eyes. But they planned to round up the expecting cows and wanted to get an early start. This might be just a little too early. Coop said there weren't many cows calving this time of the year, so that was a plus. Births were usually in the spring and fall.

After brushing her teeth, she thought of calling Walker, but it was too early. She'd call at lunch. She shimmied into jeans and stuck her arms into one of Cait's pearl-snap shirts. Luckily they were close to the same size. After tucking her shirt into the jeans, she zipped and buttoned them, then deftly wove a tooled leather belt through the loops.

She sat down to tug on her boots. Wiggling her toes, she was reminded how different her attire was from her Philadelphia wardrobe: suits, silk blouses and Jimmy Choo heels. Oh, yeah, she missed those shoes, but that was another life. Today she was a cowgirl, and work waited for her. Gathering her hair into a short ponytail, she jogged for the stairs, which she figured was a good way to wake up.

She met Etta as she was going out the back door. "Good morning, lazy bug," Maddie mocked with a smile.

"Don't get smart," Etta replied, handing her something wrapped in tin foil. "Breakfast taco. I made them for Rufus and Cooper and I saved one for you."

"Thanks, Etta."

"Get some juice from the fridge."

Maddie grabbed bottled water. "This will do."

"Now, lunch will be ready at twelve and I expect

everyone here. You can't go all day without a proper meal."

"Yes, ma'am." Maddie kissed her cheek. "Please look after Gran. I'll check on her later."

"I always look after Miss Dorie." Etta pushed her toward the door. "Go. Coop and Ru are waiting."

By noon Maddie's butt was numb and her body ached, but they had a penful of expecting mamas. She leaned on the fence beside Cooper. "How do you know these cows are ready to give birth?"

"Look at their udders."

"Oh, they're swollen."

"Yep. Full of milk, and their…"

When he stopped, she glanced at him. "What?"

Cooper removed his hat and swiped back his hair as if he was thinking about his answer. "Their tail ends are swollen, too."

"Oh." She playfully slapped his shoulder. "You thought I'd be embarrassed."

His sun-browned skin darkened. "Maybe."

"Ple-ease." She pushed away from the fence, placed her hands on her hips and bobbled her head in a what's-up-with-you movement. "I really am made of tougher stuff."

"Well, you surprised the hell out of me," he admitted. "I thought you'd do your share of the work from the house."

"Not on your life, buster." She started toward the house. "Let's go have lunch. I'm starving."

She had thought of just doing the paperwork. Cooper could run the ranch without her help, but something about being part-owner made her take an active role. Cait had. And she enjoyed the physical exercise. And she needed to feel useful. And she craved the mind-numbing tiredness that kept her from thinking *what if?* What if the cancer came back?

That fear never left her.

IT WAS A TEACHER'S workday so Walker had both kids at home. He'd received a call from Lois Willham. Her husband had just gotten laid off from his job in Rockdale. He'd bought a six-pack of beer and was in the yard drinking and firing a gun. She was afraid he was going to hit an unexpected bystander.

Walker didn't want to take the kids on that kind of call, so he left Haley in charge. He thought she would be happy, but she seemed more nervous than anything.

He didn't plan to be gone that long, so he didn't worry, which was an understatement. Worry was his constant companion.

When he reached the Willhams', Roy was sitting in a lawn chair, a beer in his hand and a shotgun resting across his lap. Walker took the gun away from him and told him to get his act together. His family needed him. Then he listened to Roy ramble on about the unfairness of life. When Walker left, Roy promised to do right by his family, even if he had to go back to farming.

In less than an hour, he walked through his back

door. Everything was quiet. Too quiet. An unexpected chill scooted across his skin. He hurried into the living room. The TV was off and the lights out. His kids were nowhere in sight.

He took the stairs two at a time. Their rooms were empty. That chill began to multiply. He dashed to the general store. They weren't there. He checked all over High Cotton. No one had seen them.

Where were they?

Could they have gone to High Five again? High Five was closer than Earl's, so he headed there first. On the way he called his part-time deputy constable to take all calls.

He had to find his children.

Etta had hamburger steaks, mashed potatoes, green beans and hot rolls. Maddie ate her fill, as did Cooper and Rufus. They had worked up an appetite.

Afterward, Coop and Ru left to check the herd. Maddie sat with her grandmother in the parlor.

"How was your visit with Cait? I got in so late last night I didn't get a chance to ask."

Gran clapped her hands. "It was wonderful to see my baby so happy."

"Mmm." Maddie had thought that Cait would never walk away from High Five. Her roots were firmly embedded here, but love had made the decision easy. Maddie hoped one day she could find a love that strong. She shifted uneasily. That was highly unlikely, though. Men didn't want damaged goods. They wanted a wife who could bear children. A sharp pain shot through her.

"I thought my baby would become a lady taking care of the house and things like that, but she's in charge of the horses while Judd manages the cows."

Maddie hugged her grandmother. "It's what Cait loves. I just can't see her knitting or crocheting or throwing parties."

"Sometimes I wonder where I went wrong. My granddaughters are so independent and live in a man's world."

"Oh, Gran." She hugged her again. "You've done nothing wrong. Times have just changed. A woman can clean, cook and make babies, but she can be the breadwinner, too. A woman is good at multitasking."

"I don't have a clue what you're talking about. Women should be pampered and loved."

"Hallelujah." Maddie stood and did a fancy tap dance, her boots clicking on the hardwood floor.

"And you're no better." Gran flung out a hand. "Out there with Cooper and Rufus in the muck and the mud."

It was no use arguing with her grandmother. Her views were from another time, another era.

She lifted an eyebrow. "Good thing I'm a Belle, then, huh?"

A smile fluttered across Gran's face. "Yes, it is, my baby."

Maddie kissed Gran's forehead. "I love you."

"And that covers for a lot of unladylike behavior," Gran replied with a touch of her true Belle spirit.

"I'll see you this afternoon," Maddie called over her shoulder. "We'll watch an old movie."

"One where a lady is a lady."

"Oh, yes, ma'am."

Maddie walked out the back door smiling. She came to an abrupt stop when she saw Walker drive up in a white car with a constable's insignia on the door and a siren on top. Oh, no, she'd forgotten to call him. But she was sure his visit had nothing to do with Ginny.

Or did it?

He strolled to her with long strides, his face set in a stonelike mask. This was not good. "Ms. Belle, are my kids here?"

She blinked, confused. "No. I haven't seen them. Isn't Haley in school?"

"No. It's a teacher's workday. Do you mind if I check your barn?"

"No. Of course not." As she followed him, a scenario was whizzing through her mind and she kept pushing it away. But she had to face it. Children's lives were involved.

After a brief search, it was clear the kids weren't hiding in the barn.

Walker clenched his jaw and she could see how worried he was. "God, where could they be? I'm on my way to Earl's to see if Ginny is home. Damn man doesn't have a phone."

As he hurried to his car, she knew she had to tell him. "Walker."

He turned swiftly, his eyes narrowed. "What? I really don't have time."

"I need to tell you something."

His face relaxed for a second. "Have you seen my kids?"

She shook her head and prayed for courage. And she prayed that she was wrong. "No, but I've seen Ginny."

"Where?"

"Yesterday at the general store."

"So? That doesn't mean anything. My kids were home until about two hours ago."

"Ah…"

"What is it, Ms. Belle? I have to go."

She swallowed the wad of cowardice in her throat. "I…I gave Ginny money for bus fare to Temple."

"What!"

The loud word ricocheted off her sensitive nerve endings. She winced. *Run* crossed her mind, but Belles didn't run. It seemed a whole lot easier than facing the angry man standing in front of her, though.

"Please let me explain."

"It had better be damn good."

She told him about the aunt and everything. "I don't believe your kids are with her. She just wanted to see a doctor about her pregnancy and to get away from her father."

"You said you had the aunt's name and number?"

"Yes. I'll get it and you'll see your kids aren't there." Oh, God, she prayed they weren't.

Maddie ran inside, grabbed her purse and hurried back to Walker, who still stood there with that same stone face, except now he had his cell in his hand.

He poked in the number and raised the phone to his ear. After listening for a second, he handed her the phone.

"Sorry, the number you've dialed is not a working number. Please try again." The message came through loud and clear. And disturbing.

"That can't be," Maddie said as fear edged its way into her voice. "I spoke to her yesterday."

"Did you dial the number?"

"No, Ginny did."

"I don't know who you were talking to, but I'm guessing it wasn't Ginny's aunt. I have a suspicion my kids are with her, and Ms. Belle—" the caramel eyes darkened "—if anything happens to them I'll…" He left the sentence hanging like a noose, and she could almost feel it tightening round her throat.

He swung toward his car, and even though Maddie had trouble breathing, she quickly followed him, jumping into the passenger's side.

His hand paused over the ignition. "What the hell do you think you're doing?"

"I'm going with you."

"No, you're not."

She stiffened. "If this is my fault, I have to help you find them."

"You've done enough, Ms. Belle. Now, get out of my car."

Her anger fired for the first time. "Stop calling me Ms. Belle. My name is Madison or Maddie."

"'Mad' is more appropriate. Now, get out of the car. I don't have time to argue with you."

She stared into his cold, cold eyes and shivered, but she didn't get out. "Sorry. I'm going with you."

He sighed angrily and started the engine. In a split second they were flying out of her driveway. For a couple of miles nothing was said.

A police radio sat on the dash, an empty coffee cup was in the console alongside a half-empty bag of jelly beans, a package of gum and a box of Kleenex. She sniffed the scent of the coffee and tried to relax.

Walker's big hands tightened on the steering wheel, and she expected it to snap from his brute strength at any minute.

She slipped her hand into her purse for her cell. She couldn't just leave without letting someone know. As she called Cait's number, Walker didn't even glance her way.

She tapped her fingers on her jeans, hoping her sister would answer and not Judd's secretary, Brenda Sue, who didn't know when to shut up.

Brenda Sue's annoying voice came on the line. This just wasn't her day.

"May I speak to Caitlyn, please?"

"Oh, hi, Madison. I'm in the office and I don't know

where Cait is and I have strict orders not to bother her or Judd. They get real angry when I do, so you'll have to just call back later. Did you know I have a boy-friend? What am I saying? Sure you do. I mean, you and Cait talk all the time and—"

"Brenda Sue," Maddie shouted, stopping the endless chatter. "Ring through to the house and tell Cait I need to talk to her. It's an emergency."

"Why don't you just call her cell?"

"Ring her!" Cait rarely carried her cell and Maddie needed to talk to her now.

"Don't get huffy. You Belles are all alike and—"

"Call her this instant." At Maddie's stringent voice, Brenda Sue put her on hold.

She glanced at Walker, and she thought she saw his lips twitch. Was he smiling? Hardly. The man never smiled.

Cait's voice came on. "What's wrong? Brenda Sue said you were rude. And I know my sister Madison is never rude."

"How do you keep from strangling her?"

"I just ignore her. So what's the emergency? Is it Gran?"

"Gran is fine. I need a favor. Could you go to High Five and tell Cooper I've been unexpectedly detained?"

"What? Where?"

Maddie took a breath and looked at Walker, who had his eyes glued to the road. "Walker's kids are missing and I'm going with him to find them."

"Why?"

"Just tell Cooper and check on Gran. I'll be back as soon as I can."

"Maddie, what's going on?"

"I'll tell you when I get back. I just didn't want anyone to worry."

"I'm worried now. Walker is more than capable of finding his kids."

"Cait, please. I have to go. I'll call as soon as I can."

"Mad—"

Maddie clicked off before Cait could do her usual grilling. At the moment she didn't have any answers. Slipping her phone into her purse, she hoped Ginny hadn't lied to her.

She noticed the car was flying down the highway, and a glance at the speedometer told her they were way over the speed limit.

"You're speeding."

That was met with a hard stare as Walker flexed his fingers on the steering wheel. He turned off the highway, tires squealing, onto a county dirt road. Gripping the door for support, she knew better than to say anything else.

Soon Walker swerved into a lane. Ahead was a dilapidated mobile home with goats and chickens in the dirt yard. Two dogs were tied at the corner and barked agitatedly at them, trying to break their chains.

"What is this?" she couldn't help but ask.

"This is where Ginny lives," he replied, getting out.

"You have to be kidding." No one could live here. The trailer was rusted and falling in.

Walker leaned down to look at her. "You may have noticed I'm not a joking type of guy." He slammed the door on that piece of news and went to open the gate.

She took several deep breaths. What had she done? Ginny would lie, cheat and steal to get out of a place like this. In that moment she knew she'd been had. Now Walker's kids were in danger.

Soon Walker was back in the car and drove up to the mobile home. He quickly got out and shooed chickens and goats away. She didn't hesitate to follow.

A foul smell greeted her. She wrinkled her nose. "What is that?" she asked Walker's stiff back.

"There's a pigpen out back," he said as he walked up the rickety steps. He banged on the screen door. It rattled from his big fist and she thought it might fall off.

A man in greasy long hair and dirty overalls opened the door, but not the screen. "Whaddya want?"

"I'm looking for Ginny, Earl."

"She ain't here."

Any hope Ginny hadn't tricked her vanished.

A woman came up behind Earl. It had to be Ginny's mother, but Maddie couldn't see clearly through the screen door. A small girl hung on to her leg.

"Where is she?"

"Don't know. Don't care."

"Earl, I'm not in a mood for your lip. I want answers and I want them now."

"She left a note saying she was leaving and for us not to worry about her." The woman spoke for the first time as she picked up the child.

"She say anything else?"

"No."

Walker stiffened beside her. "Do you have any idea where she might have gone?"

"No."

"What about your sister Thelma?"

There was a long pause and then the woman replied, "I don't have a sister named Thelma."

"Thelma Jenkins is not your sister?"

"No." The woman giggled. "Thelma Jenkins is that ol' mama goat in the yard. My boy named her that after a teacher he didn't like."

Walker glanced at Maddie with a you're-so-gullible look. And she was. She'd trusted Ginny and now she felt like a fool. Walker had every right to be angry with her. She was angry at herself.

"Does Ginny have any friends?"

"No, not now. Her friend moved away about a year ago."

"Who?"

"Tara Davis."

"Where did she move to?" Walker kept firing the questions as the dogs kept up an incessant bark. Two boys came from around the trailer and tried to quiet them.

Maddie shivered inside her Carhartt jacket, but that was preferable to going inside the trailer.

"I don't know," Verna replied.

"That's it," Earl snapped. "We don't know where the girl is."

"She's your daughter. Aren't you worried about her?" The words came out before Maddie could stop them.

"Good riddance, I say. One less mouth to feed." Earl slammed the door.

"Oh." Maddie stomped her boot. "What a deplorable man."

Walker wasn't listening to her. He went down the steps and over to the boys, who eyed him warily. Their clothes were filthy, and their long, stringy hair hung in their faces. One boy had a severe case of acne and he picked at a pimple. The other boy held a dog by the collar. The dog growled, baring his teeth, as Walker neared.

"When was the last time you saw your sister? And don't lie to me."

The boy stopped picking at the pimple and his face turned redder at Walker's tone. "She snuck out early this morning before anyone was up."

"Was someone waiting for her?"

"I don't know."

"Did you hear a car?"

"No."

"Did you see lights?"

"No. She packed her backpack and left. I was

sleeping on the sofa and saw her leave. That's all I know, mister."

"Thanks." Walker swung toward his car and ran smack into Ms. Belle, literally. He grabbed her before she toppled into goat crap. Beneath the jacket her arms felt soft, inviting, touchable. As annoyed as he was with her, he couldn't quell that reaction. A light scent of lavender didn't help, either.

"Watch where you're going." His words were rough and he didn't bother to sugarcoat them.

"I didn't realize you were going to turn so quickly."

He didn't respond as he hurried to his car and got in. Ms. Belle was still sidestepping crap to get to the car. He should just drive off and leave her here. Why didn't he? She was screwing up his whole life and messing with his emotions. From the first moment he'd met her at the party, he'd known she was trouble for his peace of mind. So drive away, he told himself. Yet he waited.

She opened the door, a frown on her face. "I stepped in it."

"You sure did," he replied, hoping she didn't miss the double meaning.

"I don't want to get this in your car." She danced around on one foot.

He tossed her the box of Kleenex. She actually caught it and then sat on the seat, wiping her boot.

Looking at him with a wad of tissues in her hand, she asked, "What do I do with this?"

For an answer he started the engine and she hurriedly crawled in. He drove to the gate and got out to open it. Once he was back inside, he noticed she'd tossed the tissues outside in the ditch.

"You're littering."

"Arrest me, then, because I'm not holding that any longer."

"Don't tempt me." He turned onto the dirt road.

"Where are we going?"

"To High Cotton. I want to know if Ginny got on a bus with my kids. The bus stopped there at ten-thirty this morning."

He clenched and unclenched his hands, trying not to think about Haley and Georgie getting on a bus bound for Lubbock to find their mother. He could strangle Ms. Belle, but when he looked at her, "strangle" wasn't exactly on his mind.

"I'm sorry. I really am." That soft, sincere voice weaved its way around his heart. And that made him mad.

"You should be. My kids could be anywhere."

"I was trying to help Ginny. She needs to see a doctor."

"You can't help everybody, Ms. Belle."

"That's very cynical."

Maybe he was. Life had done that to him. And Trisha.

"It's reality, Ms. Belle."

She turned toward him. "If you call me Ms. Belle in that tone of voice again, I'll smack you."

He met the blue heat of her eyes. "You've never smacked anyone in your life."

Her eyes crinkled. "Is it that obvious?"

"Yes."

"Doesn't mean I can't or I won't."

"Listen." His hands were perpetually clenched on the steering wheel. "When we reach High Cotton, you're getting out. I'll be moving fast to catch up with my kids."

"I can keep up."

"You're getting out!"

"Please, I really need to see this through."

That soft voice ran through him like a shot of tequila, warm, tingly and potent.

No, he wouldn't weaken. He'd had enough of Ms. Belle. "You're getting out."

Her chin lifted. "No, I'm not. You'll have a hell of a time getting rid of me."

CHAPTER SIX

NOT ANOTHER WORD WAS SPOKEN on the ride into High Cotton. Walker preferred it that way. He pulled into the convenience store where the bus stop was located. Once a week on Fridays a small bus took people who'd bought passes into Giddings to buy tickets for their destination. The town of High Cotton provided the service.

Ruth was at the counter in the store where the passes where purchased.

"Hey, Walker, what can I do for you?" Ruth was divorced and raising four kids by herself. She tended to be overly friendly.

"Did my children buy a pass for the bus this morning?"

"I wasn't on duty this morning. Woody was but he's not here now."

"Look in the book, Ruth. This is important."

"Sure. Anything for you." She reached beneath the counter and brought out a worn book. "Do you think your kids ran away or something?"

"Are they listed?"

"Nope." She chewed on a fingernail. "Just Opal Hinz, Willard Tobias, Juan Garcia and Ginny Grubbs."

"How many passes did Ginny buy?"

"I don't know. Woody would."

"Why isn't it written down?" He couldn't keep the anger out of his voice.

"Now, don't get your shorts in a bind."

"More than that's going to be in a bind if better records aren't kept around here."

"It's not a crime, is it?"

"It's just sloppy." He took a breath to control his temper. "When will Woody be back?"

She shrugged. "I don't know. He worked from 5:00 a.m. to one, so I guess he's probably home sleeping if you really need to talk to him."

Walker turned quickly and bumped into Ms. Belle again. "Look, call your sister or call Cooper. I'm leaving you here."

"You're not…"

"Madison." Joe Bob Shoemaker walked in and she paused. "I was looking for you. I need hay. Do you have any at High Five to sell?"

"No, I'm sorry. With the hurricane damage and the fire we need all we have."

"Damn the luck." Joe Bob chomped down on his chewing tobacco, eyeing Walker. "What are your kids up to?"

"What do you mean?"

"I saw them get on the bus this morning all huddled in their jackets like they didn't want anyone to see them, but there's no mistaking that gal of yours with that boy on her hip."

Walker hit the door at a run, jumped in the car and headed for Giddings. His mind was in such turmoil he didn't even realize Ms. Belle was in the car with him. He didn't have time to deal with her. He had to get to his kids.

Ms. Belle didn't say a word on the fifteen-minute trip. Walker figured she must value her life because he was in no mood to be patient with her. What was she thinking giving Ginny money?

He swerved off U.S. 290 where the convenience store/bus stop was located. The place was old, decaying from age and wear. He killed the engine and made a run for the front door. The place was just as bad inside, with outdated neon beer signs and dirty chipped tiled floors. He showed the woman behind the counter his badge.

"My name is Walker and I'm the constable from High Cotton." He pulled out his wallet from his back pocket and placed a photo on the counter. "I'm looking for these two kids. Have you seen them?"

The woman pushed her glasses up the bridge of her nose and peered at the photo. "Yes, yes. I saw them earlier. They were with an older girl. She was pregnant."

"That's them. Did you sell them a ticket?" He found he was holding his breath as he waited for the answer.

"The older girl wanted to buy tickets to Temple, but the bus had already left. I told her it would run again tomorrow, but she said that was too late."

"So where did they go?"

"They went outside."

"These were kids. Didn't you think something was wrong?" He held his temper in check.

"I was keeping an eye on them, but I got busy and when I looked up they were gone."

"Why didn't you call the police?"

"Like I said, I was busy."

"Too busy to get involved." His temper snapped.

"Now, listen—"

He cut her off. "Did you see them talking to anyone?"

"The older one was talking to a man. The next thing I knew they were gone."

Walker's blood ran cold. "What did he look like?"

"Probably in his fifties. He was wearing a brown jacket and a Dallas Cowboys baseball cap. That's all I noticed."

"Have you seen him before?"

"No."

He took a breath. "Did any of the kids say anything?"

"The little boy kept saying he wanted Daddy. The girl holding him told him to be quiet, that they were going to see Mama."

Damn! He turned toward the door and bumped into Ms. Belle again. The woman was like gum on his shoe, irritating and hard to get rid of. This time he didn't bother with a response. He was too worried about his kids.

When he got in the car, she was there. Without a word, he backed out and headed for FM 448, where the new sheriff's office was located.

On the way, he called Trisha's sister, Doris, in Lubbock to see if she'd heard from Haley. She hadn't. He told her to call immediately if she did.

When they reached the sheriff's office, he had a talk with Roger, the deputy in charge. He introduced Maddie. Walker knew all the people in law enforcement, so he had no problem getting an Amber Alert issued with Haley and Georgie's pictures. Roger then took more information. Walker gave him everything he knew, including Tara Davis's name. They would do a background check on her to see if they could locate her.

Now he waited. He let the officers do their jobs. Someone had to have seen them and he prayed he got to them before anything happened. His kids were with a total stranger. The dangers were just too many for him to contemplate and still keep his sanity.

Walker was restless. He couldn't sit still, but he knew he had to wait. The deputies were checking the bus stop again. Calls would start to come in. They had to.

He made himself sit in a chair by a water cooler, but he kept glancing at his watch. Where were Haley and Georgie? Who had them?

A hand touched his arm and he tensed, staring into

pure blue eyes. There she was. The woman he couldn't shake. Her fingers were warm and he needed that human contact.

"I'm sorry."

"I know." And he did. He really couldn't blame her. "Ginny would have gotten the money somehow for Haley. My daughter was determined to leave, so it was just a matter of time." It wasn't easy to admit that.

"I'm too trusting. My dad always told me that."

His eyes held hers. "I knew that about you from the start when you were wearing that white-and-pink dress and looking so innocent, so trusting."

They just stared at each other, and Maddie didn't know what to say. Did he still see her as a child? What a downer for her ego.

For lack of something to say, she waved toward a counter where a pot and cups stood. "Would you like a cup of coffee?"

"No, thanks. I'm wired enough."

"They'll find them."

"But will it be in time?" The words seemed to come from deep inside him.

She touched his arm again, and he didn't tense like the last time. The stern man she knew had disappeared. This man was hurting and unable to hide it. Even though most of the ordeal was her fault, she felt close to him at that moment.

"I've endangered my life many times in the line of duty. As a fighter pilot the risks were high, and I gladly took every one for my country. After my stint in the marines, I became a police officer in Houston. I put my life on the line every day. Trisha hated my job and was constantly on me about all the risks I was taking, so I quit and took on an air marshal's job. Again Trisha complained about me being gone all the time. I then became a member of a search-and-rescue team in Houston. My life was always in danger, but I never thought about it. I was just doing my job."

He took a long breath. "Now it's so different. My kids' lives are at risk and I feel that pain deep in my gut."

Roger walked over. "We've located Tara Davis."

Walker was immediately on his feet. "Where?"

"She lives in Temple with her boyfriend."

Temple. Ginny wanted to go to her friend's, not an aunt.

"Let me have her address and I'll be on my way."

Roger pulled the paper away. "Walker, calm down. A Temple police unit is on the way to the apartment. We'll know in a few minutes if your kids are there. Take a deep breath."

Walker swung away and gazed off down the hall. Maddie knew he was trying to get his emotions under control. Suddenly he swung back.

"If Ginny put my kids on a bus to Lubbock, I'll…"

She took his arm. "Let's sit. We'll have information shortly."

Like a spring, he bounced up again and paced. She had to get his mind on something else.

"Do you have any idea where your ex-wife might be?"

"No." He stopped pacing. "Her note said she was sorry but she loved this Tony Almada guy, her high school sweetheart, and she had made a choice. The kids would be better off with me because he didn't care for children. She told me to send the divorce papers to her sister in Lubbock. She loved Haley and Georgie but she had to go. At the bottom she wrote 'please forgive me.'" He removed his hat and stared at the creases. "How do you forgive such selfish behavior?"

"By loving your kids."

He raised his head, his eyes filled with pain. "I'm trying, but my kids barely know me. My jobs took me away from them and sadly I was never there." He jammed his hat on his head. "Haley and Georgie should have come first. They should have been my top priority, but I left their raising to Trisha. They have two selfish parents."

"You're there for them now. That's what counts."

He sat beside her and some of the tension seemed to leave him. "When Trisha left, I brought them home to High Cotton. I thought it would give us a new start, but Haley hasn't adjusted. She thinks I don't want them and that I'm only putting up with them because I have to."

"Have you told her differently?"

"Yes. But she doesn't trust me."

"You have to show her."

"I'm trying. I'm really trying." He closed his eyes and nothing else was said.

It was surreal sitting in the sheriff's office and talking to Ms. Belle. His main goal had been to get rid of her, but now he was glad she was here. She had a calming effect that he found strange. Other times she'd been like a steely point of a knife embedded in his last nerve.

Opening his eyes, he noticed her cowboy boots. "Are you really running High Five?"

She turned toward him with a lifted eyebrow. "You don't think I can?"

"No offense, but I see you as an indoor lady."

"Fragile and weak?" The eyebrow arched further.

"Far from it."

"You saved your butt there." She smiled, and his whole world seemed brighter. "Being raised in Philadelphia, I was an indoor person. When I visited my father and sisters at High Five, that changed. I enjoyed the outdoors."

Walker glanced at Roger, who was still talking on the phone. What was taking so damn long? To keep his nerves under control, he concentrated on the woman beside him.

"What did you do in Philadelphia? You said something about being a counselor."

"Yes. At a major hospital in Philly. Before that I was a teacher. I went to an all-girl's Catholic school and then to Duquesne University. Nothing prepared me for public schools. It was a challenge and stressful. With a degree in education and a minor in psychology, I searched for something else. The position at the hospital seemed perfect."

A shadow crossed her face. He waited for her to continue, but she didn't. She just stared at her clasped hands in her lap.

"Walker." Roger motioned him over.

He sprang to his feet. "Did you find them?"

The deputy held his hand over the mouthpiece. "I have Officer Campbell on the line. He's at Davis's apartment."

"And?"

"Your children aren't there and neither is Ginny Grubbs."

He gulped a breath. "May I speak to her?"

Roger spoke to the officer and handed Walker the phone.

"Ms. Davis, this is Walker, the constable of High Cotton. I'm looking for Ginny."

"She's not here" came the response. "Like I told the officer, she was supposed to be here, but she never arrived."

"Did you speak with Ms. Belle yesterday?"

There was a long pause.

"Don't lie, Ms. Davis. This is serious."

"Yes. I spoke to the lady. Ginny asked me to lie and I did. She said it was the only way she could get the money."

"What did she have in mind for Haley and Georgie?"

"Who?"

"Ginny has my two kids with her."

"She didn't mention any kids. My boyfriend said Ginny could stay until she found a job. That's it. He'll have a fit if she brings anyone else."

He dragged in a breath. "Just let us know when she arrives. That's important if you want to stay out of trouble."

"Yes, sir. I have a nine-month-old baby. I can't get in trouble. I was just trying to help a friend."

"Don't let Ginny talk you into anything."

"Yes, sir."

Walker handed the deputy the phone and started to pace again.

"What happened?"

He turned toward the soft feminine voice that was becoming like a tranquilizer. "They're not at the friend's. At least not yet. She was expecting Ginny, but not Haley and Georgie." Walker turned toward Roger. "Ginny might have put my kids on a bus to Lubbock."

"We'll check it out. And a policeman is watching the apartment."

"Good." He walked to the chair and sat. His fears were ping-ponging off his nerves. Removing his hat, he ran both hands through his hair. "I feel so helpless. I'm used to being in the action. It's hell waiting."

Maddie didn't say anything. Office sounds went on around them. Phones rang, faxes beeped and voices murmured in the background. The clock slowly ticked away precious time.

She got up and poured two cups of coffee. She handed Walker one and he took it. Sitting again, she asked, "What's your first name?"

"Just Walker." He took a sip and leaned over, his forearms on his legs, the cup between his hands.

"Everyone has a first name."

"Not me."

She poked him in the ribs. "You're lying, Mr. Walker."

He glanced at her, trying to hide a smile. "Maybe. But you'll never know."

"Mmm."

"Listen." His eyes went to the window. "It's almost dark. Why don't you call someone to pick you up, or maybe Roger can arrange a ride."

Her eyebrow lifted again. "You're not getting rid of me. I'm sticking to you like glue."

"Yeah. I'm beginning to realize that."

A warm, welcome feeling passed between them.

"Were you raised in High Cotton?" she asked, sipping coffee.

"Yeah. Judd and I were in the same grade. We were friends and had a lot in common."

"Like what?"

"We were both raised by our fathers."

"Oh."

He could almost see the wheels turning in her head, but being a proper lady she wasn't going to ask.

He gripped the foam cup. "When I was born it was a difficult birth and my dad said my mother was never the same afterward. She'd disappear for weeks and come home as if nothing was wrong. My dad divorced her when I was eight. I never saw her again and I lost track of the number of times she was married. I met my half brother and half sister at her funeral fifteen years ago."

He'd never shared his life story, not even with Trisha, yet here he sat as if it was the most natural thing in the world.

"Is your father living?"

He swirled the dark liquid in the cup. "No. He died when Haley was three. He thought the sun rose and set on her. Georgie is named after him."

Until this moment he never realized how much he missed his dad. He could always talk to him. How he wished he was here now. Instead, Ms. Belle…

"Walker," Roger shouted.

He was on his feet like a shot.

"We found them."

"Where?" Walker placed the coffee on the desk as his insides rolled.

The deputy was talking on the phone and raised a hand. Walker tried to wait patiently, but his heart was about to pound out of his chest.

Roger slammed down the phone and handed him a piece of paper. "A truck driver just called. He picked them up here in Giddings. The older girl told him they were trying to get to their mother in Temple. Then he heard the Amber Alert on the radio and knew she was lying. He couldn't call until he reached Milano. They're at the Shell station there. Hal Tibbetts, the truck driver, said he'd hang around until someone arrived."

"All three of them are there?"

"Yep, Walker, all three of them." Relief ebbed its way through him. His kids were okay.

"Figured you'd want to be the one to pick them up."

"I'm on my way." He turned and ran into Ms. Belle. Somehow he was getting used to that. "Let's go."

"I'm right behind you."

He didn't insist she go home. It felt right having her along. Maybe a little too right.

CHAPTER SEVEN

THE SUN WAS SLOWLY SINKING in the west as they sped down U.S. 77.

"You seem to know where you're going," Maddie said. "And you're not speeding."

"I know they're safe. I just want to get to them as fast and as safely as possible. Being raised in Texas, I know all these roads. It's a straight shot on U.S. 77 to Rockdale. Milano's about eight miles from there. It's about a forty-five-minute drive."

She watched as he clenched the steering wheel with his big hands. "I may be out of line, but please be patient with them when we arrive. They're probably scared to death."

He glanced briefly at her, his eyes guarded. "You want me to be patient with Ginny?"

"I'm sure she's scared, too."

"She kidnapped my kids, and I'm not in a mood to be lenient or patient with her. She'll be lucky if I don't arrest her."

"That's going to help the situation immensely," she said, tongue in cheek.

"She didn't kidnap your kids."

"I don't have kids." At the words, she felt an ache inside but quickly ignored it.

"You know what I mean. Why are you taking up for her? She lied to you and played on your good nature."

"She's just a kid looking for a better way of life."

"You're such a patsy. You're just asking for trouble." She wasn't offended by his words, because they were playful, almost teasing. "My sisters tell me that all the time."

"They're right."

"Cait, Sky and I have different personalities."

"I don't know Sky very well, but Cait wouldn't let Ginny off easily."

"I'm just thinking about her situation and living in that awful mobile home. She's fighting to survive."

He sighed. "And she's breaking the law and taking my kids along for the ride. When we get there, Ginny's going to get a stern lecture and she's going back to High Cotton."

"Then you won't file charges against her?"

He sighed more strongly this time. "You just don't give up, do you?"

"She's a pregnant teenager."

"If she agrees to leave my daughter alone, I might agree not to file charges. I really don't think she belongs in jail."

"Now we're thinking alike."

"Heaven help me."

Despite herself, she laughed. "That's not funny."

As they rode, Maddie noticed how capable he was, handling the car with very little effort. The temperature was now in the forties, but the car was warm. Maddie felt warm and safe just being with Walker. They'd only been together a few hours, but it seemed as if they'd been together for days. And the feeling was the best thing she'd felt in a long time.

They reached U.S. 79 and Walker turned right. "We're almost there. The Shell station will be on the left."

When they reached Milano, darkness had settled in for the night. It wasn't long before they spotted the lit-up store with gas pumps. An eighteen-wheeler was pulled to the side and a man stood by it huddled in a jacket and wearing a Dallas Cowboys baseball cap. It must be the guy the woman at the bus stop saw Ginny talking to. Thank God he was a good man and not capable of taking advantage of children.

Walker stopped by him and pushed the button to roll down his window.

The man hurried over. "Are you Walker?"

"Yes." Walker got out and shook the man's hand. Maddie quickly followed. "This is Madison Belle."

"Nice to meet you, ma'am." He tipped his cap.

"I'm so glad you called," she said, shaking his hand.

"Yes," Walker added. "Thank you. I've been worried sick."

"I thought something was a little strange with the young girl's story, but I was headed to Temple so I gave them a ride before she asked some unsavory character."

"I appreciate that. Are they okay?"

"They're fine, but the boy's been crying a lot. He wants his daddy."

Walker's gut tightened. "I'll take it from here."

"I've already lost a lot of time. I need to be on my way. The young'uns are inside eating burgers."

They shook hands again. "Thank you. Do I owe you anything?"

"Not a cent. Just take care of those little ones." He tipped his cap at Maddie again. "Ma'am."

Walker looked toward the entrance to the store. People were going in and out. Maddie placed a hand on his arm and felt his taut muscles. "Just be calm."

"I was in such a hurry to find them, but now I'm not sure how to handle this situation. If it was someone else's kids, I'd know. But I don't want to drive a wedge between Haley and me."

She wrapped her arms around her waist from the chill. "Just take it slow and go with your heart on this one."

He pulled his hat low, but not before she saw his ghost of a smile. "I'm listening to a woman who's a patsy."

As Walker strolled toward the entrance, he was glad Ms. Belle was with him. He needed a woman's touch tonight. His mind rejected the notion that he meant that in every way possible. The last thing he needed was getting involved with a woman, especially a woman like Ms. Belle who believed in good, fairy tales and happily ever after. He'd left that behind a long time ago. He had to concentrate on his kids. They came first.

His thoughts came to an abrupt stop as he entered the store. The place was neat and clean. Aisles with goods were straight ahead. A man was paying a bill at the counter to the left and there was a deli area lit up with neon signs. Coolers wrapped around to the back, where he glimpsed a restroom sign. He glanced right and saw the eating area.

There they were. Haley, Georgie and Ginny sat at one of the white tables. Drinks and half-eaten burgers cluttered the small table.

He took a few steps and Georgie spotted him. "Daddy," he screamed, and jumped out of his chair and ran to Walker.

Walker grabbed him in a bear hug and held on for dear life.

Georgie's tiny arms trembled around Walker's neck. "I 'cared, Daddy."

He swallowed. "It's okay, son. I'm here."

"I wanna go home."

Walker patted Georgie's back, and he was grateful he could touch his son again. "We will, but first Daddy has to talk to Haley."

"'Kay," Georgie mumbled into his shoulder.

Walker turned Georgie's face so he could look at

him. His heart took a hit at his son's red and swollen eyes. He had to force his anger down.

He kissed Georgie's wet cheek. "Stay with Ms. Belle while I talk to Haley."

"No. No." Georgie buried his face in Walker's shoulder. "I want my daddy."

Walker rubbed his back to console him. "I'm right here and I'm not going anywhere without you, but I need to talk to your sister. Go to Ms. Belle. She'll buy you some candy."

"Candy." Georgie's head popped up. "I want candy."

Maddie held out her hands. "Come with me, then."

"But…"

"I'm right here. You can see me at all times."

He went to Maddie, his eyes on Walker.

Walker reached in his wallet and handed her a five. Their eyes met. Locked. *Be patient. Be calm.* He saw her message clearly and he banked down his anger again.

Taking a deep breath, he turned toward the girls sitting at the table. Two pair of eyes filled with fear stared at him.

Be patient. Be calm.

He walked over, picked up Georgie's jacket from the floor and took his seat. Removing his hat, he placed it on the table, taking his time, making them sweat. But he was sweating, too, searching for the right words.

"I'm sorry, Mr. Walker." Ginny spoke first.

"You should be. You took two minors and put their lives in danger." He surprised himself by his controlled tone.

"I promised Haley I'd help her get to her mother. Things just didn't go right."

He looked her straight in the eye. "I could arrest you for kidnapping."

"What?" Her face paled. "You mean, like, go to jail."

"Yes."

"But…but I…"

"I wanted to go, Daddy." Haley spoke for the first time. "I have to see Mama."

He clenched his jaw. "Do you know how worried I've been?"

"If you'd just let us go, you wouldn't have to worry about Georgie and me anymore."

Taking a long patient breath, he knew he had to do something drastic to get Haley's attention. She wouldn't listen to him, but she might listen to someone else. This called for some tough love. He reached for the cell on his waist.

He fingered the phone for a moment. "I'll make a deal with you. I'll call your aunt Doris and you can talk to her. If she'll let you stay with her, we'll catch the next flight to Lubbock. If Doris knows where your mother is, I'll take you to her. I'll do whatever it takes to see you happy again."

"Oh." The hope in her eyes twisted his gut. He knew what Doris was going to say, and it was going to break Haley's heart. But he had no other choice. Her ploy today proved that.

"But—" he held up a finger "—if Doris says no and she doesn't know where your mother is, you have to promise to settle down and give High Cotton and me a chance. You have to stop running away."

The light dimmed for a second. "I promise."

Yeah, right, he thought, but he punched out the number, praying Doris was at home. She was.

"Doris, this is Walker."

"Hi. Have you found them?"

He didn't answer because he didn't want Haley to know he'd talked to Doris. He hoped Doris caught the hint. "Haley would like to talk to you."

"Why?"

His fingers gripped the cell. "She just wants to talk."

"Give me a hint. Oh, she doesn't know we spoke earlier."

"No. Here's Haley."

He handed Haley the cell and watched her face as she spoke to her aunt. Suddenly she slammed the phone on the table and ran into the bathroom.

He stood and jammed his hands through his hair. God, he hated hurting her. Pointing a finger at Ginny, he said, "Stay right there. Don't even think about running or I will arrest you."

"Yes, sir." Ginny shifted in her seat. "Is Haley okay?"

"No, she's not, and I want you to stop giving her hope where there is none."

"What do you mean?"

"Haley's mother has run away with an old boyfriend and no one knows where she is, not even her sister. And her aunt has a house full of kids and doesn't want any more. I'm all Haley has and she has to accept that."

"I didn't know," Haley murmured.

"Haley's a kid but she wants to believe otherwise, so please stop encouraging her."

He walked off to where Ms. Belle stood with Georgie, who was stuffing gummie worms into his mouth. Juice ran down his chin. He hurried back to the table, grabbed napkins and wiped his face.

"How's Haley?" Maddie asked.

"She has a nervous stomach and I'm sure she's throwing up."

"Oh, my. That's why she's so thin."

"Haley sick," Georgie muttered, seeming very comfortable in Ms. Belle's arms.

He glanced toward the restroom. "I better check on her. Take care of Georgie and please keep an eye on Ginny. Do not let her sneak out."

"I won't."

Georgie grinned, back to his old self. "I'm good, Daddy."

"I see you are." Ms. Belle had gummie worm juice on her Carhartt jacket. Without thinking, he rubbed it with a napkin. The spot was right over her breast, and he felt that softness, that lure of something… He pulled away and headed to the counter, his emotions slipping and sliding like a bar of soap on a tiled floor. But he reined them in quickly.

"My daughter is in the bathroom," he said to the young boy at the counter. "She's sick and I'm going in to check on her."

"What? Oh. Okay, I guess."

"Could you make sure no one comes in?"

"I don't know. Like, I…"

"I'll stand watch," Maddie offered.

"Okay. Cool," the clerk replied.

Walker headed toward the small hallway that led to the restroom. There wasn't a door, just another hallway that angled into the room. Walker then tapped on the wall and called out, waiting in case someone was in there besides Haley. No one answered, so he went in. The stench reached him, but that wasn't keeping him out. Haley was sitting on the floor in a stall with the door closed.

"Haley, it's Daddy."

"Go away and leave me alone."

"That's not happening, sweetheart. Open the door."

"No. Leave me alone."

"Haley…"

"No. I want to die, so leave me alone."

He looked around and went over his options. He had to get inside and there was only one way to do that. Tight places were nothing new to him. He stepped up on the sink and then swung himself over the top of the stall and into it.

"What are you doing?" Haley's eyes looked huge in her pale face.

"You wouldn't open the door so I had to come in."

"Why can't you just leave me alone?" She buried her face on her knees.

The stall was small and he had a hard time just turning around, but he managed to ease to the floor beside her.

"What did your aunt say?" His knees pushed toward his face in the cramped space, but he tried to be the father he should be. The father he should have been years ago.

"She doesn't want me. Nobody wants me."

"I want you."

"You don't have a choice."

"Sure I do." He tried to get comfortable but found that impossible. "I could have walked away just like your mother. You and Georgie would have gone into the system, into foster care."

She raised her head. "Really?"

"Really."

Her face puckered. "Why won't you tell me where Mama is?" Tears streamed down her face and his heart contracted.

"Sweetheart, I've told you all I know. Honest. Let's go home and we'll talk. I'll try to answer all your questions."

She sniffed and stood, wiping at her eyes with the sleeve of her knit top.

He pushed to his feet as best as he could. The stall wasn't made for a big man. No matter how many ways he turned they couldn't open the door.

"We have a problem."

"You're not supposed to be in here," Haley said, and her eyes weren't so sad. "You're a man and you're too big."

"I have a plan." He smiled at her. "I'll stand on the toilet and that way you can open the door."

He placed one foot on the seat and hopped up.

Haley glanced up at him. "You look silly."

"I feel silly. Open the door so we can get out of here."

As she pulled on the door he heard a slight giggle. Maybe there was hope for them. God, he hoped so.

Outside the restroom, Maddie, Georgie and Ginny waited. Ginny ran to Haley.

"Are you okay?"

"Yeah." Haley hung her head.

"Get your coats," Walker said. "We're going to High Cotton."

"Mr. Walker, please," Ginny begged, "let me go to Temple. I can stay with a friend. Don't make me go back to that awful place."

"You're a minor. I have to take you home." He tried to remain strong. "And after what you did, you don't deserve favors." He avoided looking at Ms. Belle because he knew what he'd see.

"Yes, sir," Ginny answered, her voice subdued. She turned toward the table to get her coat. Haley followed. Georgie wiggled from Ms. Belle's arms to get his.

That left him and Ms. Belle alone.

She placed a hand on his arm and he froze. Damn, he didn't want her to touch him. He couldn't think straight when she did that. No way was she going to change his mind.

"Think about what she has to go back to."

"I told you from the start I wasn't inclined to be lenient with her. She put my kids in danger."

"She's just a teenager trying to survive. She needs understanding."

"Listen, we're not going to agree on this. Until you have children, you won't understand my point of view."

She tensed and he sensed something was wrong. Her blue eyes darkened. "I don't have to be a mother to know when a child needs help instead of brute force."

He frowned. "Brute force? I'm not using brute force on anyone."

"No, you're just a brute." With that declaration, she marched off to where the kids stood waiting.

Where the hell did that come from? He was doing the right thing. Following the law. Then why did he feel like the brute she'd called him?

CHAPTER EIGHT

MADDIE GOT INTO THE CAR seething. Why did he have to be so structured, so by-the-book? She clasped her hands and took a calming breath.

While Walker had been in the bathroom with Haley, she'd talked to Ginny and the girl had apologized, even offered to give back what she had left of the money. She wanted to keep her baby, and Maddie didn't see anything wrong with that.

Evidently Walker did. Maybe she should try to see his point of view. No. Why did she always do that? Look for the best in people. This time he was wrong, and wrong was wrong no matter how you looked at it. She was sticking to her point of view. But…no, don't do it. Walker loved his kids and… She pulled her jacket tight around her.

"Are you cold?" Walker asked, backing out of the station and turning onto the highway.

"No. I'm fine."

"I can turn up the heat."

She looked at him. "I think the heat's already turned up."

"Yeah." He didn't miss her meaning as that gorgeous ghost of a smile visited his lips. "You may not believe it, but I'm doing the right thing."

Before she could reply, Georgie said from the backseat, "I'm mad at you, Haley."

"I know," Haley replied.

"I'm staying with Daddy."

There was a long pause and then Haley said, "Me, too."

"Maybe some good has come out of this awful night," Walker whispered to her.

She hoped it had, but she couldn't stop thinking about Ginny and her life. And the life of her baby.

"Oh, oh, oooh…"

Maddie turned to Ginny in the backseat. "What's wrong?"

"My stomach is cramping."

"Are you having contractions?"

"I don't know. I…oh…oh…it hurts."

"It's wet everywhere," Haley squealed.

"Her water has broken," Maddie said to Walker. "You have to stop."

"Dammit." He pulled over to the side of the road and Maddie jumped out to check Ginny.

From the car light she could see Ginny slumped down in the seat, her hand on her stomach and her face etched in pain. "Help me, Ms. Belle, please."

Maddie stroked back a strand of Ginny's hair. "Just relax and take deep breaths. We need to get you to a hospital."

"Daddy, please help Ginny," Haley yelled.

"Daddy, I 'cared," Georgie piped up.

Walker stuck his head in from behind Maddie. "Calm down, everybody."

His face was an inch from hers, his hat brushed her hair and a tangy masculine scent filled her nostrils. Her stomach fluttered with awareness—a welcome, stimulating awareness of the opposite sex. She turned her head, as did he, and their lips were inches apart. For a man, he had beautiful lips, not thin like most men's. His lower lip was full and inviting, and she wondered what it would be like to kiss him.

"What do you think?"

His breath fanned her face, and she soaked it up like a starved woman needing a man. In a split second reality hit her in the gut like a balled fist. What had he said? Oh… "We…we need to get her to a hospital."

"Ginny gets her wish, then. Temple would have a hospital and better facilities than the small towns."

Maddie stroked Ginny's hair again. "Keep taking deep breaths and stay calm. We're going to Temple."

"Thank…thank you…Ms. Belle."

Maddie and Walker jumped into the front seat and Walker turned the car around, heading for Temple. He reached for his cell and called information for the

Scott and White Hospital. He then phoned the hospital and informed them they were coming.

As they reached Texas 36, Ginny began to scream. Gut-wrenching sounds bounced off the interior of the car.

"Ms. Belle, please…please help me. It hurts."

"I know. Just hang on."

Haley and Georgie were quiet and pale.

Suddenly, a bloodcurdling scream erupted. "Something's…happening. The…baby…is coming."

"You just think it is," Walker told Ginny. "We'll be there soon."

Another nerve-shattering scream. Maddie couldn't stand it anymore. "Pull over. We have to help her."

Walker swerved into the ditch and stopped. Maddie stepped out into the cold winter night. The moon was full and bathed them in a warm glow. Walker got his kids out and Ginny lay down on the seat.

"Oh, no. It's coming. I feel it," Ginny said.

"Do you know anything about delivering babies?" Walker asked from behind her.

"Absolutely nothing. I'm scared for her."

"There are blankets in the trunk. Get them and wrap my kids up so they're warm and keep them far away. I'll need a blanket and I'll call the hospital for instructions."

Maddie was on autopilot, taking the keys, opening the truck and searching for blankets. She carried one to Walker and hurried to Haley and Georgie, who were standing in the dried grass of the ditch, looking scared. She guided them some distance away, sat them down and wrapped a blanket snugly around their cold bodies.

"Stay right here. I'm going to check on Ginny."

"Ms. Belle. Is…is…" Haley was trembling, so she couldn't get the words out.

Maddie tucked the blanket tighter. "She's having the baby. Take care of your brother. I'll be right back."

As she reached the car, she heard Ginny screaming, "I want Ms. Belle."

"Madison," Walker shouted.

Finally, he knew her name.

She stuck her head in. "What can I do?"

Walker was kneeling on the edge of the seat and Ginny was sprawled, her legs apart with a blanket beneath her.

"She has to take off her jeans and panties and she won't do it."

"I want Ms. Belle."

Maddie crawled in on the floorboard. "Come on, Ginny. We have to remove your clothes."

"It's embarrassing and I…this can't be happening."

"Well, it is, and Walker is here to help you. Let's get rid of your jeans."

Her denim jeans were wet, and she and Walker tugged and pulled until they were off. The panties were next. Maddie removed the Windbreaker, but let Ginny keep on her T-shirt.

"It's dark so don't even think about it." Maddie

tried to make Ginny feel comfortable. "Just concentrate on the baby."

Walker had the cell to his ear. "The ambulance is on the way."

"Stay with me, please, Ms. Belle." A scream followed the words as Ginny arched her back.

Maddie stroked Ginny's face. "I will." She glanced at Walker through the darkness. "Can you see?"

"Just enough. I see the head," he shouted. "Damn. This baby is coming—now."

"Help me. I can't do this."

"Stay calm." Maddie gripped Ginny's hand.

"I can't…it's too painful. Do something."

"Ginny, listen to me. This is part of being pregnant, so grit your teeth and bear it. It's time to grow up. You're fixing to be a mother."

A tear slipped from Ginny's eye as cars whizzed by on the highway and lights flashed inside every now and then, offering some illumination. Ginny continued to scream and push.

"Come on, just one more push and the baby will be here. Come on. You can do it." Walker kept coaxing as he talked to the person on the phone.

Ginny groaned and moaned and Maddie's hand grew numb from the girl's grip.

"It's coming, coming and…and there it is," Walker said as he reached for the baby as it slid out.

"It's a girl. I need something to wrap her in."

Maddie grabbed Ginny's backpack from the floor and pulled out a small multicolored blanket.

"That's for the baby," Ginny said, her voice weak.

Walker gently wrapped the bloodied baby, the umbilical cord still attached, and placed her on Ginny's chest. A siren echoed in the distance.

"She's beautiful," Maddie said, and used a blouse to mop Ginny's forehead.

"I have a baby and…"

The lights of the ambulance flashed on the car, and in a second several paramedics gathered round. Maddie slid out and her legs buckled. Walker caught her and she leaned on him.

"The baby's not crying," she whispered for his ears only.

"I know. The medic is clearing her throat."

She reached for Walker's hand and he gripped it with cold, steellike fingers. Suddenly a wail pierced the silence.

"She's okay," Maddie cried, and reached up and hugged Walker. Everything faded away as the night wrapped around them and he hugged her back. His hard, muscled body pressed into her and she soaked up every nuance of this strong man.

"Daddy."

Walker let her go as Haley walked up carrying a sleeping Georgie.

He gathered his son into his arms. "Everything's

okay, sweetheart. Ginny had the baby and the ambulance is taking her to Temple. You can say goodbye."

Haley walked to the stretcher. "Bye," she said in a sad tone, staring at the baby in Ginny's arms.

"Bye, Haley, Georgie, Mr. Walker and Ms. Belle. Thank you."

"We have to go," the paramedic said.

They rolled the stretcher into the ambulance, and with lights flashing and siren blaring, they sped away.

Silence replaced the sirens. Cars kept whizzing by, but they hardly noticed. They were spellbound by the events of the night—the birth of a new life.

"Time to go home," Walker finally said. "We have to sit in the front. The backseat is a mess."

Haley crawled in and Walker placed Georgie in her arms.

Maddie hesitated. Oh, she hated this part of her nature. She just couldn't walk away and leave Ginny alone. And Haley needed to see her friend was fine. How did she get that across to Walker?

She moved to where he was standing at the back of the car. "Don't you think it would be best to go to Temple to check on Ginny?"

"No." He swiped his hat from the ground. "She has friends and I'm sure she will call them. I'm taking my kids home and putting them to bed. They've been through enough tonight."

"But Haley needs to see her friend is okay."

"Haley needs to go home."

"You know, sometimes you can be a stubborn ass—an unfeeling stubborn ass."

"Listen, you've been on my case since I've met you. I said something about you looking as young as my daughter and you got your nose bent out of joint. Hell, I thought women wanted to look young."

"Maybe I didn't want you to see me as a girl, but as a woman." Cheeks flaming, she marched to the car and squeezed in beside Haley and Georgie, which was a feat, since they had to sit on one seat.

Walker jammed his hat on his head. What the hell did *that* mean? He didn't care. He just wanted to take his kids home.

The lady was starting to get to him. Why couldn't she see that the world wasn't all lily-white? Oh, no, everything to her had to have a happy ending. Ginny Grubbs was another statistic of teenage pregnancy. There was no happy ending for her. She would now become dependent on the government for her livelihood and she would milk it for all it's worth. That's the way it worked for girls like Ginny.

God, when did he get so cynical, stubborn and narrow-minded? Maybe when Ms. Belle made him so aware of his faults.

See her as a woman? How else would he see her?

He got into the car. Ms. Belle was holding Georgie and he was asleep in her arms. Haley leaned into her, almost asleep. It was against the law for them to ride like that and he worried about their safety.

"Can you buckle up, please?"

She shot him a thousand-watt glare. "Are you serious?"

"Yes."

"Good grief." She struggled with the belt, and he reached over and looped it around all three of them. The glare didn't change. He was getting sunburned.

His hand hovered over the ignition. God help him. No! No! But he was powerless to stop the words forming in his throat. "Haley, would you like to go see Ginny?"

She lifted her head. "Oh, Daddy, could we?" The excitement in her voice told its own story. Maddie was right. He was wrong. Glancing at her, he caught that gleam in her eyes.

Dammit. She knew.

GEORGIE WAS OUT FOR THE NIGHT, so Walker carried him as they went into the emergency room. In the bright light he could see that he and Maddie had blood all over them. He'd worry about that later. Maddie sat with the kids while he went to check on Ginny and to wash his hands. He was told Ginny was being attended to, so he went to wait with Maddie and the kids.

As he relayed the message to Maddie, he gathered his son into his arms. Taking a seat, he added, "I really need to get my kids to bed."

"Just let Haley see her and then we'll go."

He looked at her and quickly glanced away. She was so damn sincere that she was making inroads into a resolve he'd mastered over the years—don't get emotionally involved.

"Mr. Walker." A nurse appeared with a clipboard in her hand.

"That's me," he said, and the nurse came over.

"Are you the responsible party for Ginny Grubbs?"

"No, I'm not. She just happened to be in my car when she gave birth. She's a friend of my daughter's."

"Oh." She scribbled something on the board. "She has no insurance and we can't keep her."

"That's insane. She just gave birth." Maddie was on her feet, ready for battle. Walker felt sorry for the nurse.

"I'm sorry, but that's our policy. We'll keep her overnight, but she has to leave in the morning."

"Surely there are programs to help her."

"I'll notify Child Protective Services. That's all I can do." The nurse hurried away before Maddie could get in another round.

"That's ludicrous."

"That's the real world," Walker told her. He stood. "CPS will handle it. Now, let's go home."

Maddie placed her hands on her hips. "You're not serious."

"Yes. I am."

"Well, tough. We're not going home. Ginny needs our help and we're going to give it to her."

"Now…"

"We are." Her blue eyes bored into him like a chisel, chipping away at his steely resolve.

"Daddy, please," Haley begged.

Now he had both of them on his case. This just wasn't his night.

"I'm sure you know people you can call who can place her somewhere. There are programs in Philly and there has to be some in Texas." Maddie kept up the pressure. As a man who always knew when he was beaten, he gave in.

"I'll make some calls, but I have to get Georgie to bed first."

"I'll hold him," Maddie offered.

"We'll get a motel room for the night, but in the morning, after we get Ginny settled, we're going home. Am I clear?"

She had the nerve to smile. "As a bell."

He lifted his eyebrow at that.

WALKER FOUND A MOTEL not far from the hospital. He paid for two connecting rooms. Maddie and Haley had one and he and Georgie took the other. He removed Georgie's clothes, leaving on his underwear and T-shirt, and tucked him under the covers.

Haley came into his room. "Daddy."

"What, sweetheart?"

"I'm sorry."

He turned to her. "I know. We'll talk when we get home. Get some sleep. I'm not mad at you."

Her face lit up. "Night."

He wanted to hold her and reassure her, but he refrained. Tonight was a step forward. They were making progress.

He took a quick shower, then dressed in his same clothes, but he felt less grimy. He had to get the car cleaned before morning. Slipping on his boots, he glanced at Georgie and saw he was out.

He tapped on the connecting door. No response. He opened it slightly and peered in. Haley was asleep in the bed. Where was Maddie? He saw the light beneath the bathroom door and knocked lightly. No response. He waited and knocked again. Still nothing. Had she fallen asleep in the tub or something?

Opening the door, he just stared. She stood there naked, towel-drying her hair. Her body was smooth, curvy and better than anything he'd ever seen in the Victoria's Secret catalogs Trisha had around the house.

At that moment, she glanced up. Her face was suffused with color. "Oh, oh…" She danced around, trying to arrange the towel in front of her. "What are you doing?"

"I…I…" he stammered, feeling like a fool. "I knocked, but you didn't answer. I wanted to tell you I'm going to get the car cleaned out. Please watch the kids."

"Oh…oh. Okay." She clutched the towel tighter.

But he didn't move. He couldn't stop staring at her. With her disheveled hair she looked sexy, beguiling, alluring, and his body was reacting accordingly.

"You're staring," she said in a breathless voice.

"It's hard not to."

"Try."

"I'd rather not." He knew he was grinning.

She took a couple of steps and slammed the door in his face. It was as effective as an icy-cold shower.

But he certainly saw her as a woman.

CHAPTER NINE

MADDIE SANK TO THE FLOOR and threw the towel over her head, letting her body heat evaporate from Walker's gaze. That might take a while, though. She was sure her skin was pink with embarrassment. But she wasn't looking. The tingles shooting through her told her enough.

She liked the way his eyes turned black as he gazed at her body. If she was a bad girl, she would have pulled him into the bathroom instead of closing the door. They could have steamed up the mirror with hot, passionate kisses and maybe more. Cait would have. Sky wouldn't have even hesitated. Maybe she was Betty Crocker sweet as her sisters called her.

Being bad required a lot more experience than she had. She removed the towel and blew out a breath. Her Christian upbringing was really ingrained in her. Maybe being bad wasn't in her. But when Walker looked at her, she felt more than bad. She felt wanton.

Pushing to her feet, she reached for her panties and put them on. Her T-shirt was all she had to sleep in, so she slipped it over her head and walked into the bedroom.

Haley was asleep. She tiptoed in to check on Georgie. He was, too. It had been a rough night for all of them. Crawling beneath the covers, she got comfy, but all she could see and feel were dark caramel eyes.

Haley stirred. "Ms. Belle?"

"Yes."

"Is Ginny going to get to keep her baby?"

She turned to face the girl. "I really hope so."

"But…"

"Don't worry. In the morning we'll see what we can do for Ginny."

"Ms. Belle…"

"Please, call me Maddie."

"Okay, Maddie. Thank you for standing up to Daddy. Nobody does that. He's like Rambo."

"He's tough, but I'm tough, too."

"Yeah." Haley curled into a ball. "Women can be tough."

"Yes, but don't expect me to leap tall buildings in a single bound."

Haley giggled. "Just Daddy."

"Mmm."

Haley drifted off and Maddie stared at the ceiling for a long time. What was she doing here instead of home running High Five? Darn! Darn! She'd forgotten to call Cait.

She slipped from the bed, picked up her purse and

went into the bathroom. The call was short. She just wanted Cait to know what had happened and that she'd be home tomorrow. From Cait's response, she got the impression Cait thought she'd lost her mind.

Maybe she had.

Or maybe she'd stepped out of that predictable mode and was taking chances. Maybe even being a little bad.

She could only hope. A smile played across her lips as she tiptoed to the bed. Closing her eyes, she saw a ghost of a smile and passionate caramel eyes. Sleep had never been this good.

TWO HOURS LATER WALKER WAS back. Everyone was asleep and he was dog tired. He felt as if he'd been on an all-night stakeout. One glance at Ms. Belle's blond hair against the pillow revived him instantly.

How could one woman turn his whole life upside down and sideways? He'd been out of the dating game too long. But back then women like her weren't on his radar screen. She was sweet, nice and known as a good girl. Girls like her made life a living hell for guys like him.

Maybe that's why he fell for Trisha. They understood each other and wanted the same things. Or so he'd thought. All the times he'd been away from home, he'd remained faithful to her. He didn't do the cheating thing. Obviously she didn't have the same principles.

Looking back, he could see they'd fallen out of love a long time ago. He enjoyed law enforcement. She hated it and bitched all the time. That was the beginning of the deterioration of their relationship. She wanted him to be a nine-to-five man in an office. He couldn't handle that. He liked action.

His unwillingness to give in had been the final straw. A gulf had formed between them, but they still stayed together—for the kids. And that turned into a disaster.

Now he was paying for his selfishness. His kids were, too. Damn, it sucked that he'd failed as a father and as a husband.

He stared at Ms. Belle a moment longer before going back to his room. The sooner he returned her to High Five, the better. She made him forget rules and principles. She just made him want her. And that wasn't happening. He was thinking about his kids this time and not himself.

As he eased in beside Georgie and closed his eyes, all he could see was her nude body. This was not going to be a good night.

WHEN MADDIE WOKE UP, everything was quiet. Traffic hummed outside and daybreak wasn't far away. Had Walker come back? She hadn't heard him.

She slipped out of bed and made her way quietly to the other room. His bathroom light was on, so she could see. She stopped short in the doorway.

Walker was on his cell, talking, with his shirt

opened and his jeans unbuttoned. His boots sat by the bed. Not an ounce of flab was visible on his broad chest. Tiny swirls of brown hairs arrowed into his jeans. Her stomach fluttered uncontrollably and she started to back out.

He noticed her and clicked off. Their eyes met, and then he glanced from her feet to her legs, then to her hips and finally up to her breasts beneath the T-shirt.

Self-consciously, she tugged the shirt lower. "You're staring."

His eyebrow lifted. "So were you."

She felt a flush as it stained her cheeks.

"Daddy," Georgie murmured sleepily.

Walker turned to his son and gathered him out of the bed. Georgie rubbed his eyes and looked around the room.

"Where are we?"

"In a motel," Walker told him. "Ginny had her baby, and this morning we're going to go see her and then go home." His eyes dared her to dispute that.

"Oh." Georgie twisted his hands and then looked at her. "Ms. Belle's got no clothes on."

"We were just talking about that," Walker said with a smirk.

"I'm just…going…to…change…" Face red, she backed away.

"I put toothpaste, deodorant and other things you might need in your bathroom," Walker called.

"Thanks."

Maddie quickly dressed before she made a complete fool of herself. She was grateful for the toothpaste and hairbrush. Walker could really be thoughtful. As she brushed her hair, she wondered what had happened between him and his ex. But that was really none of her business, as she was sure he would tell her.

Thirty minutes later, they sat in a diner eating breakfast. Since they hadn't eaten the night before, they were hungry. They all had pancakes and sausages except Walker. He had eggs and bacon.

Haley picked at hers.

Walker watched his daughter. "Sweetheart, you can eat pancakes. They don't upset your stomach."

"I'm not hungry." She laid her fork down.

"Sweetheart, please eat."

Maddie's heart twisted at the pain in his voice. It was obvious he didn't know how to help his daughter.

She drew upon her time at the hospital. Children were all different, but usually they had something that sparked their interest. Haley's was Ginny keeping her baby.

Leaning over, she whispered in Haley's ear, "If you eat, I'll kick Rambo's butt today."

Haley smiled—a big smile—and picked up her fork.

Walker frowned. "What did you tell her?"

Maddie wagged a finger at him. "Oh, no. That's our secret, right, Haley?"

"Right." Haley stuffed a bite of pancake into her mouth.

Georgie had syrup running down his chin, and

Walker had to attend to him. He didn't ask again, but she caught him staring at her a time or two.

After breakfast, they made their way to the hospital. Georgie ran ahead and Haley hurried to catch him.

"Did you find out about any programs that might help Ginny?"

"Yes, Ms. Belle…"

"Maddie, please. When you've seen someone naked, you have to call them by their first name. It's a rule, and you're big on rules."

"Didn't know that." She heard a smile in his voice.

"It's a fact."

Haley held the door open and they walked through to the hospital.

"Well, Maddie, I talked to an old friend in Houston, a CPS worker. She contacted someone here and we're supposed to meet her in the lobby at nine."

"That's wonderful." She couldn't hide her joy.

"You better wait until you hear what she has to say. Usually these homes have a long waiting list."

"But you can pull some strings?"

"Haley," Walker called and the girl ran back. "There's a fish tank around the corner. Take Georgie there while we talk to the CPS lady and don't let him get away."

"I won't, Daddy."

"You didn't answer my question."

Walker glanced at his watch. "Let's sit over here. It's almost nine."

They sat by windows looking out to the parking lot.

The lobby was almost empty, just people hurrying to make their appointments.

She placed her purse on the floor. The temperature was in the high sixties today, so she didn't wear her jacket. It was stained, anyway.

"I can't pull strings. We'll just have to wait and see what the woman says."

"Would you if you could?"

He adjusted his hat. "That might take a bribe."

"Like what?"

"Like another preview in nothing but a towel." He cocked an eyebrow, the gesture loaded with meaning.

She slapped his arm. "Don't be ridiculous."

"I'm not," he said, deadpan.

"First of all, you should apologize for invading my privacy."

"I'd be lying if I said I was sorry."

She shook her head. "You're hopeless."

"No. Just haven't seen a naked woman in a while." His lips quivered with amusement.

"Will you stop. I was embarrassed."

"I know. You blush beautifully."

She settled back in her chair before she blushed again. It was easy to talk to him and her embarrassment soon left.

A tall, thin woman carrying a briefcase walked up. "Mr. Walker?"

"Yes, ma'am." Walker stood and shook the woman's hand. "And this is Madison Belle."

"I'm Reba Sims. Jennifer Haver phoned about a girl—" she looked down at a notebook in her hand "—Ginny Grubbs."

"Yes. She's sixteen and had a baby last night in the back of my car."

Ms. Sims took a seat, juggling purse, briefcase and notebook. They sat, too, one on each side of the woman.

"Are you related to the girl?"

"No, she's a friend of my daughter."

"Where're her parents?"

"In High Cotton, and they've basically washed their hands of her. Her father wants to give the baby away, and I'm guessing he's hoping to receive some compensation for that. Ginny wants her baby."

"I see." Ms. Sims scribbled notes.

Maddie couldn't stay quiet. "They live in deplorable conditions, and Ginny's just trying to get out and keep her child."

Ms. Sims straightened her glasses. "Are you related to her?"

"No. She's all alone."

"I oversee a home for unwed mothers outside of Round Rock. We take mothers with babies, too, but we don't have any vacancies. We screen these girls to see if they will fit into our program."

"What type of program is it?"

"We offer the girls a home and a job. We have a restaurant and a laundry where the girls work. They have to get assistance from the government, which goes to the home. We help them get their GED and teach them a skill so they can support themselves and their child. We have very strict rules."

"What kind of rules?" Maddie asked.

"No drugs, no drinking, no smoking, no dating. Most of all, good behavior. The girls are there to learn to take care of themselves. After six months we reevaluate them to see if they're ready to leave."

"How long can they stay?"

"Depends on their age. We have a fourteen-year-old who's been with us three years. She'll turn eighteen soon and she's ready for the outside world."

"Oh, my." Maddie couldn't even fathom a fourteen-year-old having a child, but she had seen it in Philly.

"Ginny needs a place now, Ms. Sims," Walker said.

"That's out of the question. We don't have room, and the paperwork will take some time. We have to know she's sincere and willing to work. Most girls don't like that and they leave quickly."

"Ginny'll do anything to keep her baby," Maddie assured her.

"I wish I could help, but I can't."

Walker rubbed his hands together. "Ms. Sims, why are you here if there's not the slightest possibility Ginny can get in?"

"I thought you might want to put her on the waiting list."

"But didn't Jennifer tell you we need something now?"

"Yes." Ms Sims fiddled with the notepad.

Walker mouthed "money" behind the woman's back.

Money? The woman wanted money? Everything in Maddie protested that.

She cleared her throat. "Ms. Sims, how does one get in immediately? And be honest."

"We have a very good reputation. That's why our list is so long. We make an exception if a donation is made. The economy is so bad, and we're struggling to help these girls and keep the home open."

"Oh."

"Why don't *you* take the young girl in?" Ms. Sims asked Maddie.

"I live in Philadelphia and I'm only here for a short while. Ginny needs a stable home."

Walker pulled a check from his wallet. "Do you have a pen?" he asked Ms. Sims.

She dug in her purse and handed him one.

What was he doing? Was he...?

He filled in the check and handed it to the woman. "Will this get Ginny a room?"

Maddie glanced over the woman's shoulder at the check. Five thousand dollars!

"Yes, sir. This will get Ginny a room, but we still have to do the paperwork."

"I'm sure you can breeze through that—by noon."

"Yes, sir. I'll go up and visit with the young lady now."

Ms. Sims gathered her things.

"Wait a minute." Maddie wasn't satisfied. This just seemed unethical and underhanded. "If you have no vacancies, where will you put Ginny?"

"I live on the premises and have a two-bedroom apartment. Ginny will have my spare room until a room on the floor becomes available."

"Oh." Maybe the woman was sincere and cared about the girls.

"Ms. Sims," Walker said. "Jennifer said this place is aboveboard and I'm taking her word on that, but I will be visiting and it had better live up to its reputation or I will close it down."

"You can visit anytime and see the good work we do. I apologize for taking the money, but I'll do just about anything to see these girls get help." She paused for a second. "I was once one of them." She strolled off down the hall.

Walker and Maddie stared at each other. She smiled. "You're just a softie in a big old wolf's clothing." She tapped her cheek with her forefinger. "Too bad I don't have a towel."

At one o'clock the paperwork was finalized and Ginny and baby were ready to go. The nurse pushed Ginny's wheelchair and they followed it out of the hospital to Ms. Sims's car.

Walker kept thinking he'd lost his mind. What had possessed him to give that much money to ensure Ginny a spot? For his daughter. This was a step in rebuilding their relationship. And, of course, Maddie had a lot to do with it, too. Maybe some of her good was rubbing off on him. Or maybe *she* was rubbing off on him.

CHAPTER TEN

GEORGIE CHATTERED MOST OF THE WAY home. He was mad at Haley, particularly because she'd forgotten his stuffed Curious George when they'd run away, and he wanted her to know it.

"George misses me," he told her. "I'm not going with you anymore."

"You've said that about ten times, Georgie." Haley was getting angry.

"You bad," Georgie kept on.

Maddie waited for Walker to put a stop to the bickering, but he didn't.

"But I love you, Georgie," Haley said, a slight quiver in her voice.

"I love you, too."

Then they were hugging.

Walker glanced at her. "That's the way they fight. The *L* word melts Georgie like a Popsicle in the Texas sun."

Was Walker the same way?

Maddie turned toward the backseat. Haley had her

arm around Georgie and her head rested on his shoulder. They were drifting off to sleep.

"They're worn out," she said.

"Mmm. This has been tiring for all of us."

Walker turned off Texas 36 and Maddie just had to ask, "Why did you pay the money to get Ginny in the home?"

"If I hadn't, I would have had to bring her back to High Cotton and Earl. That baby deserves better than that."

"Mr. Go-by-the-Book relented and did a nice thing. It made me very happy."

He looked at her, a gleam in his eyes. "For five thousand I get to see the towel thing how many times? Quite a number by my calculations."

"There's not going to be a *towel thing* again." She ruined the stern declaration by smiling.

"A pity." His hands tightened on the steering wheel. "But you're right. A woman who looks at the world through rose-colored glasses is not my type."

"I do not."

His eyes opened wide in dispute.

"Oh, okay, maybe a little."

"A lot. No one else would have given Ginny Grubbs a second chance. She tricked you, lied to you, and still you fought for her."

"I want that baby to have the best start possible."

"Jennifer said the rules are strict, and if the girls break one, they're gone. The home is only for girls who want help."

"Ginny will behave. She won't break the rules."

"You hardly know her."

"It's something I feel." Maddie stared at the cars whipping by on the sunny afternoon as they traveled toward home.

"Mmm" was his response.

They didn't say anything for a couple of miles. She kept thinking about what he'd said—*not my type.* Who was his type? Don't go there, she told herself. It was nice flirting with him, but her life was very precarious. If the cancer came back...

"How did you get Haley to eat her pancakes?" he asked, breaking into her haunting thoughts.

"Oh, that was easy. The night before she thanked me for standing up to you. She said you're like Rambo and no one does that."

He moved restlessly. "She thinks I'm a troubled man?"

"I believe she thinks you're strong and don't back down from anything."

"Mmm." His brow creased in thought.

"Haley was worried about Ginny, so I told her if she ate I would kick Rambo's butt to ensure Ginny kept her baby."

He grunted, but his forehead relaxed.

"Will Haley be okay?"

"I don't know. I'm hoping she'll trust me and settle down."

"Have you taken her to a doctor for her nervous stomach?"

"Yes, numerous times. The doctors have run every test imaginable, and they've concluded it's from stress. When she gets upset, it's worse. We watch her diet closely. Spicy and acidic foods make it worse, too. She can tolerate meat if it's not real greasy. Since the divorce she seems to be wasting away in front of my eyes. Most everything she eats comes back up."

"Then you have to find a way to keep her stress-free."

"Don't you think I've tried?" he snapped, and she knew Haley's problem was a touchy subject. His hands tightened again on the steering wheel. "Sometimes life isn't easy."

"I'm aware of that."

He glanced at her. "It's well known that Dane Belle spoiled his beautiful daughters. Even though your parents were divorced, I doubt if there was anything in life you wanted that you didn't get."

Except one thing.

A huge pain balled up like a fist in her stomach. She drew in a deep breath and looked up. They were crossing the cattle guard to High Five.

"You don't know me well enough to say that."

"No, I don't," he admitted. "But my daughter is my business."

"You've mentioned that a time or two."

He pulled into the driveway at the house and she

reached for her purse. "We're ending this trip just like we started."

"How's that?"

"You being an ass and me wanting to smack you." On that, she opened her door and glanced in the backseat. "Bye, Haley, Georgie."

Georgie blinked and looked around. "I wanna a cookie." Evidently he remembered the last time he'd been here.

"We have cookies at home, son," Walker replied.

She closed the door, walked toward the house and forced herself not to look back. Goodbye to you, too, Mr. Know-Everything Walker.

You don't know me.

As the car drove away, she stopped. Her companion, loneliness, returned, filling every corner of her aching heart. For the past twenty-four hours she hadn't felt alone. She'd felt needed.

Now she was back to the same ol' same ol'.

Predictable Maddie.

MADDIE STOPPED SHORT in the parlor doorway. Cait and Gran were in tutus, very old tutus with stiff skirts that fell to midcalf. Gran had most definitely been in her trunk from Broadway again.

As a young girl, Gran's father had sent her to New York to train to become an actress and dancer. It was Gran's dream, but a man named Bartholomew Belle derailed it.

Gran gave up her dream for love, but that year in New York left an indelible impression. Play-acting was Gran's favorite pastime.

The two women were bent over, their hands on the floor, butts in the air.

Maddie cleared her throat. Cait jerked up and straightened with a wince.

"Having fun?" Maddie asked with a grin.

"Gran said we needed some exercise, and, of course, she had just the thing in her trunk for us to dance in—" she held out the stiff cotton skirt "—tutus from the forties."

"Don't make fun, baby," Gran said, still in the bent-over position. "I danced *Giselle* in this tutu."

Cait's black hair was in a bouncy ponytail. She'd had it cut after her marriage. Maddie surveyed her sister in the outdated costume.

"I need a camera."

"Oh, no, you don't." Cait grabbed her arm as she headed for the study.

"Someone help me, please," Gran called.

They both ran to her.

"I can't get up."

They each took an arm and helped her stand up straight.

"Oh, my." Gran wiped her brow. "I used to do these exercises all day."

They guided her to the sofa. "You were younger then, Gran," Cait said.

Gran's eyes narrowed. "Are you saying I'm old?"

Cait kissed her cheek. "You'll never be old. You're ageless."

"Yes, I am." Gran stroked the skirt. "Your grandfather used to love me in this. He used to love to dance, too. Sometimes we'd dance until the wee hours." She stretched out on the sofa. "I'll rest for a bit and then we'll start again."

"Gran, I have a husband waiting. I have to go."

Gran waved a hand. "Go. Go. You don't have to watch over me like a mother hen."

"Yes, Gran." Cait kissed her again. "See you tomorrow."

Cait pulled Maddie toward the stairs. "You may have to pry me out of this thing."

"Why don't you let Judd do that?"

"Not on your life." Cait opened the door to her old bedroom. "He'd laugh himself silly." Cait pulled at the tutu. "Gran must have been a tiny, tiny woman back then because this thing is cutting off circulation in some vital areas."

Maddie laughed and helped her sister out of the tutu. Cait quickly dressed in her jeans.

Slipping on her boots, Cait asked, "So what's up with you and Walker?"

"Nothing." She kept her voice neutral.

Cait stopped pulling on a boot and looked at her. "Oh, please, I'm not Gran."

"I helped him find his kids and we did. Ginny

Grubbs had her baby in the backseat of his car, so it's been a very stressful night."

"Wow. Where's Ginny now?"

"We found a home for her."

"That quick?"

"Yes. Now she has a chance and so does her baby."

Cait watched her for a moment. "You know, if you had worked it right, she would have given you that baby."

Maddie bristled. "I don't want her baby. She needs to raise her own child."

"Oh, Maddie." Cait stood and hugged her. "Any other woman would have worked it to her advantage."

"I couldn't do that."

"I know." Cait stuffed her shirt into her jeans. "You're one in a million."

Maddie thought for a minute. "Not a million, I'm sure." She was sure there were a lot of barren women in the world, but sometimes it felt as if she was the only one.

"That's not what I meant." Cait grabbed her belt. "How did you and Walker get along?"

"Like oil and water. He's so…ah…"

"That bad, huh?"

"He's strict and structured. At times I didn't know whether to smack him or to kiss him."

"When in doubt, always do the kissing."

"I'll try to remember that."

Cait reached for her purse. "Walker's a really nice man who's been dealt a bad blow."

"His ex must have been something."

"Yes. He could use a little of Maddie's magic."

She scrunched up her face. "I don't think he wants Maddie's magic."

"Oh, you can fix that. Call Sky. She'll give you some pointers."

"Ple-ease. I don't need pointers."

Cait looked up. "Okay. Now I have to run. I can't wait to see Judd. We'll probably skip supper tonight." Smiling, Cait picked up the tutu and shoved it into Maddie's hands. "Your turn."

"Oh, no…" But her sister was gone.

Maddie sank onto the bed, thinking about the towel incident. Where would she be now if she had pulled Walker into the bathroom? Probably right here wondering how she could have been so foolish. The double standard was ripping her in two.

Walker wasn't in love with her. He might desire her… She stopped her thoughts. She'd been with the man twenty-four hours and most of the time they'd argued. Springing to her feet, she marched toward the door and headed for the barn. Work would get her mind on other things.

SOLOMON MET HER BEFORE she reached the barn. She rubbed his face and led him to the corral for feed.

"Hey, you're back," Cooper said, coming out of the barn.

"Yeah. I'm just going to feed Solomon."

"I did that about an hour ago."

"Well, then. He's not getting any more." Maddie stroked the bull's neck. "How are things around here?"

"Fine. All the cows fixing to calve are in the pen. Rufus and I are checking the herds regularly. Last night the dogs got one of Mr. Carter's calves. Everyone is keeping a lookout for them."

"I guess that's all we can do."

Cooper removed his hat and gazed into the afternoon sun. "I was thinking in January we could cultivate that piece of land on the west we're not using. Come spring we could plant corn and sell it or have it ground for feed."

"Did you talk to Cait?"

"No. I thought it would be your decision."

"Well, dang, Coop. You see me as the boss."

He settled his hat on his head. "Yes, ma'am, I sure do."

She leaned in and whispered, "I don't know a thing about planting corn."

"You're in luck. I do."

"Thought you might. If it will cut back on expenses, I'm all for it. But first, let's work up an estimate of what it will cost versus the benefits to the ranch."

"Damn, gotta love a woman with a brain."

"Ah, shucks, you gonna make me blush."

He grinned. But Cooper's smile wasn't the one she was beginning to love.

LATER THAT EVENING, MADDIE WAS wondering how to get the blood off her jacket. She showed it to Etta.

"Put some hydrogen peroxide on it, and then we'll wash it and see what happens."

Maddie checked the pockets before tossing it into the washing machine. She found the change from the five Walker had given her to buy Georgie candy. She'd forgotten to give it back.

She thought about it for a minute. "Etta, I have to go out for a little while. Can you please stay with Gran?"

"Sure. We'll watch a movie, but I'm not putting on one of those ancient tutus. I draw the line at that."

"You don't have to worry. Gran is worn out."

She dashed upstairs, showered and changed into clean jeans and a black pullover sweater. She had no idea why she was going to Walker's, but at least she had an excuse. One minute she was mad at him and the next...

Only one problem remained. Where did he live? That was easily solved by asking Etta. She knew everyone in High Cotton.

MADDIE HAD NO PROBLEM finding Walker's house. It was around the corner from the general store, and his car was parked in front of the garage. The house was very similar to the house at High Five—same half Doric columns with a wraparound porch. Walker's ancestors had been here forever, too.

She parked in front and went up the steps. Tentatively she knocked.

A TV blared inside, but no one came to the door at first. Then slowly it opened. Georgie stood there in his underwear and socks, Curious George clutched in one arm.

"Hi, Georgie."

He raised a hand. "Hi."

"Is your father home?"

"Yeah. Haley's locked in her room and Daddy's trying to get her out."

Before she could say anything else, Walker called, "Georgie, who's at the door?"

"Maddie. And she's got clothes on."

She was glad of the darkness. The blush that warmed her cheeks was unnoticeable. Hopefully.

Walker immediately appeared and he was frowning. "Maddie!" She thought of just backing away, but that was silly.

Luckily he noticed his son. "Georgie, where're your clothes?"

Georgie pointed to the TV where they lay in a heap.

"Why did you take them off?"

"I'm hot."

The phone rang, interrupting this discussion. Walker reached for it and she stood there feeling foolish.

Georgie looked up at her. "Wanna come in?"

She stepped in and closed the door.

"I'm gonna watch TV." Georgie went back to his spot in front of the set.

She took in the room. It was functional, Maddie

noted. Besides the large TV, there was a bookshelf with an assortment of movies, a sofa, a recliner, some odd tables and an area rug covering hardwood floors. An old piano stood in one corner. No curtains, just blinds. No flowers, no frills, nothing feminine. A man's room, a man's home.

"I'll be right there," Walker said, and hung up. He ran both hands through his hair.

"Is something wrong?"

"I have to go on a call. Haley's locked in her room and I'm at a loss as to how to reach her."

Maddie sat her purse in a chair. "Go on your call. I'll watch the kids and try to get Haley out of her room. I owe you a favor."

"You'd do that for a stubborn ass?" That light in his eye was making her dizzy.

"Yes" came out all squeaky.

He reached for his hat. "I'll make it short. Georgie, Maddie's staying with you for a bit. Behave and put on your clothes."

"'Kay."

Walker paused at the door, his eyes holding hers. "This doesn't cover the bribe. That involves a towel and nothing else."

CHAPTER ELEVEN

MADDIE FELT THE WARMTH in her cheeks, and she knew why she was here. Walker irritated and annoyed her, but she was attracted to him. On their quest to find the kids, she'd seen a different side of him, a side he rarely showed: his soft, compassionate nature. It was evident in the way he loved his kids and would do anything for them, even making sure Ginny had a fair chance at life.

Of course, she might be looking at him through rose-colored glasses, as he'd accused her. But that was okay. She was stepping out of her cautious world. Predictable Maddie would not be here. Predictable Maddie did not take risks.

She noticed Georgie staring at her.

"Where's Haley's room?" she asked.

He pointed to the stairs leading to the top floor. "I show you," he said, darting for the stairs with his Curious George and a blanket in tow.

She trailed after him. With the blanket, he reminded her of Linus from the *Peanuts* cartoon. They reached the landing and Georgie pointed to a door.

Maddie tried the knob, but it was locked.

"She does that a lot," Georgie told her.

"Is she sick?"

Georgie shrugged. "She locks herself in and won't talk to Daddy."

"Oh." Even though the thought of Haley in pain was breaking her heart, she decided to give her some time.

She bent to Georgie's level. "Have you had your bath?"

He shook his head vigorously. "I don't like baths."

This stopped her, but only for a moment. "You have to get ready for bed."

"I don't like going to bed."

This wasn't going to be easy. "If you're bathed and tucked in bed, Daddy will be so happy. You want to make Daddy happy, don't you?"

"Ah…uh-huh, but you can't wash my eyes or my ears."

"Deal." Maddie suppressed a smile. "Let's get your jammies."

Thirty minutes later Georgie was bathed and in his Spider-Man pajamas. She managed to wash his ears and eyes without him really noticing.

"You bath good," he told her. "Daddy gets soap in my eyes." Evidently Walker gave an energetic bath.

Georgie yawned and his eyes fluttered. He was half asleep. She gathered him, Curious George and the blanket and headed for his room.

Pulling back the covers, she tucked him in. "Mama," he murmured, clutching his stuffed animal.

How could Walker's ex leave these precious children? She would never understand that.

She turned and saw Haley standing in the doorway. Her Hannah Montana pajamas hung on her thin body, and her long blond hair was limp around her pale face.

"I can put Georgie to bed," she said.

"He's already in bed and out for the night." Maddie glanced toward Georgie's sleeping form.

"Does he have his Curious George?"

"Yes, and his blanket." Maddie flipped off the light and they left the room.

As Maddie made to close the door, Haley said, "You have to leave it half open."

Maddie did so and they walked out into the hall. "Would you like to come downstairs for a minute?"

Haley didn't answer, but she followed Maddie to the living room. "I'm not sure what Georgie was watching but…"

"*Finding Nemo*. He loves that movie." Haley settled on the sofa. Maddie clicked off the DVD player and picked up Georgie's clothes.

Sitting by Haley, she folded them neatly in her lap, taking her time, hoping Haley would talk.

"Why would a mother leave her children?"

The words were spoken low but Maddie caught them. She juggled them in her head before answering, searching for a magic answer that would help Haley.

"I'm sure it wasn't an easy decision."

"He came to our house all the time when Daddy was gone."

"Who?"

"Tony. Mama's boyfriend. I told her I didn't like him and she got mad and… She said he was only a friend, but when Daddy was gone she'd leave us at the neighbors' and stay out all night. I wanted to tell Daddy, but I…" Tears streamed down Haley's face and she wiped them away.

Maddie gave her a minute. "You're not responsible for what your mother did."

"If I had told Daddy… I needed to tell Daddy."

"What would have happened?"

"Maybe he could have stopped her. I mean, he can do anything. Then we'd still be a family."

"Do you really believe that?"

"I want to." She hiccupped. "But…she left and didn't even say goodbye and… Georgie cried himself to sleep for two weeks."

"Did you cry, too?"

Haley twisted her hands. "Yeah. I thought it was my fault and…that's why I have to see her."

"It's not your fault," Maddie told her.

"But I made her nervous when I threw up and…and I did bad things. I…made Mama mad."

Maddie rubbed her thin arm. "Sweetie, your mother's leaving had nothing to do with what you did or didn't do."

"Aunt Doris said Mama's lost her mind and we're better off with Daddy." Haley gulped a breath. "But he doesn't want us, either. Nobody wants us." A flood of fresh tears followed that statement.

Maddie took the girl in her arms. "I don't know your father very well, but I spent twenty-four hours with a man who was worried out of his mind about his kids. Everything he did showed how much he loves you and Georgie. He even paid so Ginny could get into a decent home. He did that for you because Ginny is your friend and he wanted you to have some peace of mind."

"Daddy did that?" the girl cried into her shoulder.

"Yes. He's feeling his way on being a single father, but I know one thing—he will never leave you. He will always be here for you and Georgie. That's why he brought you home to High Cotton and took the constable's job. He may have not been there in the early years, but, sweetie, he's in your life to stay because he loves you. Please believe that."

More tears followed and Maddie just held her. Haley seemed to carry the weight of her parents' marriage on her shoulders and Maddie's heart broke for her.

Walker was right. Maddie never had this kind of stress in her life. After the divorce, her parents got along so much so that her mother allowed her only child to spend every Christmas at High Five with her father and her sisters. That must have been a tremendous sacrifice for her mother. But Dane and Audrey always did what was best for Maddie. She never realized what a gift that was until now.

The door opened and Walker stood staring at them.

"Haley, sweetheart, what's wrong?" Worry was carved into every word.

Maddie got to her feet and relinquished her seat to Walker. He took his daughter into his arms and Haley gripped him tightly.

"I'm sorry, Daddy. I'm sorry."

Maddie picked up her purse and quietly left. Walker needed time alone with his child.

THE NEXT MORNING, MADDIE was up early, ready to get back into the swing of ranching. As she was coming down the stairs, the phone rang. She hurried to her office to get it.

"Mornin', Maddie." It was Walker, and her name never sounded so good. So sensual.

"Morning."

"You left so quickly last night I didn't get to thank you."

"You needed time with Haley."

"We had a long talk. I never dreamed she blamed herself for not telling me Trisha was seeing Tony behind my back."

"I got that impression, too. Poor kid has been carrying around a lot of guilt and making really bad decisions."

"I owe you for getting her to open up. I think we're making a turn for the better."

"I hope so. And if you ever need a sitter, just call me."

"Don't you have a ranch to run?"

"Yes, but I can take Georgie wherever I go. Just so long as he's not scared of cows or horses."

"The only thing he's afraid of is a bath. How did you get him to take one last night?"

"I asked very sweetly."

"Ah. That might work on me, too."

Her heart kicked against her ribs. "I don't know if 'sweet' works on you."

"Try it tonight."

"What?"

"I'm doing burgers on the grill. Have supper with us."

"Oh. Okay." He didn't have to ask her twice.

"See you at six. Oh, did you come for a reason last night?"

"Yes. I forgot to give you your change."

"What change?"

"From the five you gave me to buy Georgie candy."

"You can't be serious."

"It's your money."

"Just keep it."

"I'll bring it tonight."

"Fine. See you then."

Walker hung up, wondering if she was for real. It was five measly bucks. But that was Maddie. What was he doing inviting her over? He wasn't ready for a relationship. His kids needed him. A friendly thank-you was all it was.

With the most gorgeous woman he'd ever laid eyes on.

With or without her clothes.

THE TEMPERATURE DROPPED into the thirties, and Maddie froze her butt off helping Coop and Ru feed the cattle. They had to cut off the water to the well pumps so they wouldn't freeze. While they were working, Maddie kept a close eye on the woods, looking for the wild dogs. If she saw one, she didn't know what she'd do. But Coop wasn't far away.

The whole time she worked she thought of Walker and the evening. She couldn't believe how much she looked forward to it.

She had to impose upon Etta again to stay with Gran.

"Don't you worry about it," Etta said. "Dorie, Ru, Coop and I are playing Texas hold 'em tonight. So have a good time. I'll be here."

Maddie had forgotten about their weekly poker game. It was hard to imagine Gran with her Southern manners and attitudes playing poker. But Gran loved it.

Tonight she wanted to look good. No, scratch that. She wanted to look bad. Sexy and unpredictable. She took her time dressing. Since it was so cold, she wore a heavy white turtleneck sweater with black slacks and boots—not cowboy ones. These were made of soft leather and had a three-inch heel. Grabbing a black leather jacket, she was on her way.

Georgie answered the door. He was fully dressed and his hair was neatly combed. He looked so cute.

"Daddy's out back and Haley's in there." He pointed inside.

She removed her coat and followed him into the kitchen where Haley was cutting lettuce and tomatoes for hamburgers.

"Can I help?" Maddie asked.

"No. You're a guest," Walker said as he came through the back door with a pan of cooked burgers. The smell whetted her taste buds. As did the man.

For a moment she soaked up his strong, manly persona. His hair was tousled and his shirtsleeves were rolled up, revealing forearms sprinkled with dark hairs. A smoky, woodsy scent filled her nostrils. He warmed her senses by just being in the room.

She was impressed with Walker's concern for his daughter's eating habits. The French fries were baked in the oven, and he patted her hamburger with a paper towel so it wasn't greasy. Haley only ate the bun and meat with mustard and she seemed to hold it down. It was a fun, relaxing evening.

After dinner, Haley and Georgie ran to watch TV. Maddie laid her napkin on the table. "Have you talked to Ginny's parents?"

"I spoke to them today. Earl said Ginny wasn't welcome at his house anymore. Her mother seemed nervous, so when Earl stomped off I told Verna where

Ginny was in case she wanted to write her. But I doubt that will ever happen."

"It's sad."

He reached across the table and lifted her chin. The gentle touch sent a warm sizzle through her. "Ginny is free and so is that baby. They don't have to live in that squalor. Isn't that what you wanted?"

"Yes." Her eyes met his. "Are you looking in on the other children?"

"You bet I am. I even called CPS, so now they're involved."

She leaned over and whispered, "You have a compassionate side."

"Don't tell anyone," he whispered back. For a moment they were lost in an attraction pulling them closer and closer. Suddenly Walker got to his feet. "Time for bath and bed, son," he called to Georgie. She slowly followed Walker into the living room.

"No. I don't wanna go to bed."

"Son…"

"I want Maddie to give me a bath. She gives good baths." Georgie ran to her, took her hand and they went upstairs. He soaked her sweater with the bathwater, but she didn't care. She wrapped him in a towel and carried him to his room. Walker helped to put his Spider-Man pajamas on and laid him in his bed.

Walker kissed him. "Night, son."

"I want Maddie to read George to me."

"Son…"

"It's okay." There was a stack of Curious George books on the nightstand. Maddie picked up *Curious George Goes to the Library.* She had barely begun George's adventure before the boy was out.

"Night," she whispered, and they walked to the door.

Outside the room, Walker said, "You're very good with kids. You should have a houseful."

She couldn't keep her expression from changing and Walker noticed.

"Did I say something wrong?"

"No, no. We better check on Haley." She hurried down the stairs and went to the kitchen. Walker was a step behind her.

"Sweetheart, you didn't have to clean the kitchen."

"It's all done." Haley turned with a smile, and Maddie thought she was actually very pretty. Too many times sadness marred her features. "I have homework, so I better go do it." She hugged Walker. "Night, Daddy. Maddie."

"Night, sweetheart."

That left the two of them, and Maddie felt nervous and she wasn't sure why.

Maddie sat on the sofa as Walker moved the wrought-iron fireplace screen and placed another log on the burning fire. It crackled and popped and bathed the room in an effervescent glow.

A romantic glow.

Walker stoked the fire and she thought the sparks might burn his forearms.

"Do you ever wear a jacket?"

He placed the poker by the fireplace and sat by her. "Sometimes. In the marines I learned to condition myself against the elements. Mind-over-matter type of thing. But the truth is, jackets are cumbersome and I don't wear one unless it's really cold."

"Like tonight."

"Mmm."

She watched the leaping flames. "Haley seems better."

"I think she's finally realized that I do want her and I don't know where her mother is."

"That has to be hard for a young girl."

He looked at her, and her nerves crackled like the fire. "You helped her."

"I didn't do anything."

"You listened with your heart and saw all Haley's pain. You said everything she needed to hear."

"That ability comes with rose-colored glasses." She felt her mouth lift into a smile.

He smiled that gorgeous grin and her knees felt weak. They weakened more as his eyes traveled over her. "Do you know how good you look?"

"I just put on warm clothes."

"They're certainly warming me up."

She thumbed toward the fireplace. "It's the fire."

"No, I think it's blue, blue eyes, a curvy body and blond hair."

They stared at each other for a long moment. Almost in slow motion his hand circled her neck and pulled her forward. His lips touched hers tentatively at first and then the warmth of the room, the warmth of each other, engulfed them.

Her arms went around his neck and she pulled him closer, their tongues and lips kindling their own hot fire. She knew he'd kiss like this—with heart-squeezing intensity and a body-numbing wildness.

Pressing her breasts into him, she heard him groan. Or was that her? It sounded delicious, evocative. And the moment spun away into feeling, touching and mind-blowing sensations she hadn't felt in forever. Her body needed this desperately.

His hand scorched her skin beneath the sweater and her hands molded the muscles of his shoulders. God, he was strong and…

"Maddie…we…have to stop this." He spoke the words between her lips, but made no move to stop.

"Why?" The one word came out as a smoky whisper. With Victor she'd never been ready, but with Walker she knew she was.

Cupping her face, he rested his forehead against hers. "My life's a mess. I can't get involved with anyone. I have my kids to think about."

His breath was hot against her face and she reveled in it. "We're kissing. Nothing else."

"Ah, when I touch you, I want it all." He pulled away and leaned back on the sofa. "And you're not a one-night stand."

She tugged her sweater down with shaking hands. "You don't know that."

His eyes pinned her. "Oh, yes, I do. It's written right there in your beautiful blue eyes—good girl."

"Looks can be deceiving." Could she tell him her secret? Very few people knew and it wasn't an easy topic to discuss. But she wanted to be honest. She wanted him not to be afraid that she wanted more than he could give her.

"Not in this case."

She tugged her fingers through her hair, fluffing it as she searched for the right words. "I'd like to tell you something about myself."

His gaze stayed on her face and it made her feel shy. But she forced out the words. "When I applied for the job at the hospital, I had to have a physical." She had to take a breath and she was glad he didn't say anything. "They found a small tumor on my left ovary and it was malignant. I won't go into details, but they said it was stage 1a. They removed it and I went through the hell of chemo. Six months later they found a spot on my right ovary. It…it was also malignant. The cancer stage was now 1b. The doctor said they'd caught it early, but to save my life, he recommended removing the other ovary as well as the fallopian tube. There's a history of cancer on my mother's side. I didn't have much of a choice."

She looked at her linked fingers in her lap. "To save my life they took everything a woman my age values—the ability to have a child."

"Oh, Maddie. I'm so sorry." He stroked her face with the back of his hand and she felt its power.

"The cancer affected everyone around me, my mother and stepfather. My friends. I saw the worry in my mom's eyes so I held off telling my dad. But he came one day while I was having chemo and Mom told him. He…"

He reached over and touched her clasped hands and it gave her the courage to continue.

"After that, Dad flew in often and he was there when I got the news of the second cancer. I didn't want to have the surgery. My dad, who was a big risk-taker, said it wasn't the time to gamble. It was time to live. So…so…I did and I've been cancer-free for three years now. But every day I wonder what if…what if it comes back?"

"The doctors gave you a good prognosis?"

"Yes. They said I was one of the lucky ones because they caught it early. Funny, I don't feel lucky."

"You look so healthy. I would have never guessed what you've been through."

"I was thin for a long time, but Etta has been fattening me up." She tried to smile but failed.

"You look gorgeous."

Her fingers were numb from gripping them so tightly. The cancer was hard to talk about, but Walker gave her the strength to say what she wanted to—needed to.

She raised her head to look at him. All she saw in

the soft caramel eyes was concern, not pity. "I haven't been with anyone since then and I'm just... trying to rediscover all those feminine emotions I thought I'd lost."

"Oh."

"I'm attracted to you and I was acting on it. I'm not looking for a long-term commitment. I'm just looking for a decent guy to have fun with. That may make me a slut—"

He laughed out loud, interrupting her well-thought-out speech. The sound released the tension in the room and in her. "Please. Don't go overboard. You're Mary Sunshine and Mary Poppins all rolled into one."

She leaned in close. "You don't think I can be bad?"

"The thought will haunt my dreams tonight, sweet lady." He tucked her hair behind her ear. "I've been burned so badly by love I'm not sure what it is anymore, but you deserve everything it entails."

"But not with you," she added.

He kissed her lips lightly. "I was married for almost eleven years and I've been divorced for seven months. I want to grab at everything you're offering, but I have to take it slow. I don't want to hurt you."

So much for pouring out her heart. She knew when to admit defeat. At least this time. She stood and slipped into her jacket. Her hand felt the money in her pocket and she pulled it out. She placed it in his hand and then kissed his rough cheek. Her lips lingered for a moment.

"Good night," she whispered.

"Maddie…" But she was walking toward the door and she didn't stop.

Rejection hurt like hell.

CHAPTER TWELVE

WALKER HAD TO RESTRAIN himself from tearing out the door after her. But what would that accomplish? They would still have the same problem. He had to focus on his kids. And she needed someone who could give her his full attention.

Then again… No strings, no commitment. Just enjoying each other's company… He was old enough to know that was a recipe for disaster.

Maddie was an emotional, loving and compassionate woman. Why was he trying to talk himself into having an affair with her? As much as she didn't want to admit it, Maddie wasn't that type of woman.

He could still taste her on his tongue, her scent filled his senses, and her touch was like a brand. He'd remember it forever on his skin. Not only from the heat it had generated in him, but from the sheer power of her gentle fingers.

God. He dragged both hands over his face. He needed something cold. He flung open the door and a blast of frigid air almost knocked him off his feet.

But it did the trick. The effects the kiss had on his body slowly eased.

He'd been too long without a woman. The last time he'd had sex was with his ex two weeks before she'd disappeared out of his life. He then went on a search mission to find a missing girl. When he'd returned, Trisha's note was waiting for him. Her betrayal, her deceit, hit him hard, and he wasn't sure he could trust another woman again.

"Daddy."

Haley stood in the doorway in her pajamas and floppy slippers. God, she was so thin.

"Did Maddie leave?"

"Yes. She just drove away."

"She didn't say goodbye."

That was his fault. "She didn't want to disturb you. She told me to tell you bye."

Liar. Liar.

"Oh." Her face brightened. "I like Maddie. She's nice."

"Yes, she is."

Too nice for a jaded man like him.

"I hope she comes back."

God help him. He did, too. But now, that was highly unlikely.

"We'll see. Do you need an extra blanket?" He quickly changed the subject.

"No, I'm fine. Night, Daddy."

"Night, sweetheart."

She stood there, hesitating, uncertainty on her face. So many times he had tried to connect with his daughter and had failed. This time he went on a father's instinct and took her in his arms, kissing the top of her head.

She didn't resist or pull away. Her arms gripped him around his waist.

"Do you think Mama's okay?"

He swallowed. "Yes, sweetheart, and now we have to go on with our lives."

Haley pushed back, nodding her head. "I'll try." She paused. "Is it bad to keep a secret?"

Walker looked into her concerned eyes. "You had nothing to do with your mother's leaving."

"But I...I...was bad...I made her..."

He cupped her face with one hand. "You have nothing to feel guilty about."

"I should tell the truth."

"Stop worrying." He kissed her cheek. "Sweet dreams."

She walked out of the room.

He let out a long sigh and realized he was clutching something in his hand. That damn money Maddie had given him. He placed it on the mantel.

Maddie.

He'd never met anyone like her before. After what she'd been through, she hadn't lost that goodness inside her. There wasn't an ounce of resentment or bitterness in her—only a touch of sadness that she hid very well.

He remembered how she'd looked when he'd told her she was good with kids. An expression of anguish had filled her eyes. He now knew why.

He ran his hands through his hair. He had to stop thinking about her. And he had to wonder if that was even possible.

THE NEXT MORNING MADDIE hurriedly dressed and refused to think about Walker anymore. She'd thrown herself at him, offering him anything he wanted. That wasn't predictable Maddie. That was foolish Maddie.

She had to admit she'd been trying too hard, yearning for Walker's touch. Had she said she was a slut? Surely not. But she remembered saying those words, and she hadn't had a drop of wine. What had gotten into her?

Now she would back off and leave Walker and his kids alone. Maybe she could find her dignity again. She had certainly misplaced it. Besides, she had work to do, and she didn't have time to continue to make a fool of herself. Usually that was Cait's or Sky's role.

Heading for the door, she braced for a new day. Her cell buzzed. Where was it? She searched frantically until she found her purse. Looking at the caller ID, she winced.

Her mother.

She clicked on. "Hi, Mom."

"Oh, Maddie, it's so good to hear your voice. I haven't heard from you in over a week."

"Sorry. But I've been busy."

"Too busy to talk to your mother." The guilt-inducing tone was like a sharp knife slicing off a piece of her backbone.

She drew a breath. "Of course not. I'm busy working. I'm healthy and I'm happy. Isn't that what you want?"

"Yes, darling. I just miss you."

"I miss you, too."

"Victor called and asked about you."

She gripped her phone. "Tell him I'm fine."

"I'm sure he'd rather hear that from you."

"Mom…"

"You were only going to stay a few days, but you've been there months."

"I own part of this ranch. I need to be here. I want to be here."

There was a noticeable pause. "Are you eating well?"

Maddie gritted her teeth, feeling like a ten-year-old. "Yes, Mom. Please stop worrying." Her mother's concern was out of love and Maddie had to remember that.

"Etta cooks fabulous meals, but you have to watch for too much fat. She tends to overdo it."

"Etta also serves fresh vegetables and fruits."

"I know. I get so angry at this happening to you. You're too young and…"

"Mom." Her head was beginning to throb. "Don't do that. It makes me sad."

"I'm sorry." Another long pause. "Anyway, I called to find out if you're coming home for Christmas."

"No. I'll be staying here with Gran."

"Since Dane has passed, you don't have to stay there."

Maddie had had enough. "Mom, I'm staying for Christmas, and I'm not sure when I'll be back in Philly. Please respect my decisions."

"You sound defensive."

You make me that way.

Maddie decided to change the subject. "Aren't you and Steven planning a Christmas cruise?"

"Yes, but I wanted to make sure you weren't coming home."

"I'm not."

"I guess that's it, then."

"Have a great time and take lots of pictures."

"I will. I know I smother you, but I love you, darling."

"I love you, too, Mom." She took a breath and hated that the cancer had made her mother so paranoid. "Tell Steven hi and that I love him."

Maddie hung up feeling once again as if she'd disappointed her mother. She didn't have a lot to complain about, though. Her mother was really an angel, but she tended to be overprotective and she pushed too hard. So what else was new in the mother-daughter relationship?

Madison slipped her cell into her pocket and headed for the door and breakfast. Cooper was still at the table.

"Morning, Coop." She slid into a chair.

Etta placed a cup of coffee in front of her. "Thanks, Etta. I'll just have one of your whole-wheat cranberry muffins."

"That's not enough to keep you going all day. How about some eggs?"

"No, thanks." She poured milk into her coffee and added sugar.

Cooper pushed a piece a paper across the table.

"What's this?" She picked it up.

"The corn estimate." He came around the table and looked over her shoulder. "If we plant about a hundred acres, we can save a lot of money." He pointed to the paper. "That's the cost of planting the corn, the diesel and such. If we have a good crop and grind it into feed, it should carry us through several months. It's a win-win for High Five."

"I'm impressed." She glanced over the figures. "There are no wages."

"You already pay Ru and me so there would be none. Ru and I can harvest it, too."

"Sounds good. Let's plant corn."

"Great." He beamed a smile she'd never seen before, and she thought Cooper loved High Five as much as Dane's daughters. "Ru and I will start cultivating as soon as the weather's a little warmer. Now, we better make sure the cows have water this morning." He reached for his hat and turned to her once again. "Ru and I are going to put up that fence by the new windmill, another one the hurricane took out. Then we can start herding cattle to that pasture." He reached in his pocket and handed her another piece of paper. "That's the supplies we'll need."

She glanced at the paper but didn't take it. Lifting her eyes, she said, "You pick up the supplies."

"Ru and I have to clear the fence row to install the new fence."

Yanking the paper out of his hand, she pointed a finger at him. "I'll do it, but next time, Mr. Yates, you're going to face Nell Walker."

"Yep." He headed for the door and she thought she heard him mumble, "When pigs fly."

The screen door banged behind Coop and Etta sat a muffin in front of her. "Eat. Dorie's still sleeping."

Maddie glanced at her watch. "Yes, and it's already seven-thirty. She's usually up by now."

"Dorie's going through a little empty-nest syndrome."

"What do you mean?" She took a bite of the muffin.

"Caitlyn's like her daughter, and she misses seeing her every day. Now, she'll never admit that, but she was happy as a child playing dress-up with Cait on Saturday. Dorie was her old self."

Maddie wiped her mouth. "I'll go cheer her up and I'll make sure Cait visits more often."

Etta waved her spoon. "Cait's a grown woman with a husband. Dorie has to adjust."

"Mmm." She took a swallow of coffee and darted for the stairs. When it came to Gran, the sisters were wusses. They loved her too much.

She found Gran lying on her lounger still in her cotton gown, staring out the window.

"Gran," she said softly, and sat by her. "Aren't you coming down for breakfast?"

"I was just thinking about Dane and how proud he'd be of his daughters."

Oh, no. Was Gran sinking into depression again? They went through this right after their father had died. Gran had had a hard time accepting his death.

"Gran, come downstairs. We'll have breakfast together. I'll call Cait and see if she'll join us. That would be fun, wouldn't it?"

"Don't bother Cait. I just want to sit here with my memories."

"Gran…"

"I'm fine, baby." She squeezed Maddie's hand. "You have work to do. Go." Gran waved toward the door.

Maddie had no choice but to leave. She'd give Gran time and then she'd check on her again. She'd even put on one of those tutus if Gran wanted her to— anything to make her happy.

THIRTY MINUTES LATER, SHE opened the door of Walker's General Store. She saw Cait and Judd at the back talking to Walker. Georgie stood beside his father.

Judd's Ford Lariat was parked outside so Maddie knew he was in the store. Seeing her sister was a surprise.

She laid her list and her keys on the counter in front of Nell. She had the ordering thing down.

Nell looked it over. "We'll have it loaded in no time."

"Thank you."

Cait came up behind her. "Hey, sis."

They embraced, and Maddie noticed Cait wasn't dressed in her usual jeans and boots. She wore slacks and a dressy blue blouse. And heels.

"Where are you going?"

"Judd and I have to testify in Albert Harland's trial today."

Harland was the reason High Five was struggling. Angry at Cait, he'd torched their hayfields and their home. He'd even tried to kill Cait. The man needed to be put away for a long time.

"Walker has to testify, too," Cait continued, "but he's having a problem finding a sitter."

Don't even think it. Don't offer.

Walker and Judd joined them and her heart did excited flip-flops at the sight of his stern face.

"Hi, Maddie," Judd said, looping his arm around Cait. Judd was one of those strong males who'd resisted love. It had taken Cait fourteen years to convince him otherwise.

Walker was on his cell. As he clicked off, Cait asked, "Did you get Mrs. Hathaway?"

"Yes. She has the flu."

"Damn."

Georgie looked up at his father and then glanced at Maddie. He smiled and she smiled back.

"I'll have to call and tell them I…"

"I'll stay with Maddie," Georgie said, and reached for her hand.

"Son…"

"Perfect solution," Judd said. "Best babysitter in High Cotton, probably the world."

Maddie made a face at him. "You sweet-talkin' devil."

Cait kissed her husband's cheek. "He is that."

Maddie squeezed Georgie's hand and avoided looking at Walker. Clearly he didn't want her to keep him.

"I don't need a bath," Georgie said, as if that might persuade her.

He was so cute she couldn't say no. His father was another matter.

"I'll keep Georgie."

"Are you sure?" Walker asked, and their eyes met for the first time and she felt light-headed. She was so easy.

"Yes," Georgie answered for her.

"Thank you," Walker said as he followed Cait and Judd out the door. "I have his car seat in my vehicle. I'll drop him at High Five."

"As soon as Luther loads my truck, I'll be right behind you."

They walked off and Georgie looked back, waving, and a warm, fuzzy feeling suffused her—so much for staying away from Walker and his kids. She really was a patsy.

"Cait," she called before her sister crawled into the pickup. Maddie hurried to her. "Do you think that later you could stop by and see Gran?"

"Why? What's wrong?" Cait was immediately concerned.

"She's a little depressed, reliving old memories and thinking about Dad."

"Oh, no."

"She's not doing anything weird like before," Maddie assured her, "but I'm a little worried."

"I'll be there as soon as I finish in court."

"Thanks, and good luck."

Cait lifted an eyebrow. "You, too."

HER TRUCK LOADED, MADDIE sped home. Walker and Georgie waited at the front door and she hurried there.

"I'm here," Georgie shouted as Etta opened the door.

"Oh." Etta looked at Georgie. "Would you like a cookie?"

"Uh-huh."

Georgie followed Etta and she turned to Walker.

"I don't know how long I'll be," he said. Her traitorous eyes soaked him up like raw cotton. In a crisp white shirt stretched across his broad shoulders and his long legs encased in starched jeans, Walker's sheer male presence made her nerves tingle.

"Ah…it doesn't matter. Just pick him up when you're through."

He nodded, but he didn't move away. "I thought about you all night."

"I didn't think about you at all," she lied, but the expression on his face was worth it.

He grabbed his chest. "Ouch." And then he looked closely at her face. "You know you get little lines around your eyes when you lie."

"I do not get little lines."

He cocked an eyebrow at her sharp retort.

"Coop's always telling me that."

He rubbed his jaw. "Mmm. Is there anything between you and Cooper?"

"Friendship."

His eyes held hers, and she couldn't look away from the warmth she saw there. "Well then, if you're willing to take this relationship one day at a time and see where it takes us, I'll meet you halfway."

"I…" She was at a loss for words. She hadn't expected this.

His arm snaked out and he pulled her against him, his lips covering hers, effectively silencing any doubts she had. The kiss went on as he wrapped her tight in his embrace.

His musky after-shave triggered her senses, and the fire of his kiss melted every other part of her. "Am I forgiven?" he whispered between kisses.

"Maybe. We might have to explore this more."

That ghost of a smile warmed her against the chilly wind.

"Later tonight." It was a promise that erased the rejection of the night before.

He picked up Georgie's backpack at his feet and placed it in her hands. "He has all kinds of stuff in there. Curious George, for sure. He wants it when he takes a nap, and I added an extra change of clothes. If he gets dirty or banged up, don't worry. That seems to be the norm for my kids. They're accident-prone, but since they're getting older, it's getting better."

"I'm such a patsy," she murmured with a smile.

He kissed her briefly. "I'm beginning to like that about you…and the lines." His eyes twinkled as he sauntered away.

She watched until his car was out of sight. She might have *easy target* written on her chest, but this time she was doing what she wanted.

And following her heart.

CHAPTER THIRTEEN

THE MORNING WENT WELL. Maddie put Georgie in front of her on Sadie to help check on Coop and Ru. Georgie was very good. He did exactly what she told him. He talked a lot, but that didn't bother her.

They rode back to the house at one. The temperature was now in the fifties, so it wasn't too cold. When they reached the barn, Solomon was waiting. At first, Georgie was a little afraid, but she let him pet the bull. Soon he was leading the animal around by his halter. She watched closely because animals were unpredictable.

When they reached the house, Etta had lunch ready. She settled Georgie at the table and hurried to check on Gran. She was sound asleep and that worried Maddie. Maybe she should call Cait, but Cait was at the trial.

In the kitchen, Georgie was keeping Etta entertained with tales of Solomon. Etta had made meat loaf and Georgie wanted lots of ketchup, which he got mostly on his face and clothes. She was washing his face and hands when the phone rang.

It was Walker. "How's Georgie?" he asked.

Her heart fluttered. "He's fine. We had a late lunch."

"I hate to ask another favor."

"But you are?"

"Yeah. I'm still waiting to testify and I'm not going to make it to pick up Haley from school. She can walk or ride the bus, but there would be no one home."

"I'll go get her."

"Thanks, Maddie. I'll let the school know you're coming. It lets out at three."

"I'll be there."

"I owe you for this."

"You certainly do." She could see him smiling as she hung up.

She finished washing Georgie's face. "Do you take naps?"

He frowned. "No. I'm too big."

"Oh, sorry, but I have to ask these things." Walker had said something about a nap, but she wasn't going to push it.

"Are we going riding again?" His voice was hopeful.

"We have to go get Haley from school."

"Oh."

"But first I have to check on my grandmother. You stay in the kitchen with Etta."

"'Kay. She'll give me a cookie." He ran for the kitchen.

Maddie headed for the stairs and stopped short. Gran was sitting in the parlor, fully dressed, her hair in a neat knot.

"Gran."

Her grandmother looked up. "Hi, baby. I thought I heard a child."

"That's Georgie, Walker's son. He's staying with us for the day."

"I was thinking about when you girls were little and how laughter filled this old house. Now it's so quiet."

Before Maddie could answer, Georgie came running in. "I got ketchup on my jacket." He held it up. "See?"

She took the coat. "Yes, I see. I'll try to get it out."

"Hi, Georgie," Gran said.

Georgie lifted a hand. "Hi."

"Do you have a Christmas tree at your house?"

Georgie shook his head.

"We need to do something about that. We don't have a tree, either." Gran glanced at her. "Contact Cooper and tell him we need to cut down a tree. Make that two trees. Right, Georgie?"

Georgie nodded vigorously.

"And we'll pick them out." Gran got to her feet.

Gran was throwing things at her from left field. She wasn't ready to put up the tree, but if it made Gran happy, then she was all for it. She just had one small problem.

"I have to pick up Haley from school."

"Then let's get going." Gran reached for Georgie's hand.

The truck was small and Maddie didn't think they'd all fit. Oh, well, they were off on an adventure.

Haley was waiting by the curb. Gran let her get in and then she held Georgie on her lap. Walker would not like this. No car seat for Georgie or seat belts. Every time she shifted the gears Haley had to move her leg. She drove slowly, hoping there were no maniacs on the road.

"We're getting a Christmas tree," Georgie told Haley.

"We are? Daddy didn't say anything."

Daddy was going to be surprised.

The ride was uneventful and they made it safely back to High Five. Gran took Haley and Georgie inside for a snack and she went to alert Cooper.

The change in Gran was phenomenal. She was chatting with the kids and making plans. She just needed an interest.

As they piled back into the truck to go choose their Christmas trees, Walker drove up. Maddie got out and Georgie was off like a bullet to his father.

Walker swung his son high in his arms. Georgie's giggles filled the afternoon air.

"Daddy, Daddy." Georgie could hardly catch his breath. "We gonna get a Christmas tree." He spread his arms. "A big one."

"What?" Walker's eyes went to Maddie. She was like a magnet, pulling him in. God, she looked great in tight jeans, and her blond hair spread out on the collar of her jacket.

He dragged his thoughts back to his son. "I haven't thought about a tree."

"That's okay," Georgie told him. "We gonna do it, aren't we, Maddie?"

"You're back early," she said instead of answering.

"Court convened early. I have to go again in the morning. Judd and Cait are still there talking to the D.A."

"I'll stay with Maddie." Georgie bobbed his head.

"Now, son…"

"Gran wanted to put up a tree and Georgie got sucked into the excitement."

"We need a tree, Daddy," Georgie said in his most pitiful voice.

"What does Haley say?" He looked to his daughter standing behind Maddie. She smiled—a real smile.

"Well, Maddie, if you don't mind some tagalongs, we'll go with you."

"Not at all." The light in her eyes sent his blood pressure up a few notches. "Except we're not all going to fit in my truck. Some will have to ride with Cooper. He has a chain saw and he'll lead the way to the cedars."

Coop strolled over and threw Walker his keys. He caught them while juggling his son.

"Take my truck. It's a double cab and has more room. Chain saw's in the back."

"Thanks," he called to Cooper's retreating back. "I think."

Cooper waved a hand over his head in acknowledgment but kept walking.

He could go home and get his truck, but that would take time and his son's patience was short. After cutting down the tree, he'd come back and get it. That way he wouldn't spoil the kid's excitement. Lord knew they had very little of that lately.

The air was beginning to get chilly again. "Let me get my jacket and we'll be on our way."

Slipping into his lined sheepskin coat, he hurried back.

Maddie smiled. "You do own a jacket."

He nodded. "Comes in handy every now and then." It was hard to look away from the teasing light in her eyes.

The group made their way over to Cooper's truck. Miss Dorie sat in the front with him, and Maddie crawled into the back with Haley and Georgie. They were off to find a perfect tree, which took more time than he ever imagined.

Georgie ran from cedar to cedar, Haley a step behind him, searching for the right one. Miss Dorie found hers quickly, and he had it in the bed of the truck in no time.

His kids had to have Maddie's opinion on everything, the same with Miss Dorie. Maddie was very patient guiding them to the perfect tree. Soon he had it in the truck, and the kids scurried to get in the warmth of the cab, as did Miss Dorie.

He made sure the trees were secure and jumped to the ground. Maddie stood there, her arms wrapped around her waist, her nose red.

He lightly touched her cold skin. "I want to kiss you so bad my lips are tingling."

"That's from the cold, silly."

"No. Don't think so. Other parts of my body are warm…very warm."

She giggled.

"Let's go before you get hypothermia. I must have been out of my mind to cut a tree in weather like this."

Or in love.

Those three words immobilized him. His wife had been gone eight months. He couldn't fall in love again so quickly. But then there was Maddie and her loving nature that went all the way to her soul. She cared about his kids. And they responded to her. Hell, who wouldn't respond to her? He felt a little giddy himself.

He had to take this slow. But everything in him was already going full speed ahead.

When they returned to the house, Miss Dorie insisted on putting up the tree. His kids begged to stay, so he attached the stand while Maddie gathered the boxes of decorations out of the attic.

The next hour was a lively affair as Miss Dorie and the kids decorated the tree. Etta made sandwiches and hot chocolate and placed them on the coffee table. Thankfully she brought him a cup of coffee.

Maddie sat at his feet looking wistfully at an ornament.

"What is it?" he asked.

She held up a crystal angel. "It's my first Christmas ornament from my father. See—" she held it up

"—my name and the day I was born is inscribed on it." She was silent for a moment. "Cait was his baby. I was his angel and Sky was his princess. That's what he called us. Although most of the time he called Sky Spitfire." She fingered the ornament. "I miss him."

He squeezed her shoulder and her hand covered his. They were quiet for a few seconds and then she smiled—a stellar one he was sure could move mountains. It sure moved his frozen heart.

"May I please have cheese and crackers?" Haley asked, staring at the sandwiches.

"You certainly may."

Haley was watching what she ate and she hadn't thrown up in days. He hoped they could keep the status quo going.

"Oh, peanut butter and jelly," Georgie cried. "My favorite." He looked at Etta. "It is grape jelly, right?"

"Of course. Don't make it with anything else."

"Daddy does. He used strawberry." Georgie made a face. "It was yucky."

"He's never going to let me forget that," he said for Maddie's ears only.

She laughed, and it felt good to be with her and in this warm family environment. He'd never seen his kids this happy. Looking into her eyes he had to wonder if he'd ever been this happy.

THE NEXT MORNING, MADDIE called Cait to let her know Gran was much better. Last night Cait hadn't made it by because she and Judd were busy with the D.A. going over details.

After a brief conversation, she hurried downstairs, hardly able to believe how excited she was that Georgie was coming. She'd fallen in love with the little boy and Haley, too. Most of all, though, she…

The doorbell rang and she ran to get it. She barely had the door opened before Georgie darted in.

"Whoa." Walker grabbed his son. "Manners, please."

"Bye, Daddy. I'll be good. I gotta go. Etta has something for me I know." Then he was gone.

"One day and you'd think he's lived here forever."

"He really is very good and everyone loves him."

"Gets that from his dad, huh?"

"Maybe." She stared into those warm, warm eyes.

"I never did get that kiss last night. Georgie was asleep on his feet."

She went into his arms as if she belonged there. Slowly he turned his head and their lips met in a fevered kiss that went on and on.

"Damn." He sighed heavily, resting his forehead against hers. "I have to go."

"I'll pick Haley up from school and we'll get started on the decorations for the tree."

"Georgie was whining this morning about the tree, so I have to get it up tonight. I don't have any decorations, though. When Trisha left I sold what I didn't want out of the house and gave the rest to our neighbor."

"We'll raid the general store."

"Oh, that should make Nell cringe."

He seemed not to want to leave, and she didn't want him to. It felt strange and right that their relationship was taking off so quickly.

"I'm going in my truck so I can bring the tree home as soon as possible."

"We'll be waiting," she called as he strolled away.

THE DAY WAS UNEVENTFUL. Georgie chattered nonstop and asked a million questions. After checking the wells to make sure they were flowing, she let him feed Solomon. Coop and Ru were installing the new fence, so she and Georgie went to the house. He entertained Gran with his childish antics.

Later they went to the school to get Haley. She was waiting in the same spot. Haley smiled when she saw them and hopped in. Maddie thought that was a good sign. Haley was better.

They drove to the general store and bought just about everything Nell had for a Christmas tree. Maddie gathered construction paper, glitter and glue so they could make decorations, too.

"We're putting up a Christmas tree, Aunt Nell," Haley said. "Would you like to come over?"

"I'm too old for that kind of stuff."

"How old are you?" Georgie asked.

Maddie quickly intervened. "If you change your mind, please come over."

"Where's Walker?"

"He's testifying at a trial."

"Shouldn't he take care of his own kids?"

As always Georgie had something to say. "I like Maddie. She doesn't hit me."

A look of anxiety crossed Nell's face.

Maddie shuffled him to the door. Unable to resist, she turned back. "If you change your mind, please come." She couldn't help herself. Nell seemed so lonely.

When they reached the house, Haley let them in with her key. They paused in the doorway. The tree was standing in the front window. Walker came from the kitchen.

Georgie ran to him. "Daddy, Daddy. The tree is up."

"Yep. Now we have to decorate it."

Maddie and Haley laid their bags on the sofa. "We have plenty. Did you get through early?"

"Yes. And I don't have to go back." He winked at her and the world was suddenly brighter.

"Oh, boy. Oh, boy." Georgie jumped up and down. "We have our very own tree."

The next hour was a hive of excited activity. Walker put on the lights while Maddie made popcorn. She and Haley made strands for the tree and cut rings out of red construction paper to make a garland.

Maddie created an angel out of construction paper, glue and glitter. She used a pipe cleaner for the halo.

Georgie in the meantime was throwing icicles on the tree in fits of giggles. Finally it was finished.

"Oh, it's pretty." Georgie clapped his hands.

"Wait," Walker said. "I have something else." He went into the kitchen and came back with a small bag. "Since I got out early, I thought I'd pick up something to remember our first Christmas in High Cotton." He pulled out two boxes and gave Haley one and Georgie the other.

Haley held up a heart ornament. "Oh, it has my name on the back and the date." She hugged her father and hurriedly hung it on the tree.

Georgie dropped his and Walker had to help him. "It's George. Oh, boy," he shouted, staring at the Curious George ornament.

Walker held him so he could hang it high on the tree, his eyes catching hers. He wanted them to remember this Christmas the way she'd remembered her father's one-of-a-kind ornament. Walker was such a special man, but she'd known that for a while.

"Now we have to turn on the lights," Haley said. "Everybody sit. I'll turn off the living room lights and then turn on the tree."

Maddie took her seat by Walker. Georgie crawled into her lap and she squeezed him gently. The lights went out and the room was in total darkness. Then the lights of the tree came on, beautiful and spellbinding.

"Oh." Georgie's voice came out low and breathless.

Haley slid into the spot next to her and they just sat in the warmth of the crackling fire and the beauty of the lights.

Haley rested her head on Maddie's shoulder and Walker's hand reached for hers. All that loneliness inside her dissipated. Ever since they'd told her she would never be able to have children, she'd been adrift. Now she was anchored and felt more love than her heart could contain.

She'd found everything she'd wanted here in High Cotton, Texas.

She'd found Walker, the man with no first name.

CHAPTER FOURTEEN

IN THE DAYS THAT FOLLOWED, Maddie was involved in Walker's life more and more. She juggled ranch duties with keeping Georgie and picking up Haley from school when Walker couldn't make it. After a day in the saddle, she'd shower and change and hurry to Walker's. She cooked dinner a lot of nights at his house, working on menus that Haley's stomach could tolerate. They were like a family except for one thing. They had no time alone.

When the kids were in bed, it was time for Maddie to go home to Gran. She couldn't continue to impose on Etta. Hot kisses at the door were creating a lot of repressed sexual tension—for both of them.

"Come on, Georgie. We have to go," she called, saddling Sadie.

"I have to give Solomon more feed. He's hungry." Georgie now considered feeding the bull his job.

"Solomon has had enough. Come on. We have to catch up with Coop and Ru."

"I'm coming. Be a good boy, Solomon. I'll be back."

Georgie was attached to the bull and the feeling was returned. Solomon was so docile with Georgie. Probably because the boy fed him anything he wanted.

In his cowboy boots and hat that she'd bought him, Georgie was too adorable for words.

She lifted him into the saddle first, which wasn't an easy thing to do since he was a solid boy. Putting her foot in the stirrup, she climbed up behind him and they were off.

Holding on to the saddle horn with both hands, Georgie said, "I like Sadie." And that started his childish chatter. She just let him talk as they galloped across the pastures.

They reached Cooper and stopped. He was putting out round bales of hay with the tractor. The cows were milling around ready for food.

Seeing them, he drove over and killed the motor. "Hey, Georgie."

"Hey, Coop." Georgie lifted a hand.

"Are you through feeding?" she asked.

"Yep, for the day. We're low on salt and minerals."

"I've already ordered them."

"Damn, can't get anything past you."

"You can pick it up at the general store."

Coop removed his hat and replaced it in a nervous gesture. "I was going to check the fence over there." He pointed. "That big Brangus cow was poking her head through the barbed wire to eat Judd's grass. I wanted to make sure she hasn't broken the fence."

Sadie moved restlessly and Maddie patted her neck to soothe her. "I'll check the fence. You pick up the minerals." Coop had to stop hiding on the ranch. People had to learn he was a good man, not a criminal. "If there's a problem, I'll sort it out."

"Yes, ma'am." Coop tipped his hat with a frown. "Bye, Georgie."

Coop started the tractor and drove away. Georgie kept waving.

"Okay, partner, let's check the fence."

"I'm helping."

"Yes, you are."

The fence was through a thicket, so Maddie dismounted and lifted Georgie to the ground.

"Oh, look." He pointed to some rocks in the grass. "I'm gonna pick out the pretty ones." The boy had a fascination with rocks. He'd done this several times when they'd been out. Maybe he'd become a geologist.

"You stay right here," she told him. "I'm going to walk through the woods to check the fence."

"'Kay." He was already sorting through the rocks. It was strange how a simple thing could make a kid happy.

She checked the fence with one eye on Georgie. She didn't want him to wander off. The Brangus had broken a wire. They'd have to fix it tomorrow before the cow broke through.

Starting back toward Georgie, she heard a deep growl and glanced to the right.

Her blood froze. The wild dogs were on the edge

of the thicket about forty yards away. The lead dog bared his teeth, growling. The other dogs answered with hair-raising howls. Their attention was on Georgie.

Oh my God!

She had to get to the boy. If she ran, the dogs would most certainly attack. If she screamed for Georgie to run, they would also attack. How much time did she have?

What should she do?

The gun!

That was the only solution.

No. No. No!

Despite her hatred of firearms, she eased slowly toward Sadie. The horse reared her head, sensing a threat. Maddie stroked her neck and saw the rifle was in the scabbard where Coop had put it.

What did Coop say? Remember, dammit! Georgie's life depended on it.

Gently sliding out the gun, she watched the dogs. They hadn't moved, but they were growing more agitated. The other dogs milled around, tossing their heads. The lead dog never took his eyes off Georgie. Thank God the boy was oblivious, engrossed in the rocks.

A light breeze stirred and danger hung in the air. Sadie neighed and sidestepped nervously.

What had Coop said?

Turn off the safety.

She was shaking inside, but her hands were steady.

Where was the safety?

In her mind's eye, she saw where Coop had pointed and she flicked it off.

Raise the rifle and line up your prey through the guide.

She did.

Coop's words played in her head. *It's automatic with six bullets in the magazine. Just pull the trigger.*

Could she do that?

She swallowed, and it felt like a golf ball going down her throat. Her eyes on the dogs, she prayed they'd retreat into the woods.

Suddenly the lead dog let out a bloodcurdling howl and leaped through the air, heading straight for Georgie. The pack howled behind him at a dead run.

Georgie jerked up his head.

"Lie flat," she shouted, and Georgie immediately fell to the ground.

Pull the trigger. Pull the trigger.

The dogs bounded closer.

Now!

Without thinking, she fired. She missed. The loud sound echoed through her head and her insides cramped, but there was no time to think. Just act. The dogs were a few feet away.

It's automatic.

Looking through the guide, she squeezed the trigger again. The lead dog flipped and lay on the dried grass, but the other dogs kept coming. She fired again and again and again, until there were no more bullets. When the last dog went down, the rest scurried into the woods.

She threw the gun on the ground and ran to Georgie. She lifted him, then headed for Sadie, who had trotted some distance away. With one hand, she reached down for the gun, jammed the rifle into the scabbard and swung into the saddle.

Not until she was in the saddle did she realize she'd mounted with Georgie in one arm. If adrenaline wasn't pumping through her veins like a gushing well, she would never have been able to do that.

Or fire the gun.

"I 'cared," Georgie mumbled into her breast. She held him against her instead of the other way. She needed to hold him.

"I got you. You're safe." She kissed the top of his head and realized he'd lost his hat. They'd get it later. In case the other dogs came back, they had to leave here fast.

"That doggie was gonna get me."

She took a much-needed breath and turned Sadie toward High Five. "Let's go home."

"I want my daddy."

She did, too.

WALKER DROVE TO THE BARN. Cooper and Rufus were inside. "Hey, Coop, where's Maddie?"

"She's—"

Gunshots echoed through the landscape.

"What the hell!" Cooper glanced out the door.

"That sounds like it's coming from where I left Maddie and Georgie."

Fear shot through Walker's heart. "Rufus, may I borrow your horse?"

"Sure thing."

He jumped into the saddle and Cooper ran for his horse. They galloped through the cool winter's day, but Walker only felt fear. Reaching a ridge, they stopped. Dead dogs lay everywhere, and Maddie was steadily headed to High Five with Georgie clutched against her.

"Shit," Cooper said at the sight.

Kneeing the horse, Walker took off at a run. Maddie pulled up and waited for him.

"What happened?"

"Daddy." Georgie held out his arms and Walker took him. "Bad doggies were gonna get me. Maddie shot 'em."

His eyes held hers. "Are you okay?"

She nodded, but he could see she was trembling.

Cooper rode over. "Damn, Maddie. You *can* use that gun."

"They…they were after Georgie and there are more. About five ran off into the woods."

For a moment there was silence. Walker sensed she was about to burst into tears. "Cooper, can you take care of this? We're going back to the house."

"Yep."

They cantered back to the barn. Georgie rattled on,

but he heard very little. He was worried about Maddie. She dismounted and began to unsaddle her horse.

"Son, go to the house and Etta will give you something to eat."

"'Kay." He sprinted away.

"Maddie." He caught her hands. She flew into his arms and he held her in a firm grip. "You and Georgie are fine. You did what you had to."

"I was so afraid. Georgie could be—"

"He's not. He's fine, thanks to you."

"I should never have let him pick up rocks. I—"

"Maddie, look at me." She raised tear-filled eyes and his heart jerked with pain. "You did nothing wrong."

"I did." She pulled away, eyes blazing. "I did. He's four years old and I should have never taken him with me. I put him in danger."

"That's life."

"No." She turned and ran for the house.

"Maddie." But she was gone.

MADDIE WENT THROUGH THE FRONT door and up the stairs before anyone could see her. She needed time alone. In her room she sank onto the bed, trying to ease her shaky nerves.

That Georgie could have died today kept running through her mind. A precious child was put into her care and…she stopped those thoughts. They were destructive.

Cait had once told her that in a crisis you did what

you had to. She had. She could still hear the loud sound of the gun, feel the sting in her shoulder, see the dogs falling, blood everywhere, and then the enormous quiet that echoed through her shaking body.

She did what she had to for Georgie. She'd give her life for him. At that moment she realized how much she loved Walker and his kids.

There was a tap at the door. It had to be Gran. She had to pull herself together. Wiping her eyes, she called, "Come in."

Walker stood there looking worried. She ran into his arms. "Don't do that to me again."

"What?" She pulled back.

"Run away from me."

"I've never known fear like that before. I'm a city girl."

He stroked her face with the back of his hand. "I don't think so. You're a true country girl from where I'm standing. A beautiful, courageous…"

"Maddie, where are you?" Georgie called a moment before he entered.

"Right here."

"We're never going to get five minutes alone," he whispered.

She picked up Georgie. "You okay, partner?"

He bobbed his head. "I want my hat."

"Coop will bring it."

He wrapped his arms around her neck and she melted. "I love you."

Her throat closed up. "I love you, too," she managed to say, trying very hard not to shed any more tears. She failed.

Walker rubbed his son's back, his eyes on her. "I called Judd and we're getting together some guys to track down the rest of the pack. When they start attacking our kids, we have to do something."

"I agree. They're not dogs anymore. They're predators."

"Can you watch Georgie a little while longer?"

"Yes, and I'll pick up Haley."

"I'll meet you at my house." He kissed her cheek. "Thank you." That one touch eased all the fear inside her.

BY THE TIME SHE PICKED up Haley she was in a better mood. She didn't have to go home early as Gran was having dinner with Cait. She assured Gran she was fine before she left so she wouldn't worry.

Georgie played with his Spider-Man figures while she helped Haley with her homework. Haley's hair was shiny and her complexion smooth. The sparkle was back in her eyes, too. She looked so different from the defiant girl she'd found in her barn.

"When was the last time you had a spell with your stomach?"

Haley looked up from her book. "Not since Ginny had her baby, and I've gained four pounds."

"You look great."

"Thanks for helping with my diet."

"I didn't do anything. Your father told me what the doctor said, no greasy or spicy or acidic foods, and that's what I cook when I'm here."

"I love your cheesecake and baked potatoes." She looked thoughtful. "It's strange that cheese and hamburgers don't upset my stomach."

"Your father buys low-fat cheese and pats the grease off the burger. Spice and grease are your enemies." And stress, which trigged most of her upsets.

"Did I tell you I got a letter from Ginny?"

"No."

"She's doing great and so is the baby. She named her Haley Madison. Isn't that cool?"

"Very." Maddie was touched.

"After she gets her GED, she's going into nursing. The government will pay for it. Isn't that neat?"

"Yes."

"Daddy said we can go see her at Christmas. You have to come with us."

The doorbell rang, interrupting her answer. Georgie jumped up to get it. Nell stood on the doorstep with a bag in her hand.

Maddie got to her feet. "Come in."

"I don't want to intrude, but I have something for the kids. Is Walker here?"

"No. He's with some men who are tracking the wild dogs."

"I heard about that."

"What you got, Aunt Nell?" Georgie was anxious.

"Haley was curious about my quilting, so I made two ornaments for you." She pulled out two quilted hearts edged with sequins and beads; the back was red satin. One had an *H* stitched on it, the other a *G*.

"They're beautiful," Haley said. "Thank you."

"They are lovely," Maddie echoed.

"We have to put them on the tree." Georgie bounced up and down.

Once the ornaments were in the right spot, Nell said, "Haley, I have my quilting frame up if you'd like to see how it's done."

"Can I, Maddie?"

"You've finished your homework so I don't see why not."

"I'm staying with Maddie." Georgie leaned against her.

Haley whispered something in his ear.

"I gotta go."

"Are you sure, Georgie?" Maddie felt he would be in the way and get on Nell's nerves.

"I'm sure." He nodded his head.

"I'll watch him," Haley said, and then they were gone.

She stood there for a moment and wondered why they hadn't asked her, which was silly. She saw Haley and Georgie all the time. Nell just wanted to spend some time with them. The woman was really lonely. Maybe she would be more lenient with them.

Plopping onto the sofa, she thought about the horrendous day and was so grateful it had turned out well.

She got comfy and it suddenly hit her—she was alone. The one thing she and Walker had been waiting for. But Walker wasn't here.

She curled up and drifted off. The door opening woke her. Walker strolled in with a rifle in his hand. "Hey, gorgeous," he said, locking the gun in a cabinet.

She sat up. "Did you get them?"

"Yes, there were six more. Now we don't have to worry about them attacking our kids."

"It seems so sad."

"Well, Ms. Bleeding Heart." He sat by her and a woodsy outdoor scent stirred her senses. "The town is going to do something about that. I spoke with Judd and we're going to have stricter leash laws in High Cotton. Strays are going to be picked up, spayed or neutered free by a vet who lives here, and then Mrs. Finney is going to keep them until someone wants to adopt them. Mrs. Finney loves dogs and she's eager to help."

She rubbed his arm. "Wow. You've accomplished a lot tonight."

He watched her hand and then glanced around the room. "Where's my brood?"

"At Nell's."

He lifted an eyebrow. "What?"

"She's being nice. She even brought ornaments for the kids." She pointed to the tree.

"Well, I'll be damned."

"Evidently Haley is interested in quilting and Nell is showing her how to do it."

"And Georgie?"

"He went, too."

"Really?"

"He didn't want to go at first and then he changed his mind."

He put his arm around her and she snuggled into him. "You mean we have the house to ourselves?"

"For a little bit."

Removing his arm, he reached for his cell. "Let's see if I can stretch that."

He talked to Nell for a minute and then hung up. "She's going to keep them until I call." He placed his arm around her again. "Now, what should we do?"

"Play Scrabble?"

He made a face.

"Cards?"

"Oh, no." He shook his head, his eyes darkening. "This is where the towel thing happens."

She jumped up and ran for the stairs, laughing all the way to the bathroom.

CHAPTER FIFTEEN

MADDIE RAN INTO THE BATHROOM and stripped out of her clothes, almost falling on her head trying to remove her boots. Quickly stuffing her things into a drawer in case the kids returned unexpectedly, she grabbed a tan fluffy towel and held it in front of her. Her heart bounced off her ribs as she waited for him.

Slowly the door opened and Walker stood there, his warm eyes holding hers with a sensual, sexual gaze.

As he devoured her with his eyes, Maddie realized being bad was easy and natural with the right man. She let go of the towel and it fell to her feet in a soft swish. She didn't think twice about the scars on her stomach.

Walker's gaze shifted from her face to her breasts and down to her legs. His eyes, darker than she'd ever seen them, came back to her face.

"Are you sure about this?" His voice was husky.

"Yes." She stepped over the towel and moved until she was almost touching him. "But I can't make love with a man unless I know his first name."

He sighed. Deeply.

"What is it?" She waited.

And waited.

She gently began to unbutton his shirt.

He moaned and then said, "Valentine."

She lifted an eyebrow. "What's wrong with Valentine?"

"Trying being a boy and defending that name. I learned how to be tough very early."

She touched his face. "I like it."

"Good" came out as a groan, and he pulled her naked body against his. "You're giving me heart palpitations. You're so beautiful." His hand slid up her back and cupped her neck, his fingers stroking her skin, driving her wild.

His lips traveled from her shoulder, to her neck, to her cheek. She was hardly breathing when he captured her lips. She opened her mouth, giving and needing to taste and feel everything that was Walker. Needing more, she pulled his shirt from his jeans.

"Wait," he said in a ragged tone. "Let's go somewhere more private." Swinging her into his arms as if she weighed no more than Georgie, he carried her down the hall to his bedroom. He kicked the door shut, then locked it.

The light was on, which was good. She wanted to see every inch of him. His lips caught hers again and she frantically finished unbuttoning his shirt. He threw it aside and whipped his white T-shirt over his head.

Her hands splayed across his broad chest, her

fingers soaking up the rough texture of his skin, the strength of his muscles and the lure of the dark spirals of hair arrowing into his jeans.

At the feel of him, liquid warmth permeated her stomach and centered between her legs. This is what she wanted. This is what she needed. Walker. Brazenly, her hand went to his jeans.

"Boots," he breathed between hot kisses.

He sat on the bed and she knelt to remove them. Yanking on one, she fell back on her butt.

He laughed—a sexy, throaty sound that rippled through her.

"Oh. I'll get you for that."

"Come and get me." His laugh deepened as he quickly jerked off the other boot, unzipped his jeans. In less than a heartbeat he was standing nude in front of her. Her breath caught in her throat. He was magnificent, muscle and sinew, strong and powerful and more man than she…

He gently lifted her to her feet, then they fell backward onto the bed. She lay on top of him, feeling the power of those muscles, feeling their effect on her. Her body tingled and yearned and…

Walker pushed the blond hair from her face and kissed her deeply. Between heated kisses, he murmured, "You said you haven't been with anyone since…"

"No. Not since the cancer scare." She kissed his chin, the corner of his mouth. "And very little before then."

Walker wanted to take it slow for her, but he was

way past that. The sight of her body and the feel of her satiny skin had sent his hormones into overdrive. And it had been eight long months. He wanted her with a vengeance. Not just the sexual part. He could have that with any woman. He wanted Maddie...the sweet, kind, good woman that drove him crazy. He wanted to be in her, deep and tight.

He rolled her over onto her back and took her lips in a fierce need. His hand caressed her breasts and traveled to her stomach and below. Oh, it was evident she wanted him, too.

Moaning, she slid her hand over his chest and gently stroked his bulging manhood. Her touch sent him into orbit and he groaned, taking her lips and sliding between her legs.

One thrust and he was inside her and the world floated away. It was just her and him, their bodies conversing in an age-old way. He heard her cry his name a moment before the top of his head almost blew off with pleasure. He'd had sex before. He'd made love before, but never like this. His life depended on pleasing her, making her realize how special she was. And in return his pleasure was tenfold.

He wanted to stay joined for a little while longer. Forever, if possible. He never wanted to be apart from her again. Finally, he eased to the side and just held her.

He stroked her hair. "I love you," he whispered.

She took his hand and kissed it. "I love you, too. And thank you."

"For what?"

"After the cancer treatment, I was afraid to find out if everything was still working." She smiled. "It is…wickedly."

"Good girls do it best," he teased.

"You bet," she murmured sleepily.

He gathered her closer. "I'm so sorry for all you had to go through, but you don't have to worry about kids. We have two who need you almost as much as I do."

She jerked up. "Oh my gosh, the time. The kids. We have to get dressed."

He pulled her back into his arms. "In a minute."

She sighed and lay against him. His world was slam-damn good for the first time in his life. Happiness was within his reach. All because of her.

His Maddie.

THIRTY MINUTES LATER they were in the living room, trying to keep from smiling as they waited for the kids. The door opened and Haley walked in carrying Georgie. Nell was behind them.

"He fell asleep," Haley said as Walker took him.

"I'm not sleep," Georgie mumbled, and scrubbed at his eyes. Looking at Maddie, he held out his arms and she took him.

"We made you something, Mommy."

Her heart stopped. She glanced at Walker and he shrugged. Georgie was just asleep and got her name mixed up. That's all. But next to Walker saying I love you, it was the very best thing she'd ever heard.

"We made you this." Haley held up a quilted heart ornament with an *M* on it. "Aunt Nell helped us. It's just like ours."

Her heart wobbled. "It's lovely." With Georgie in her arms, she placed it on the tree and hugged Haley. Haley hugged her back with a smile.

She then hugged Nell, who stiffened. "Thank you." And she meant that in more ways than one.

"I'm really not a bad person," Nell whispered.

"I know," she whispered back, and hugged Nell again. This time she made an effort to return the embrace.

"Time for bed," Walker said.

"Mommy has to give me a bath."

There was that word again. Maddie looked at Walker, but neither knew what to do about it.

"Son…"

"I'll give him a bath." She kissed his soft cheek. "And then I have to go."

"'Kay."

"Bye, Maddie," Nell called.

"Bye, and thanks." She winked.

"Anytime."

Georgie went to sleep as she dried him. Walker helped her get his pj's on and then Walker carried him to his bed. They tucked him in.

"He's had a rough day," Walker said.

"Yeah."

His arm slipped around her. "None of it was your fault."

"It's hard to get it out of my mind, except…you know…when we were…"

His hand slid up her side to her breast. "We'll have to 'you know' more often."

She smiled, feeling warm, safe and loved. He flipped off the light and they went downstairs.

"Why do you think he's calling me mommy?" she asked, slipping into her coat.

"Is that a problem?"

"No. It's just…"

"What?" He looked into her eyes.

"Too good to be true."

He grinned. "I thought it was impossible to fall in love again and I resisted like hell, but now I'm accepting everything that you and happiness can bring."

"Daddy." Haley walked through from the kitchen eating an ice cream bar and they drew apart. "I'm going to bed."

Walker hugged and kissed her. "Night, sweetheart."

Maddie embraced her, too. "Ace that test tomorrow."

"I'll try." She darted up the stairs.

Walker watched her go. "It's so good to see her eating."

"Her life isn't in an upheaval and neither is her stomach. And now I have to go. I have to pick up Gran at Cait's." She reached for her purse and Walker's arms slid around her waist.

"That bed is going to be awful lonely now."

She turned in the circle of his arms. "I'll be back tomorrow." Standing on tiptoes, she kissed him lightly, but one kiss led to another and then another.

She ran from the room laughing, feeling young, alive and so in love.

THE BUSY DAYS OF LATE December were the happiest of Maddie's life. She took time to call Victor and wish him a Merry Christmas. The conversation wasn't an easy one since she had to tell him about Walker. He advised caution, but wished her the best.

Hanging up, she knew she was taking a risk. She was Dane Belle's daughter, though, and he'd always told her if she wasn't taking risks she wasn't living.

Every now and then *what if* would run through her mind. Then she'd remember her father's words. But still that anxiety was there. What if the cancer returned? Predictable Maddie would certainly turn away from this happiness. But the new Maddie held on to it. Cherished it. Embraced it.

With Nell's help, she and Walker continued to have time together, which they both needed. It was getting harder and harder to leave. And *what if* faded into the background.

Nell was helping Haley make a baby quilt for Ginny, and Georgie had to help because the gift had to be from both of them. Maddie knew Haley was tricking her brother so she and Walker could have time alone.

A week before Christmas they went to see Ginny and the baby. Maddie was impressed with the home. It was up-to-date and clean, the girls and babies very well taken care of.

Ginny was different, more mature. She'd cut her dark hair, and she seemed to have shed her childhood. Her parents were not mentioned. The future and her daughter were her focus.

They took her out to lunch and then shopping, buying clothes for her and the baby. It was a happy day for all of them.

But the tears came when it was time to leave. Ginny hugged her tightly. "Thanks, Ms. Belle. I'd be stuck in High Cotton if it hadn't been for you. And—" her voice broke "—I wouldn't have my baby."

"You're welcome, and call me Maddie."

Ginny turned to Walker. "I'm sorry I made you worry. And thank you for delivering Haley Madison."

He should be angry at this young girl for putting his kids' lives in danger, but he didn't feel anger. He was relieved Ginny now had a life worth living.

Clearing his throat, he said, "Just don't do anything like that again."

"I won't."

Maddie was holding the baby and his eyes were drawn to her as always. A look of rapture was on her beautiful face, and he hated what had been taken from her. She deserved a child of her own.

WHEN THEY DROVE UP AT High Five, an old car Walker had never seen before was parked out front.

"Oh, Skylar's home," Maddie shouted, and jumped out and ran for the house.

"Who's Skylar, Daddy?" Haley asked.

"Maddie's sister."

They got out and followed more slowly. Maddie was hugging Sky in the parlor. A little redheaded girl about three sat on Gran's lap. Maddie gently lifted her into her arms and motioned for them to come in.

"Sky, this is Walker, Haley and Georgie."

"I remember you," Sky said, shaking his hand. "I danced with you at the ball at Southern Cross. Mainly because Maddie wouldn't and I never miss dancing with a handsome guy."

"Maddie and I got off to a bad start."

Sky glanced from him to Maddie. "But that's changed, huh?"

"Yes, it's changed," he admitted with a grin.

"He's mellowed," Maddie added, sitting on the sofa with the little girl.

Georgie eyed the girl in Maddie's arms. "Who's that?"

"This is Kira. She's my niece."

Georgie frowned. "Why you holding her?"

Georgie didn't like for Maddie to hold anyone but him. He took after his father.

Maddie reached out with one arm and pulled Georgie onto her lap beside Kira. "There's room for both of you."

"No," Georgie shouted, and pushed Kira with his hand.

Before anyone could react, Kira pushed back.

Sky scooped Kira into her arms. "What can I say? She takes after her mother."

Walker knelt by Georgie. "Son, we don't push girls."

Georgie twisted his hands. "She sat on Mommy's lap."

The room became quiet. Very quiet.

Maddie kissed his cheek. "That doesn't mean I don't love you."

"It doesn't?"

"No. You're my partner."

"Now, apologize," Walker said.

"Sorry." Georgie eyed Kira. "But you can't sit on Mommy's lap."

Walker lifted the boy into his arms. "This may take more time than we have." He looked at Maddie. "Visit with your sister. I'll take the kids home. Nice to see you, Skylar, Kira. Bye, Miss Dorie."

Maddie followed them out. When Haley and Georgie were in the car, he lingered outside, staring into her beautiful eyes.

"I'll call you later," she said. "Don't punish Georgie."

"Mmm. You've spoiled him, just like you've spoiled me. We can't live without you."

She linked her fingers with his. "The feeling is mutual and I'll miss you tonight."

"Roughing it is going to be hell."

She squeezed his hand. "I love you." She waved to the kids and ran into the house.

CAIT ARRIVED AND THEY TALKED until after midnight. It felt good to be back together.

"How long are you staying?" Maddie asked Skylar.

"I don't know. I just wanted to be here for Christmas." She flipped back her red hair. They sat in the parlor with the fire crackling and the Christmas lights burning. "A detective showed up asking my neighbors questions in the apartment complex where I lived, so I got the hell out of there."

"Sky, why don't you just stop running and fight this?" Her sister had been on the run since Kira was born, trying to keep her out of her boyfriend's parents' clutches.

"With what? I don't have any money and Todd's parents are loaded. They'd hire the best attorney possible and I'd lose Kira. I can't let that happen. She needs me."

"I can't tell anything's wrong with her," Cait said, curled into a corner of the sofa. "But when she falls I notice she winces."

"The doctor said she might outgrow the juvenile arthritis, but she might not. I have to be there for her."

"You've come to the right place. No one will get near Kira," Maddie assured her. "Cait and I will see to that."

"Hey, I hear you've become Annie Oakley…or Cait." Sky grinned. "They're the same woman, I believe."

"Shut up, Sky."

"You shut up."

They burst into giggles as if they were teenagers.

Sky sobered. "Gran seems a whole lot better than the last time I was home."

"She has some bad days, but Walker's kids have had a positive effect on her. She's just lonely and misses her baby Cait."

"Don't start, Maddie."

Sky turned to Cait. "I guess you know about Walker."

"Oh, yeah."

"Betty Crocker has found her man." Sky poked Maddie in the ribs, and for the life of her Maddie couldn't stop the smile that played across her face.

"Whoa. That looks like Betty Crocker sweet is being oh so bad," Cait added.

"And bad never felt so good." Maddie laughed.

Sky leaned her head back against the sofa. "I haven't had sex in so long I've forgotten what it's like."

"It's like riding a bicycle," Maddie told her. "It comes back to you quickly, in Technicolor and surround sound."

Sky looked at her. "Are you for real?"

Cait's cell beeped. "That's my hubby. I have to go." She rose to her feet, said a few words to Judd and clicked off. "I'll be back tomorrow and we'll talk about the ranch."

"Do you ever stop worrying about High Five?"

"No, dear sister." Cait hugged Sky, blew Maddie a kiss, and she was gone.

Maddie and Sky walked up the stairs arm in arm.

"I'm glad you're home," Maddie said before going into her room.

"Me, too."

MADDIE COULDN'T SLEEP and it was ridiculous. She just wanted to see Walker. Fifteen minutes later she opened his front door with the key he'd given her and let herself in. This was bad, but it felt delightful.

She tiptoed through the dark house, hoping not to bump into the old piano and wake the whole house. She slithered up the stairs like a thief. Quietly, she opened his door and went in, locking it behind her.

Sliding into bed, she curved her hand under his T-shirt and across his stomach and lower.

He caught the wandering hand. "This had better be who I think it is or I'm going to arrest you."

"Oh, Valentine."

CHAPTER SIXTEEN

MADDIE SNEAKED THROUGH her back door at five in the morning. Sky was leaning against the kitchen counter in her T-shirt, terry-cloth bathrobe and fuzzy slippers. Her arms were folded across her breasts.

"Have a good time?" The words were laced with humor.

"Why isn't the light on?" Maddie asked instead of answering.

"I saw your headlights and didn't turn it on. I wanted to see what you were up to and the moon is full tonight. I can even see the color creeping into your cheeks."

Maddie grabbed her face. "You can not."

Sky laughed. "Oh, Betty Crocker, if you're going to be bad, you have to do it with bravado."

"As Cait said one time, I missed that course in college."

"Mmm."

"What are you doing up?"

"Kira woke up crying and I came down to get her some warm milk. Sometimes that helps her sleep."

"Is she hurting?"

"I never know. I just watch for the swelling and try to keep her comfortable."

Of the Belle sisters, Sky was the party girl, the outgoing, outspoken, fun-loving one. And she had a mouth on her that could curdle milk. *Fight* was her middle name. Maddie spent most of her summers on High Five separating Cait and Sky. Two strong sisters, neither willing to bend. It was wonderful to see this caring, motherly side of Sky.

"Where's Kira?"

"She's in my bed with her Elmo. She loves that ugly-looking thing."

"Georgie has a Curious George."

Sky turned from pouring milk out of a pan. "You're really in love."

"Yeah." She wrapped her arms around her waist. "It happened so quickly. I'm afraid my bubble's going to burst."

Sky poured the milk into a glass. "The way Walker looks at you, I don't think so."

They went upstairs together, and Maddie fell into her bed for an hour's sleep.

MADDIE WAS IN THE KITCHEN at seven drinking coffee, lots of it. She and Coop talked about the day's work. In the wintertime it was constant feeding.

"Ru and I are herding the cows in the pen back to the pastures. The wild dog threat is over."

"I'll find you later," she said.

"There's nothing much to do. I still have to pick up the minerals and put some out." With a twinkle in his eye, he added, "You have my permission to take the day off."

She threw a biscuit at him. He fielded it like a pro, took a bite and was gone.

Maddie went to the study to get the books ready for Cait and Sky. An hour later, they sat together, the door closed.

Walker had called and dropped off Haley and Georgie. They were in the parlor with Kira and Gran. Georgie was in a better frame of mind, and she felt sure he wouldn't hit Kira again. But she kept her ears open.

Cait crossed her legs. "The D.A. called late last night and said Harland was found guilty on all charges."

"That's great." Maddie clapped her hands.

"The sentencing is later, but the D.A. said he'll be put away for a long time."

"Glad we have that behind us." Sky scooted forward in her chair. "Let's get this meeting started."

"The ranch is struggling, but we're managing to keep our heads above water." Maddie opened the books. "Oil prices have dropped and that's cutting into our cash flow."

"Judd's not happy about it, either," Cait said. "The economy sucks."

"It's not all bad," she continued. "We received the insurance money from the fire in the house. It went toward the new windmill, which is up and running.

Coop did a lot of the work and it saved money, but this month we're breaking even." She glanced at Sky. "Sorry, but there won't be a check this month."

"Damn. What the hell happened?"

"The economy. Winter. Taxes. Life." She pushed the book toward Sky. "There are the figures."

"Maddie, you're the most honest person I know, and I'm not double-checking the figures." She sighed heavily. "I guess I'm stuck here."

"Next month should be better. The expenses won't be so high and Coop purchased more cows so the calf crop will be larger. And in the spring we're planning to plant corn. Maybe even sorghum. I checked this out on the Internet and this could be good for High Five."

"I hope you're not letting that ex-con make decisions."

Maddie bristled at Sky's tone, but she tried not to let it show. "Coop knows more about ranching than I do, and I trust his instincts. I trust him."

"I do, too," Cait said.

"Well, isn't this dandy? You're ganging up on me."

"I manage High Five and I'm doing what's best for it," Maddie stated.

"That can change," Sky fired back.

"Like hell." Cait shot to her feet. "Maddie agreed to run this ranch and that's the way it will stay."

"You're not the boss, Cait."

"I gave my life to High Five, and if you think—"

Maddie picked up a glass paperweight and threw it

at the wall. It hit a lamp, which crashed to the floor. No one made a move or spoke.

Maddie rose. "I'm tired of you two constantly bickering. I run High Five and what I say goes. Got it?"

Her sisters stared at her, as if they'd never quite seen her before.

"Damn," Sky said. "When did you get balls?"

"When I constantly have to put up with Bossy and Bitchy." Those were nicknames for her sisters.

"Well, I think you had a little tequila with your oatmeal this morning."

"I could use some now," she shot back, and they started laughing.

"Okay, okay, do not sidetrack me," she said. "This month there are no profits to split. Next month there will be. We just have to roll with it."

Sky looked at Cait. "I think we have to change Betty Crocker's name."

"Yeah. Maybe Brave."

"Bad," Maddie said.

This caused another round of laughter.

But they were feeling better and agreeable.

"I'm not cleaning up that mess." Sky pointed to the lamp.

"Would you like Maddie to make you?" Cait asked.

"No. I'd like for her to make you."

"Let's all do it." Maddie walked toward the lamp and her sisters helped. Then they went into the parlor. They stopped and stared.

Everyone was in costume. Gran wore a long gossamer dress and held a wand in her hand. Haley's hair was in pigtails and she wore an old gingham dress with red shoes. Georgie had on a lion's suit and Kira a dog suit. "Over the Rainbow" played on the stereo.

"Hi, my babies," Gran said. "We're doing the *Wizard of Oz*. We need a tin man, a scarecrow and a wicked witch."

"Why did she look at me when she said 'wicked witch'?" Sky whispered.

"If the shoe fits…"

"Shut up, Cait."

Before they knew it they were pulled into make-believe.

WALKER RANG THE DOORBELL, but no one answered. He knocked loudly, but still no one came to the door. Music vibrated through the walls, so he knew they were here. He tried the doorknob and it was unlocked. He went inside.

In the parlor he stared at the show that was going on. Everyone was in costume. Haley was lip-synching the words to "Over the Rainbow" and dancing in red shoes. Georgie growled, leaping around the room, followed by Kira barking.

He'd never seen his kids so happy. They were having the time of their lives. His eyes zeroed in on the scarecrow. His Maddie.

"I love you," he mouthed

"You better," she mouthed back.

CHRISTMAS ARRIVED AND Maddie had presents to wrap, plans to make. Nell watched the kids so she and Walker could go shopping. They bought Haley a new computer system with video games. They settled for a motorized truck for Georgie, one he could drive himself, a Thomas the Train set, books and more Spider-Man toys. They picked out clothes for both of them.

On Christmas Eve Maddie planned to spend the night at Walker's. She wanted to be there when Haley and Georgie opened their gifts. Sky was with Gran, so she didn't have to worry. They would exchange gifts and eat dinner at High Five on Christmas Day.

The kids were in their rooms, supposedly asleep. They carried all the presents she'd wrapped into the house and put them under the tree. Walker drove the small truck from the garage. They were ready.

Sitting on the sofa, they snuggled together in front of the fire. Walker picked up a cookie Haley and Georgie had left for Santa and handed it to her.

"We better eat these."

Nibbling on a cookie, she enjoyed the quiet moment of being together. Walker reached for the milk and took a swallow.

"I know this is quick, but I thought we should make it official."

"What, Valentine?"

"You love saying that, don't you?"

"Yes." She took the milk and drank.

"Now I'm not going to tell you."

"Ah, please." She kissed him with a milk mustache and then licked it off his lips.

He groaned. "You're driving me crazy, you know that?"

"Yes." She giggled and placed the glass on the coffee table.

His arms went around her and he kissed her deeply. He tasted of milk, winter cold and heat…hot melting heat that made her limp.

"Do I have your attention?" he whispered against her lips.

"Y-yes." She sat up and tucked her hair behind her ears. "What?"

He stuck his hand behind a cushion and pulled out a small gold-wrapped box.

She stared at it. Could that be a…?

Her heart pounded. "Christmas is tomorrow."

"I wanted to do this tonight when we were alone."

"Oh." Suddenly she was nervous. For so long she'd resigned herself to a single life. She never thought she'd find a man to love her the way she was. Then she'd found Walker.

He pushed the box into her hands. "Open it."

What if… No. Don't listen.

"I'm a little nervous."

What if…

He leaned over and kissed her slowly. "That help?"

"Yes." She ripped off the paper and paused a moment before she flipped open the lid. She gasped at the sight of the white-gold ring with a round solitaire diamond.

"Will you marry me?" he whispered.

What if...

"Maddie?"

She fingered the diamond. "I can't help but think what if the cancer comes back."

"Oh, honey." He cupped her face. "It won't. But if it does, we'll face it together."

"Walker..."

He kissed the tip of her nose. "Dane took risks every day of his life. Now I'm asking you to take one—take a risk on me. On us."

The promise of his words buffeted her, gave her strength. "Yes," she breathed, afraid to move or speak loudly. The moment might disappear.

He took the box and removed the diamond. Taking her left hand, he slipped it on her third finger. "I love you."

She threw herself into his arms then. "I love you. I love you." He gathered her close and they lay entwined on the sofa. The fire crackled, and the warmth of the room enveloped them in a cozy world of their own. Only love and happiness lived there.

He lifted her into his arms and strolled to the stairs and his bedroom.

CHRISTMAS MORNING ARRIVED early with screeches of delight. Haley and Georgie tore into their packages like little hurricanes. There were a lot of "ahs," "ohs" and smiles. They were so different from the kids she'd first met.

Walker helped Georgie drive his truck out in the yard and she helped Haley set up her computer.

"I can't believe I have my own computer." Haley hopped around with glee. "I made a new friend. Her name is Cara and she has a computer. Now I have one. Wow!"

Georgie came running in his pj's and slippers, his nose and ears red. "It's cold outside, but I drive good, huh, Daddy?"

Walker ruffled his son's hair. "Like a pro."

"You need your coat and cap," Maddie said. "They're by the door." She waved a hand toward them.

"What's that?" Haley asked, pointing to Maddie's diamond ring.

"Well—" Walker sat down and pulled Georgie onto his lap "—I asked Maddie to marry me and she said yes."

"Oh, boy. Oh, boy," Haley shouted. "I got my Christmas wish. Oh, boy."

Haley and Georgie danced around the room holding hands. Nell walked in. "I see the excitement is over."

"Aunt Nell." Haley grabbed her hands and pulled her into the room. "Daddy and Maddie are getting married."

"Go figure that."

Maddie walked over and sat by Walker. He pulled her

close and Georgie crawled onto her lap. They would become a family—the family Maddie always wanted.

It wasn't a risk at all.

IT WAS A RUSH TO GET to High Five on time. They dressed for Christmas. Maddie wore a black dress trimmed in red, and high heels. When she came downstairs, Walker stared at her for a long time.

"You look gorgeous."

"So do you, Valentine." Her gaze slid over his body in Dockers and white shirt and came to rest on his cowboy boots. "Mmm, sexy."

"Later," he murmured.

Haley came down in her new plaid skirt and sweater. Georgie trailed behind her in his slacks and a new blue shirt.

Haley hugged Maddie. "Don't we make a good family?"

"Yes, we do, sweetie." Her gaze caught Walker's and she'd never been happier in her life.

The whole family was at High Five for dinner, including Nell and Renee, Judd's mother, Chance, Judd's foreman, and Etta and Rufus's nephew. They opened gifts and enjoyed the company and the holiday.

They were exhausted when they returned home. Haley ran to her computer and Georgie played with his train set. Maddie made ham sandwiches, but no one was really hungry.

"I'm playing with my computer all day tomorrow," Haley announced.

"I'm driving my truck," Georgie said, taking a bite of sandwich.

"Daddy has to be home for you to drive your truck," Walker told him.

"'Kay."

"Can I have cheesecake, please?" Haley asked.

Maddie opened the refrigerator and placed it on the table. It was one of the things Haley could eat, and it was loaded with calories, so Maddie cut her a big piece.

As she placed it in front of Haley, the doorbell rang, interrupting the quiet evening.

"I'll get it," Maddie said. "Georgie, eat your sandwich."

"I want cheesecake."

"In a minute."

She swung open the door and a pregnant blond woman stood there. A woman she'd never seen before. Her hair was in a ponytail, and she held a hand over her stomach. She wasn't beautiful, but she was pretty with a natural look. She seemed nervous and looked past Maddie as if she was looking for someone.

"May I help you?"

"I'd like to see Walker."

Maddie thought it had to be someone in trouble, needing help.

"He's in the kitchen." She stepped aside so the woman could enter. She smelled faintly of cigarette smoke.

Walker stood in the kitchen doorway, Haley and Georgie behind him.

"Hello, Walker."

"Trisha."

CHAPTER SEVENTEEN

TRISHA!

Walker's ex.

Maddie's happy heart fell to her feet and she had trouble breathing. She closed the door and realized her hands were shaking.

"Mama," Haley breathed, but made no move to go to her mother.

Georgie wrapped himself around Walker's leg and buried his face against Walker.

"What do you want, Trisha?" Walker's voice was cold enough to freeze water.

"It's Christmas. I want to see my kids."

"Maddie, please take Haley and Georgie outside."

Maddie quickly grabbed their coats and herded them out the door. The kids didn't hesitate or look back.

They sat at the picnic table in the backyard. The late evening bite in the air was echoed in her heart.

A barbecue pit and redwood chairs sat among live oak trees, their gnarled roots poking through the ground. A few feet away Georgie's bright red truck rested in the brown, stiff winter grass. But Georgie had no interest in it now. He was glued to her lap, his face buried in her chest. Haley shivered beside her, and Maddie wrapped an arm around her. This was no way to end Christmas.

Haley leaned against her. "Why is she here?"

"She said she wanted to see you."

"I don't want to see her," Haley said, her hands clenched tight in her lap.

"Me, neither," Georgie muttered, not raising his head.

Maddie knew this was a normal reaction. Their mother had hurt them and they were leery of her feelings. But that would change. Kids forgave easily.

"She's pregnant," Haley whispered almost to herself.

"Yes." Maddie certainly recognized that. What did the woman really want? She wished she could hear what was being said inside.

"YOU'RE NOT SEEING HALEY or Georgie," Walker said, trying to keep his anger under control.

"They're my children. I have that right."

"You have no rights. You signed those away when you ran off with your boyfriend. You didn't even have the decency to say goodbye to them."

"I couldn't." Trisha looked down at the floor. "Once I made the decision, I just had to go."

Her selfish attitude angered him more. "Then you don't deserve any consideration. Georgie cried for two solid weeks for his mama. Haley, God, Haley threw up so much she was wasting away before my eyes."

"She only does that to get attention."

Get attention! Had he ever really known this woman?

"Get the hell out of my house! You've seen the last of them."

"I think you'll change your mind once you calm down and hear what I have to say."

"I don't want to hear anything you have to say."

"Damn, my back is killing me." Trisha walked to the sofa and sat down as if they were having a normal conversation. She removed her coat and pushed up the sleeves of her knit top. His eyes were drawn to the butterfly tattoo on her forearm. That was new. As was the pregnancy, which he was trying to ignore.

"Don't get comfy. You're leaving," he warned.

"Who's the blonde?"

"None of your business."

She looked around the room and wrinkled her nose in distaste. "I can't believe you brought the kids to this hick town."

"I wanted to give them some stability. A new beginning."

"I take it you gave up your job, which I begged you to do for years."

He gritted his teeth. "How else would I be able to care for Haley and Georgie?"

"And it helped that your dad left you a bundle."

His patience snapped. He wanted her out of his

house, out of his life. "You have five minutes to tell me what you want."

"Well." She leaned back, the mound of her stomach very evident. "Tony and I were having Christmas with his mother in Houston."

"How nice. Get to the point."

"She was surprised I was pregnant. Seems Tony had a bicycle accident when he was a kid and he wasn't supposed to be able to father a child. The bitch." Her face darkened in a way he'd seen many times. "She just had to bring it up. That put the wheels in Tony's head to spinning, and he wanted to know if the baby was his." She paused and raised calculating eyes to his. "Or yours."

A sucker punch hit him in the gut and he had to catch his breath. His hands balled into fists. "And?" came out as a groan.

"I'm not sure." She shrugged. "Tony knew the diagnosis from the accident, but he figured over the years that it had changed. Now he wants the truth. I want it to be Tony's, but I did sleep with you before I left." She shifted uncomfortably. "Tony's pissed about that."

"I know the feeling."

"Walker—"

"He kicked you out?" Walker cut her off, feeling his insides coiling into knots.

"Not exactly. We decided to part ways until the baby is born and a paternity test is done."

"Which is…?"

"Any day."

"God." He swung away. "I can't believe your audacity. Your gall. You selfish, selfish bitch."

"Damn, Walker, you love kids so much I thought you'd be happy to learn you might be a father again."

He pointed to the door. "Get the hell out of my house."

She pushed to her feet. "What about the baby?"

"When it's born and the test is done, give me a call. Until then I don't want to see you."

"I can't go through this alone." Her voice quivered and he didn't feel one ounce of sympathy.

"Haley and Georgie felt the same way when their mother bailed on them."

"Why do you have to keep bringing that up?"

"Because you have to realize what you've done to their lives. You destroyed them. They're in a stable, secure home now and that's the way it will stay."

"I want to see them."

"No." He remained firm.

"Walker…"

"The only way that's going to happen is if they ask to see you. Then I might relent."

She frowned. "You always were hard and unrelenting. You never cared about us. It was work, work—"

"Get out of my house."

She reached for her coat and purse. "I'll call when the baby comes. Please bring the kids."

On the entry table at the door she placed a small

sealed box. "This is a DNA swab testing kit. Just follow the instructions inside and mail it. The address is on the return packet. When the baby is born, we can get the results quickly." She pulled a piece of paper from her purse. "That's my phone number. Whether you believe it or not, we have to talk about our children. And the future."

WALKER SANK ONTO THE SOFA and buried his face in his hands. Could it be his child? No. No. Not now. He rejected the mere possibility.

He felt Maddie's presence and glanced up. She was everything he'd ever wanted in a woman. But he'd known from the start that he shouldn't get involved with her. She was special and needed someone special. He couldn't resist her, though. Now his life was messed up and it was worse than ever.

How did he tell her?

How could he break her heart?

"Is she gone?" Maddie asked, her voice anxious.

His eyes met hers. She looked great in that black dress. It brought out the blue of her eyes and the shine in her hair. He cleared his throat. "Yes."

Haley and Georgie charged around her and into his arms. He held them in a viselike grip.

"Daddy…"

"Let's talk," he said, settling back. "Your mother wants to see you, but I told her it was up to you. It's your decision."

"No," Haley said rather too quickly. "I'm going up to play on my computer."

"I need a bath," Georgie said to Maddie.

"Since when do you like baths?" Walker ruffled his son's hair.

Georgie shrugged and took Maddie's hand. Together they bathed his son and soon tucked him in.

"I don't want to see Mama," Georgie mumbled as he dozed off.

Walker and Maddie went downstairs. He could feel the tension in her. Sitting on the sofa, she straightened her skirt over her knees. He thought how beautiful she was and how it permeated everyone around her. She deserved everything that was good on this earth, just like she was.

"What did she really want?" Maddie asked.

He wanted to take her in his arms, but he refrained. He had to tell her the truth.

"She wants to see Haley and Georgie and…"

The blue wave of her eyes caught his. "And what?"

"This isn't easy, Maddie."

"But we have to face it whatever it is." His sweet Maddie was holding on to her control very well. It was evident in the way she clenched her hands and kept her gaze on him.

"First, I want you to know how much I love you. How much the kids love you."

She bit her lip. "It must be bad if you have to preface it with that."

"Maddie." Her sad face broke his heart.

"Tell me."

He ran both hands through his hair. "She said I might be the father of the baby."

"Oh…" The one word seemed ripped from her throat.

He went to her then, but she wouldn't let him take her in his arms. "Is that a possibility?"

His stomach churned. "Yes."

Getting up, she walked into the kitchen to get her coat. As she shrugged into it, she said, "I don't think we should see each other anymore. It's too hard. Your kids need you."

"Maddie, I don't even know if the baby is mine."

"But you have to prepare yourself and Haley and Georgie. It's better if I'm not in the picture."

"They don't even want to see Trisha."

"That will change. She's their mother." She reached for her purse. "I have to go."

He caught her before she reached the door. "I don't love Trisha anymore."

She leaned against him, her face beneath his chin. A faint hint of Chanel teased his senses. He kissed her forehead, her cheek and took her lips with all the passion he was feeling. She returned the kiss with equal fervor for a moment and then tore out of his arms and ran out the door.

He sighed heavily as the chilly air surrounded him. But he didn't feel it. All he felt was her pain. A pain he had caused.

"Goddamn it!" He slammed the door so hard the sound echoed through the house with a ring of goodbye.

He wanted to go after her, to tell her they had a future. But he didn't know what the future was and he couldn't keep her hanging on. He wouldn't do that to her.

Goodbye, sweet Maddie.

MADDIE REFUSED TO CRY. She refused to think. It was too painful. She drove steadily home. When she went inside, the house was quiet. Good. She couldn't talk to anyone.

As she headed for the stairs, she heard voices. Sky and Kira were in the parlor. Kira was playing with a baby doll she'd gotten for Christmas, dressing and undressing it. Sky patiently watched her daughter.

A mother's love. A mother's… Maddie stared a long time, lost somewhere between a dream and a nightmare. Unable to speak to them, she ran to her room.

Stripping out of her clothes, she reached for her big T-shirt and curled up in the bed. When she stayed at Walker's, she didn't even need the T-shirt.

Walker.

A whimper left her throat, but she stoically held back the tears. From the moment she knew who the woman was, she inexplicably knew life would never be the same.

Trisha might be having Walker's baby.

No. *She* should be having Walker's child.

But that was impossible. She couldn't have any man's child. And she couldn't claim Trisha's kids, either. Maddie loved Walker. She probably always would. That's why she knew she had to walk away. Walker and Trisha had to have the opportunity to re-connect—for their children and especially for the baby.

Trisha didn't deserve her consideration, but Haley and Georgie did. She couldn't break up a family if there was the slightest chance for reconciliation. Her Christian upbringing was kicking in big-time. This was no time to be bad.

She hated that side of her personality.

Clutching a pillow, she saw her engagement ring. It sparkled with the promise of tomorrow. But there was no tomorrow. She should have given back the ring. When she felt stronger, she would.

There was a tap at the door and Sky stuck her head in. "Hey, what are you doing home?"

Maddie pushed up against the antique headboard that had been hers since she was a child. Their father had let them choose from a collection of furniture that had belonged to their ancestors. She'd loved the dark oak and intricately carved headboard that seemed to reach to the sky. Her father had said she would get lost in the bed.

How she wished he was here now. She needed his shoulder to cry on.

"Are you crying?" Sky asked when Maddie remained silent.

"No." She wiped away a tear and realized she was.

Sky sat on the bed in flannel pajamas. "You're

wearing flannel?" Maddie hiccupped. Flannel and Sky did not go together. Her sister was known to prefer silk and cashmere. Or she used to.

"Yeah. So what? I have to get up so much during the night with Kira and they're warm."

"Remember that time we went shopping in Austin and you bought that sexy teddy? It was black with white lace and you wore it to bed. Dad had a fit and made you throw it away." She dropped her voice. "No fifteen-year-old daughter of mine is wearing something so skimpy."

"I loved pushing his buttons." Sky ran her hand over the soft flannel. "I miss him. I miss his calls."

"Me, too."

There was silence for a moment as they remembered a father they both loved. All the pain in Maddie welled up and tears stung her eyes.

"Walker's ex is back."

Sky's head jerked up. "What?"

"She's pregnant and she says it might be Walker's."

"Shit!"

"It's Christmas. How could she ruin our Christmas?" She didn't want to cry, but she was slapping tears away like crazy.

"You didn't just walk away, did you?"

"Yes." She sniffed. "What else was I supposed to do? I can't come between Walker and his family."

"That bitch abandoned those kids. She doesn't deserve your selflessness."

"But Haley and Georgie do."

"You're such a bleeding heart. If you want Walker, fight for him."

"I have to give them a chance to reunite. I couldn't live with myself if I didn't."

Sky narrowed her eyes. "If it were me, I'd be hiring a hit man."

Despite her pain, she smiled. "You're crazy."

"But I made you smile."

Maddie pulled up her knees. "My life was so bright, but now I feel as if I've been drop-kicked through the goalpost of life. I don't know what I'm going to do."

"The last I heard, and very strongly I might add, is that you're running the ranch. Pick yourself up and go on. That's what Belles do. Isn't that what Dad said?"

"Yes."

"And Cait and I will be there to catch you when you land on the other side of that goalpost."

Maddie leaned over and hugged her sister. "I know. That's what I love about coming to High Five. Family, love and sisters. Though we weren't raised together we have a strong sister bond."

She twisted the ring on her finger. "I forgot to give Walker my engagement ring. It has to be the shortest engagement in history. Twenty-four hours." She couldn't keep the quiver out of her voice.

A wail pierced the silence. "Kira. I have to go." Sky paused at the door. "Keep the ring until you know the baby is really Walker's."

Maddie lay back on the bed. Something about being the good sister made her angry. She should refuse to step back and let Trisha reclaim her family. She didn't deserve it, but Haley and Georgie were her children. They weren't Madison's children.

That one thought kept running through her mind. It kept her from charging back to Walker. It kept her embedded in the worst misery she'd ever felt.

She pulled the pillow into her arms and held it against her. "Walker," she murmured as she fought the waves of sleep tugging at her.

CHAPTER EIGHTEEN

LIFE WENT ON. MADDIE FOUND that out quickly. Even though she had a broken heart, the world had the audacity to keep turning. She had only one option—to throw herself into running High Five.

She made sure all the fences were in good shape and repaired those that weren't. The new windmill worked like a dream and the cattle had plenty of water, though they didn't drink much in the winter months.

Coop and Ru were busy cultivating the hayfields so they'd be ready to plant when the worst of the winter was over. In Harland's anger at Caitlyn and Judd, he had burned their fields and now they had to start over. They could wait to see if some of the coastal and alfalfa sprouted, but that was taking a risk. They needed hay, so their best course was to make sure they had it.

One day as she was crossing Crooked Creek, she dismounted and sat in the grass. The ground was hard and cold and the wind seemed to go right through her. But she didn't move as she tried to piece together her broken life. She'd survived cancer. Surely she could survive this.

Her mother and stepfather had put their lives on hold to help her deal with the debilitating process. She had great family support. She had it now, too. But she just wanted to be left alone. That's why she worked fourteen-hour days. She had to. It was the only way to deal with everything she was feeling.

As she sat there, she noticed the towering pecan trees that grew along the bank. She walked over to investigate. The ground was covered with pecans. Cracking two in her hand, she noticed they were paper-shell ones and they tasted great.

When she reached the house, she made several phone calls to see if she could sell the pecans. She found a buyer. The next day she filled two twenty-pound sacks and took them into Giddings. Even though the pecan season was over, people were still buying.

As long as the store wanted the pecans, she kept gathering them. Cooper started to help her. Once they had the truck loaded, he leaned against it, looking at her.

"You're killing yourself," he said.

She dusted off her jeans. "I'm stronger than you think."

"You Belle sisters are going to kill me with your love lives."

She slammed the tailgate. "Ah, you can take it."

"Maddie, please talk to Walker."

She ran her hand along the top of the tailgate. "Do you see him here?"

"No."

"That should tell you a lot." She walked around the truck. "Walker's a go-by-the-book type of man. He'll do the right thing by his ex and his kids. That's just who he is. We love each other, but that doesn't matter. Walker has to do what's right and so do I."

"Sounds complicated when it should be simple."

She pointed a finger at him. "Wait until you fall in love."

He grunted. "When pigs fly."

"Yeah." She hopped into the driver's seat. Coop slid into the passenger side. "For a man who hardly ever leaves the ranch, you'll never find a woman."

"That's what I'm hoping. Love is highly overrated and I think you'll agree with me."

"You'd be wrong, buster."

Love was the best thing that had happened to her. Soon she'd have to find the strength to let go of Walker and all the love she felt for him. And soon she'd have to return his ring.

Soon being eons from now.

WALKER TOOK THE DNA test and mailed it. After that he spent his days listening for the phone. And missing Maddie. He missed her smile, her touch, her sweetness. He wanted to call her so many times, but he forced himself not to. It would only hurt her more.

He was caught between two women—one he loved, the other he detested. The one he detested was the mother of his children. He couldn't ignore that, although neither Haley nor Georgie wanted to see Trisha. He asked every day and he got the same answer. A sharp "No."

He didn't understand that. Haley had run away so many times to find her mother, but now that they knew where Trisha was, Haley had done a complete one-hundred-and-eighty-degree turn.

Sorting this out was taking more patience than he had. His kids asked about Maddie every day and he thought about taking them to visit. But that wasn't fair to Maddie.

Haley was in her room and Georgie was outside driving his truck in the backyard. Walker glanced out the kitchen window and saw Georgie ramming the small vehicle into a tree over and over.

He ran outside and yanked Georgie out of the truck and turned it off. Georgie started to scream and cry, flailing his arms at Walker.

Grabbing his hands, Walker walked stoically to the house and sat Georgie on the sofa. He pointed a finger in Georgie's face. "Stop it." Georgie cried louder.

Haley darted down the stairs. "What happened?" She went to Georgie and picked him up. "Did you hit him?"

He was taken aback by the question. "No. I've never hit you or Georgie."

"It's okay, Georgie." She patted his back. "Haley's here."

As they went up the stairs, Walker ran his hands through his hair. What the hell had just happened? His kids were changing right before his eyes. They were becoming sullen and defiant, similar to the kids he'd picked up from his neighbor months ago.

He had to do something, but he wasn't sure just what yet.

New Year's Eve arrived and he spent it nursing a glass of bourbon, wondering where Maddie was, what she was doing. He took a couple of sips and went to bed.

The call came the first week in January. The baby had been born and it was a girl.

"She looks just like Haley," Trisha said.

His last vestige of hope seemed to squeeze from his lungs. He took a deep breath. "Is the baby okay?"

"Yes. The doctor said she's healthy."

"When will they do the paternity test?"

"It's already been done. We should know something in a week or so."

"Call me then."

"Walker?"

"What?"

"I want to see Haley and Georgie."

He hung up, not able to deal with her request. Right now his kids weren't in a mood to see her and he wasn't going to push them. School started on Monday and he couldn't wait for that. Maybe they could get back into a normal routine.

He might have another daughter. The pain and joy of that ripped through him.

That night he told Haley about the baby.

"I don't care," she said, and ran to her room. She wouldn't talk about it and that was the problem. No one was talking.

Oh, God, he needed Maddie. They all needed Maddie.

MADDIE WORKED HER BUTT off until she couldn't think and she couldn't feel. That's the only way she could get through each day.

Cait and Sky tried to talk to her, but she resisted. Talking wasn't what she needed. Gran was worried about her, and she made a point of reassuring her grandmother that she would be fine. They both knew she was lying.

The one thing that kept her going was the ranch. She had to make it succeed. The pecans brought in a good chunk of money, and Mr. Bardwell was going to start buying their sand and gravel again. By the end of January, High Five would be in the black.

Even though that was her goal, it wouldn't make the pain in her heart go away.

WHEN THE CALL CAME, he didn't want to answer, but he forced himself.

"Walker, I have the results." He could tell Trisha was crying.

"And?" He hardened his heart.

"You're the father."

And just like that the life he wanted came to an end. It took a moment before he could speak.

"Give me the name of the hospital. I'll be there as soon as I can."

After rattling off the name and address, she added, "Please bring the kids."

He hung up without answering. His kids had to make that choice, not him. And the mood they were in continued to get worse. Haley was throwing up again. Their lives were turned upside down and they were reacting out of fear. He had to do something about that, but first he had to see his new daughter.

He called Nell for help. She knew the turmoil the kids were going through and she agreed to take the day off and stay at his house so Haley and Georgie could be in their own home.

In the past few weeks Nell had changed. Because of Maddie. That good in her spilled over into others.

His job was now a problem. He couldn't keep the peace to the best of his abilities. He put Lonnie on full-time until he got himself sorted out.

Then he dressed and headed for Houston and the nightmare that was his life. But first he had something he needed to do.

MADDIE, CAIT, SKY AND GRAN sat in the parlor.

She looked at them. "What? I have work to do."

"That's the point, my baby." Gran patted her hands. "That's all you do."

"It's what I need right now. Please respect that."

Sky crossed her legs. "You start throwing around the word *respect* and it makes me nervous 'cause you know I'm going to ignore it."

Cait shot Sky a glance. "Don't listen to her, sweetie. We just want you to be happy again."

Maddie shuddered. "It's almost an alien emotion to me now. Without Walker…" Her voice wavered and she jumped to her feet. "See. I don't want to go through this. I'm going back to work."

As she swung toward the hallway, the doorbell rang. "I'll get it."

"Maddie…"

She ignored Cait's call and opened the door. Walker stood there with his hat in his hand. Her heart hammered so hard against her ribs it resonated in her ears. Oh, how she'd missed him. She just wanted to throw herself in his arms and hold on until the pain stopped. But the somber look in his eyes prevented her from doing that.

"May I speak to you, please?"

"Yes." She stepped out and closed the door, remembering another time they had talked on the porch—when Haley had run away. He was stiff and unyielding then and she felt it in him now.

She was two feet away from him, and his tangy after-shave pulled her into a vortex of memories, him touching her, kissing her, making love to her. She'd been keeping them at bay, but now they were free and running rampant.

Walker twisted his hat. "The baby's been born. It's a girl."

"Oh." The word scratched her throat.

"I wanted to tell you before you heard from anyone else."

"Thank you."

"The paternity test has been done." He squeezed the hat until the brim creased. "I'm the father."

"Oh." This time the word was barely audible, but it scorched her throat with a burning finality.

"I'm on my way to Houston. I'm sorry, Maddie. I don't have any choice now. I have to do the right thing."

"I understand."

"I don't want you to understand," he shouted. "I want you to be angry. I want you to be furious at what I've done to your life. At what I've done to us."

She bit her lip and pulled off her beautiful ring. Without a word, she handed it to him.

"Maddie…"

She shoved it closer. He stared at it for a moment and then he took it. Their fingers touched and an electrical shock bolted through her. The tears weren't far away.

I love you. The words were in her heart, but she didn't say them. It would only complicate things.

"Goodbye, Maddie," he said, and slipped the ring into his pocket. Turning, he placed his hat on his head and walked to his car.

Goodbye.
It was over.

MADDIE RAN INTO THE HOUSE, up the stairs and into her room. Slamming the door, she slid down the wall like a wet noodle.

Pulling her knees up, she wrapped her arms around them to stop her body from shaking. And to keep from crying. It didn't work. The tears burst forth like a fountain and she cried for everything she'd lost, for everything that would never be.

From the moment Trisha reappeared in their lives, Maddie had known Walker was the father. Walker had known it, too. And so had Trisha. That's why she had come on the pretense of seeing the children. She was paving the way to get Walker back in her life.

Who would tell a man he *might* be the father unless the woman knew the truth? Trisha had a devious plan and it had worked. She gave Walker time to let the news of a new baby sink in. Trisha knew Walker as Maddie did. He would not abandon his child even at the expense of his own happiness.

The door opened and Cait and Sky slipped in and sank down by her. Sky lifted a bottle of wine. "Want to drink away your sorrow?"

"It won't help."

"We saw Walker drive away," Cait said. "What did he want?"

Maddie grabbed the bottle and took a swallow. "The baby is his."

"Dammit." Sky stretched out her legs, and Maddie noticed the Crocs she was wearing. Maddie had a pair in Philly, and that's where she wished she was now. But…

Taking another swallow, she added, "He's going to do the right thing by his kids. He wouldn't be the man I love if he didn't. It's just…"

"Hard," Cait said, finishing the sentence.

Maddie nodded, took another swig and handed the bottle to Sky.

"I can't. I have a three-year-old downstairs who depends on me being in my right mind."

"Kira's out of luck on that one," Cait said tongue-in-cheek.

"Don't push your luck, big sister." Sky made a face at Cait.

Maddie tipped up the bottle and handed it to Cait.

"No, thanks. Judd and I are trying to get pregnant and that damn sperm is taking forever to get to the egg, so that means no liquor. I'm on good behavior."

Maddie took a big swig and burst out laughing, spewing wine all over them. "Sorry," she muttered.

"You can't get drunk that quick." Sky brushed wine from her clothes with a frown.

"It just hit me that you two have finally grown up. I'm the only one still in limbo, so I guess I'll drink myself silly."

Sky jerked the bottle from her. "It's time to face some hard facts. The ex is a bitch. She left Walker and the kids and she doesn't have any right for a second chance." Sky dropped her voice. "It's time to be a Belle and stand and fight for what you want."

Maddie yanked the bottle back. "Dad said that when I was sixteen and Becky Thomas ran against me for class president. She was my friend, or I thought she was, and I didn't want to run against her."

"But Dad made you," Cait said. "And you won."

"And lost a friend."

"You didn't lose squat," Sky snapped. "But you will now if you let the ex take control by using the baby."

Maddie stared at the bottle and saw a lonely empty life ahead of her.

"I don't say this often." Cait linked her arm through Maddie's. "Hell, I've never said it. But Sky makes sense. If you want Walker, you have to make some hard choices. Just like the Becky incident, it's a matter of what you want. And I personally believe you're best for those kids. Think about it, Maddie, that's all we're saying."

"Hot damn, Cait." Sky raised her hand for a high five. "You're right for a change."

They slapped hands like they did when they were kids. Maddie raised the bottle. "Here's to shattered hearts, lost love and whatever the hell comes next."

She didn't really know, but with her sisters' help she could now face it. The more wine she consumed, the more an idea began to take hold.

Was she willing to fight for what she wanted?

CHAPTER NINETEEN

WALKER DROVE STEADILY toward Houston. Country-side of gently rolling hills, farms and ranches flashed by, but all he saw was the pain in Maddie's eyes. He'd probably see it for the rest of his life.

As he neared Houston, traffic became congested and slowed to a crawl. He was glad to see the Bel Air exit and turned off the freeway, heading for the medical center.

He parked in a parking garage and walked through to the hospital. It didn't take him long to find the nursery floor. The curtain on the picture window was open and he could see the babies inside, six girls, two boys.

His eyes scanned the name plates until he found Baby Walker. He moved closer. She was sound asleep, and the only thing visible was her face. Her head was covered in a pink cap and her tiny body was lost in a sleeper covered by a white-and-pink blanket.

He stared at the precious round face, bow mouth and upturned nose—just like Haley's. She was the spitting image of her sister.

His hand touched the glass. *Hey, little one. Your daddy's here.* His heart contracted, and he had a hard time looking away.

A nurse waved at him and mouthed something he didn't catch. She then closed the curtain. Otherwise, he probably wouldn't have moved from the spot.

He took a long breath and walked down the hall to Trisha's room. A woman at the front desk had given him the number. He tapped on the door and went in.

Trisha sat up in bed flipping agitatedly through a magazine. Her blond hair hung limply around her face and she wore a hospital gown. She looked up.

"Walker." She glanced past him. "Where are the kids?"

"At home."

"Dammit." She threw the magazine across the room. "You're doing this to hurt me."

"It's their choice. I've asked every day and they say they don't want to see you."

"You could make them." She jerked her fingers through her already tangled hair.

"I'm not going to do that."

"Oh, yeah. Mr. Perfect who never does anything wrong."

He let that slide and sat in a chair not far from the bed. Removing his hat, he studied the texture of the beaver felt for a second. "I don't understand why the kids don't want to see you. Haley ran away so many times to find you. It doesn't make sense."

"I just need to see her, talk to her. Can't you understand that?"

"Frankly, no I don't."

She glared at him with a look he knew well. She was about to lose her cool.

"I saw the baby," he said to segue into something they needed to talk about.

"Isn't she adorable?" Trisha's whole demeanor changed—the tense lines of her face eased.

"Yes. She favors Haley a lot."

A shadow crossed Trisha's face, and he was becoming more and more puzzled at her reactions and her attitude.

"I want to see the paternity test."

Her eyes shot open. "What? Don't you trust me?"

He looked her straight in the eye. "No."

"And you have to have those i's dotted and those t's crossed?"

"Yes."

She waved toward the door. "They're at the nurse's station."

He stood. "If everything checks out, you and the baby can come back to High Cotton with me. We can try to put our family back together." The words tasted like sawdust, but he meant every one.

"I'm not living in that hick town," she declared.

"That's your choice." He placed his hat on his head. "But the baby comes with me."

"No, Walker, please. She's all I have. Let me think

about this." She jerked the sheet to her neck, her hands trembling. "I need a damn cigarette."

"You're still smoking?" She'd quit years ago. Or at least he had thought she had.

"Don't preach. I don't need a lecture. Tony said he was bringing them, but he hasn't showed."

Tony was back in her life. Walker was making a huge sacrifice and she was playing him and Tony against each other.

Before he could form a reply, the door opened and a man he'd never seen before stood there. Instinctively, he knew it was Tony.

The man was completely different from what Walker expected. Medium height, slightly balding with a long ponytail and full beard, Tony wore faded jeans and a black T-shirt. The short sleeves of the shirt were rolled up and a cigarette pack was hidden in one. Tattoos covered his arms, a snake on one and a dragon on the other. Biker man screamed through Walker's mind.

"What took you so damn long?" Trisha yelled.

Tony eyed him for a moment, and then walked over to Trisha. "Calm down. You can't smoke in here."

"Like hell." Trisha reached for Tony's hand. "C'mon, baby, I need a smoke. I'm coming apart at the seams."

Tony reached for the pack in his sleeve and tapped out one against his palm. "Be quick."

Walker watched this scene in a daze. He played by the rules and did what he was supposed to. There was a right and there was a wrong. This was wrong. He could clearly see that—wrong for him and for his kids.

He'd been willing to do the right thing, but... He moved toward the door on feet that felt like concrete.

"May I have a word with you, please?"

Walker turned to look at Tony. "You have nothing to say that I want to hear."

"Listen, man…"

"Tony, no." Trisha took a drag on the cigarette and pulled on the man's hand, stopping him.

Walker stared at the woman who used to be his wife and wondered if he had ever known her. "I'm going to confirm the paternity results and then I'm calling a lawyer. I'd advise you to do the same."

"Walker, Walker…" Trisha screamed after him.

But he didn't even pause in his stride.

He spoke to the nurse at the station, and he had to show his driver's license and sign before he could see the test. Ninety-nine point nine. The baby girl was definitely his. He thanked the nurse and then strolled to a small sitting area.

Having lived in Houston many years, he had a lot of friends here. One was a lawyer, and Walker sat down to call him. He fingered the cell in his hand, staring at the beige tile on the floor. There was no way he and Trisha could reconcile and become a family again. Too much had happened. And he didn't love her.

He loved Maddie.

Thinking back, he wondered if he'd ever really

loved Trisha the way he loved Maddie. He'd met Trisha when he was on leave from the marines. They had a whirlwind week of hot sex and then he received a letter saying she was pregnant. Of course, since doing the right thing was his modus operandi, he had married her. God, how could one man get his life so screwed up?

He called his friend and told him what he wanted— full custody of the baby. He wanted the papers at the hospital as soon as possible. Come hell or high water, Trisha was not getting his daughter. Once he made that decision his life seemed to right itself.

"Hey, man." Tony ambled in and sat across from him.

Walker clipped his phone onto his belt. "I don't have one thing to say to you, Tony, except get a lawyer. This is going to get nasty."

"Trisha said you were going to get back together."

"For one insane moment I was willing to, for my kids. Trisha knows the kids are my weak spot, but she's not playing me anymore."

Tony nodded. "I think you're doing the right thing. The kids need to be with you."

He frowned. "Why? Because you don't want them?"

"Man, I'm not good with kids." Tony shook his head, a vein working overtime in his neck. "I had a stepson once and I took him riding on my motorcycle. A car slammed into us and he died instantly. He was seven years old." He took a deep breath. "That was it for me. I'm not taking responsibility for anyone else's kids."

"Then convince Trisha to let go of the baby and things will go a lot smoother."

Tony ran his palms down his thighs. "Man, I don't want to get into this, but I think you need to know."

"What the hell are you talking about?"

Tony clasped his hands between his legs. "Trisha and I have been friends since grade school. We were going to get married, but I wanted to see the world on my motorcycle and she didn't. I ended up in California and I have a motorcycle shop. I sometimes do stunts for some of the studios. But no matter how far away I got, Trisha and I stayed in touch."

"Funny she never mentioned your name."

"There was nothing but friendship between us then."

"Evidently that changed." Walker couldn't believe he was talking to this man. He should just walk away. But he found he couldn't.

"After my divorce, every time I came to Houston to visit my mom, I'd see Trisha. I love Trisha, but she didn't feel that way about me until last year. My mom was ill and I stayed in Houston for a long time." He paused. "Things just happened—you know."

"It's called adultery."

Tony moved restlessly. "Yeah. But Trisha needed me and I was glad to help her with her problems. We've always been kindred spirits."

Walker's frown deepened. "Problems?"

"I don't know how to say this."

"Then maybe you shouldn't."

"Yep. I should get up and walk away. Trisha's going to hate me for this."

An icy chill slid up Walker's spine. Yet he waited.

Tony flexed his hands and the snake tattoo seemed to wiggle up his arm. Walker watched as if fascinated.

"Man, have you ever noticed your kids have a lot of accidents?"

The question took him by surprise. "Kids are kids and they get bumps and bruises."

"That's one way of looking at it." The snake wiggled faster and Walker knew something bad was coming. "Have they had any lately?"

"No, why?"

Instead of answering, Tony said, "They seemed to have a lot when they were with Trisha."

"What are you getting at?"

Tony raised his head. "I made Trisha leave to protect your kids."

Walker clenched his jaw. "You'll have to explain that."

Tony clamped his hands onto his knees. "Okay, man, here it is. Trisha has a temper. You know that."

"Yes."

"Haley didn't fall off her bike and break her arm. She was whining about something she wanted. Trisha told her no, but she kept on. Finally Trisha slapped her hard and she fell against the kitchen table. That's how she broke her arm. The bruise on Haley's shoulder happened the same way. As did Georgie's concussion. The boy's always yakking and not listening and it makes Trisha angry. His head bounced off the tile floor. That's how he got the concussion. Your kids were being abused. It's not all the time but lately it's gotten worse. Trisha can't control her temper."

Walker leaped to his feet, his hands locked into fists. Everything in him denied what he was hearing. But he knew it was true. The bruises on the kids when he returned from a mission. When he'd questioned Trisha, she'd say, "Haley fell again today," or "Georgie jumped off the swingset and hit his head. He's clumsy." *And he'd believed her!* Everything started to make sense.

Did you hit Georgie?

I don't want to see her.

But one thing didn't. "Haley ran away many times to find Trisha. Why would she do that?"

"Trisha told Haley if you ever found out, that you would have her arrested and thrown in jail. Then Haley and Georgie would be put in foster care because you didn't want them."

"But once Haley was with me and her mother out of her life, she never said a word."

"You'll have to ask Haley about that."

"And the school watches for signs like that. A teacher would have noticed." He was searching for excuses. It couldn't be true.

"She did, but Trisha told the teacher that Haley gets really weak when she throws up so much, and she falls. The teacher believed her because Haley was throwing up at school."

Oh my God!

I have to see Mama.

You know where Mama is. You just won't tell me.

You don't want us.

Is Mama okay?

Haley's words tortured him. It had been a cry for help and he hadn't heard it. His legs felt weak and he sank back into the chair. The hell his kids must have been going through and he'd been oblivious to it all. Believing Trisha. Their mother.

The chill turned to an icicle that pierced through to his heart. It was clear now why Haley had befriended Ginny—because of the abuse. Haley knew how that felt.

He'd blamed Ginny for putting his kid's lives in danger. But he had done much worse. Every time he walked out the door of his home and went on a mission, he'd threatened Haley's and Georgie's lives by being oblivious as to what was happening in his own house.

How could he not have known? Not suspected? He was their father and should have been looking out for them, seeing the signs.

You were helping other people when you should have been helping us.

Haley's words drove the icicle further into his heart. He'd failed his kids. He'd let them down. What kind of father was he?

"Man, I'm sorry." Tony's voice penetrated his thoughts. "But Trisha was very good at covering up, and she was so sorry afterward. She really didn't mean to hurt them. She just loses control every now and then."

Walker raised his eyes to Tony's, anger shooting through him like an electric current. "That bitch will pay for making their lives a living hell."

"Ah, c'mon, man, take your kids and leave her alone. Despite her faults, I love her and I'll take care of her."

Walker stood. "She will never see her kids again, including the baby."

Tony got to his feet, rubbing his beard. "Well now, Trisha's gonna fight that. She sees this baby as her redemption."

"It's not going to happen."

"I can talk Trisha into letting go, but you have to promise not to press charges."

Walker stepped closer, his body rigid. "You're not in a position to make deals."

Tony took a step backward. "You need me, man. Admit it. Leave Trisha alone and I'll make sure she gets help."

"All I see is a man who stood by and let her abuse my kids."

Tony held up his hands. "Whoa, man. I was in Hollywood most of the time. Trisha called when something bad happened and she was always sorry and promised it wouldn't happen again. Just like you, I believed her."

Walker took off at a run. He had to get away from Tony, Trisha and the guilt that was ripping through him.

As he ran from the hospital, his boots thumping on the tiled floor, people stared at him. But he kept going.

His heart pounding, his lungs tight, he sank onto a bench, realizing he was never going to outrun the guilt. It was branded on his heart.

Failure as a father.

Maddie.

The one word brought calm to his shattered mind. He'd never needed anyone in his life. He was strong, able to handle whatever life threw at him. But he needed her.

What would she think of a man who failed to protect his children?

MADDIE WOKE UP ON HER BED fully clothed in the afternoon. What? She sat up and her head pounded with a reminder. Jeez! She'd drunk too much wine. And she wasn't a drinker. Holy moly.

She swung her feet to the side and sat there for a moment as she thought about the conversation with her sisters.

Fight for what you want. That was easy for them, but she was different. She was raised to be kind, gentle, loving and to never hurt anyone. That was her nature and it sucked most of the time. People took advantage of her, just like Becky had in high school. She knew Madison would not run against her friend.

Becky had been wrong.

Maddie's father had made her.

But Maddie had not felt good about the situation. The tension, the catfighting and the ugly words got to her. But she was a Belle and would not bow to adversity. Those were her father's words and she'd always thought he was right and that he knew everything.

This time he didn't. She couldn't stay in High Cotton and watch Walker with his wife and kids. It would be too painful. She had no recourse but to return to Philadelphia. Her mother was home now and would be excited to see her.

She walked to the closet and pulled down her suitcase. Methodically, she neatly placed undies and bras inside.

You're running.

Belles don't run.

She glanced at the photo of her father and her sisters on her nightstand. "Stop talking to me."

Gathering blouses, the voice kept taunting, "You're running. You're running."

She sank onto the bed, the blouses in her arms. She was running. From the pain. And she was letting everyone down, including herself.

The cancer had taken her ability to have children, but it hadn't taken her ability to love. She loved Walker. And she loved Haley and Georgie.

Could Trisha love them more than her? She'd been Walker's wife and she was Haley and Georgie's mother. But she'd tarnished that love when she'd left them.

Walker didn't love Trisha. Maddie was certain of that. So what kind of marriage could they have without love? A turbulent one, she surmised. And that wasn't good for the kids.

Without even realizing it, she was hanging the blouses back in the closet. She wasn't leaving. Trisha couldn't make her leave. This time Madison Belle was fighting for what she wanted. And she wanted Walker, Haley and Georgie. The new baby was another matter. But until Walker told her they had no future, she was still in the game.

She quickly dressed in black slacks and a cobalt-blue cashmere sweater. Nell would know where Walker was in Houston, and Maddie planned to find him there. She may get her heart broken all over again, but it was a risk she was willing to take.

Hot damn, her fighting spirit had finally been awakened. Sometimes certain things were worth fighting for.

Grabbing her purse, she headed for the door with a spring in her step.

There was something about being bad that made her feel very, very good.

SHE KISSED GRAN AND TOLD her where she was going and for her not to worry. Sky had gone into Giddings, and Maddie didn't have time to wait for her. Gran would give her the message.

Her head was still aching and she'd meant to take some Tylenol, but she didn't have time. She had to talk to Coop. He was probably wondering what had happened to her.

Coop wasn't in the barn, so she had to leave him a note. It would take too long to find him. She searched for a pen and pad in her purse and was scribbling an explanation when she heard a noise. Was that ol' tomcat chasing a rat?

She finished the note and propped it by the bridles where she knew Coop would go when he unsaddled for the day. Turning, she heard the noise again and glanced toward the horse stalls. Two sets of sneakers were visible under one. Her heart picked up speed. She knew exactly who they belonged to.

Haley and Georgie.

Before she could move, the door flew open and Georgie ran to her. "It's me. It's me, Mommy."

She caught him and just held him. Oh, how she'd missed them.

Haley leaned into her and Maddie wrapped an arm around her.

"We miss you," Haley murmured.

"I miss you, too." She set Georgie on his feet. "Does your father know you're here?"

Haley shook her head.

"Let's talk." Maddie led them to a bale of hay and sat down, one child on each side of her.

As she started to speak, her cell buzzed and she fumbled in her purse for it.

"Maddie, have you seen Haley or Georgie?" Nell's

frantic voice came on the line. "Georgie and I were watching a movie and I fell asleep. When I woke up, they were both gone. Walker's going to be so mad."

"They're here, Nell, and they're both fine."

"Oh, thank God."

"Where's Walker?"

"He's still in Houston seeing Trisha."

"Which hospital?"

Nell told her and then said, "I'm so relieved. They've been so deviant lately and it's hard to deal with them. I'll be right there."

"It's okay. I'll keep them."

"Are you sure?"

"Yes, and I don't think Walker will mind. If he does, I'll explain it to him."

"Okay. I know you'll take good care of them."

Maddie looked at Haley. "Now Haley would like to say she's sorry for worrying you." She handed the girl the phone.

Haley talked for a minute, tears swimming in her eyes, and then handed the phone back. Maddie slipped it into her purse.

"I am sorry, Maddie, but I didn't know what else to do. Daddy is going to make us see Mama."

"And you don't want to?"

Haley shook her head.

"Tell me why, sweetie. When I first met you, you were running away to find her."

"Do I have to?"

Georgie crawled into her lap and buried his face in her chest. Maddie patted his back, and Haley burrowed into her as if she wanted to disappear. It wasn't hard to recognize that they were both afraid.

"Tell me, sweetie."

"You can't tell Daddy," she murmured against Maddie.

Maddie stroked her hair. "We don't keep secrets from Daddy. Tell me and I promise I will help you. Trust me, sweetie."

All her life Maddie had been a calm, patient person, but as Haley talked, anger consumed her and she wanted to physically hurt Trisha. For them she kept her emotions in check, wondering how they'd managed to survive.

She clutched their small bodies, telling them that no one was ever going to hurt them again.

"Sweetie." Maddie rubbed Haley's arm. "When your mother left, why didn't you confide in your father? You knew the foster care threat was over."

"I was scared," Haley hiccuped. "I didn't know if Mama was really with Tony or in jail. I came home from school and she was gone. Georgie and I stayed at the neighbors' until Daddy arrived. He wouldn't tell me anything and I asked and asked. Mama said he didn't want us and I thought he didn't."

"But later when you knew your daddy loved you and wanted you, why didn't you say something?"

"I was too scared. If Daddy found out, he might hurt Mama 'cause…'cause…"

"She did a bad thing."

"Uh-huh."

"And you love your mother?"

Haley nodded. "And it was my fault. I threw up and made her nervous and angry…and I didn't behave. I…"

"No. No. No. It's not your fault."

"It's not?" Haley's eyes opened wide.

Maddie hugged her. "No, sweetie. You did nothing wrong."

"But…but I don't want to live with Mama anymore and Daddy might make us."

"He won't, but you need to see your mother and tell her how you feel."

Haley drew back, wiping at her eyes. "Will you go with me?"

Maddie tucked wet strands of hair behind Haley's ear. "Yes. But you need to see her with your daddy. Do you think you can do that?"

Haley nodded.

"Then let's go find your father."

A few minutes later, they were in Gran's old Lincoln headed for Houston. First they had to stop by Nell's for Georgie's car seat and then they were off.

To find Walker.

CHAPTER TWENTY

AFTER WALKER HAD HIMSELF under control, he went back into the hospital. He wanted to talk to Haley, but he couldn't do that on the phone. He had to do it in person. His lawyer called and he met Mike in the cafeteria.

They had coffee and he listened to his options as he watched people eating, laughing and talking as if his world hadn't been shattered for the third time.

"Walker."

He looked at his friend, who was starting to go bald and had a spare tire around his middle. But to Walker he was the guy in the marines who'd always had his back. With effort, he brought his attention to the conversation.

"I only have one option. No way am I letting Trisha walk out of this hospital with the baby."

"Well, then." Mike patted his briefcase. "Let's see if you can get Trisha to sign papers relinquishing her parental rights. As the father you will have full custody."

"Can you get a court order to prevent her from removing the baby from the hospital?"

"You bet I can."

Now Walker just had to persuade Trisha to sign the papers.

How in the hell was he going to do that?

ON THE WAY TO HOUSTON, Georgie fell asleep and it wasn't long before Haley did, too. Two young lives torn apart by a mother who couldn't control her anger. She knew Walker wasn't aware of any of this, and he had to know as soon as possible.

Again, she was sticking her nose into his business, but this time she hoped he didn't mind. It was almost five when they reached the hospital. She asked at the desk for Trisha's room number and she kept looking for Walker. He was nowhere in sight, but it was a big place.

She got snacks for the kids from a vending machine. Since she couldn't find Walker, she was unsure of what to do next.

Settling the kids in chairs down the hall from Trisha's room, she said, "Stay here and I'll see if I can find your father."

"I'll be good," Georgie replied around a mouthful of an Oreo cookie.

"I'll watch him," Haley told her.

"Do not leave this spot."

"Maddie…"

"And don't worry."

Haley nodded, but Maddie could clearly see the worry in her eyes.

She tapped on Trisha's door and heard a faint "Come in."

Trisha sat up in bed, her hair hanging around her face. She'd aged since Maddie had seen her a few weeks ago. Dark rings shaded her eyes and her face was drawn.

"What do you want?" Trisha asked in a defensive tone.

"I was looking for Walker."

"He just had to call you, didn't he?"

"No. I haven't heard from him."

"Then what are you doing here?"

Maddie took a seat in a straight-back chair, even though she hadn't been asked to. Her knees were feeling weak. Trisha's anger was hard to confront, but it didn't stop her.

"I had a talk with Haley."

Trisha's features tightened. "So?"

"Do you really have to ask that question?"

Trisha pleated the sheet with her fingers. "It's not as bad as she said."

"When you hit a child hard enough to break her arm or give him a concussion, it's bad any way you look at it."

"They were accidents."

Maddie set her purse on the floor. "I firmly believe every woman has a right to raise her own children, but you don't deserve Haley or Georgie."

Trisha pointed a finger at her, her eyes blazing. "You're not getting my kids."

"I'm just trying to protect them, something you should have been doing since the day they were born." It crossed Maddie's mind that she shouldn't be talking to Trisha without Walker. But if she was going to fight, this was where she started.

"No one understands me," Trisha said in a low voice.

"Help me to understand." Heavens, what was she doing?

To Maddie's surprise, Trisha wiped away a tear. "I love them, but I have a hard time controlling my temper. I…I—" she blinked away another tear "—had a rotten childhood. My father died when I was little. I don't even remember him. After that, my mother was an angry woman who went into violent rages. My sister and I lived in fear every day of our lives. I swore I would never do that to my kids but…"

Maddie tried to harden her heart, but she couldn't. She felt sorry for the woman.

"I can be a good mother. I just need a chance."

Maddie took a moment before she replied. "You've had your share of chances. Do what's best for your kids."

Trisha looked straight at her. "Do you want them?"

She reached for her purse and stood, knowing she'd already said too much. "I would love them, care for them and protect them with my life."

"But they love me," Trisha said in that same low voice, the anger not so evident. "Walker said when I left Georgie cried for two weeks for his mama."

"Kids are like that. They love you no matter what, and you're the only mother Georgie has known. He missed you and he didn't know where you were."

As if Maddie hadn't spoken, Trisha added, "Walker said Haley ran away trying to find me."

"Yes, she did. She was scared. She thought Walker had put you in jail and it was her fault because she threw up and made you nervous and angry. She thought it was her fault that you hit her repeatedly. And you made it worse by forcing her to lie."

Trisha pleated the sheet into a knot. "I had to. If Walker found out…"

"He would have insisted you get help and made sure that you did. He would have been there for you and the kids."

Trisha looked up, her eyes skeptical. "You don't know that."

"Yes, I do. I know Walker. He would be angry, but he would do the right thing by you."

The door opened and a man in a leather jacket strolled in. He looked as if he rode with the Hell's Angels. She thought he had the wrong room until Trisha screamed at him.

"Get out of here, Tony. I told you to leave. I thought you loved me, but then you went and told Walker behind my back. Get out, you bastard."

The man glanced at Maddie, seemingly unmoved by Trisha's tirade. "Hi, I'm Tony Almada."

"I'm Madison Belle."

"She's Walker's new love," Trisha said. "And she's trying to make me feel guilty."

"Is it working?" Tony quipped, and Maddie instantly liked him. But she had to wonder what he was doing here.

"Go away, Tony," Trisha shouted again.

Tony walked to the bed. "C'mon, babe, you know I'm not going anywhere."

"How could you tell Walker?" Trisha's voice was softer. Relenting. Maddie knew it was time for her to go.

"I have to find Walker."

Trisha scooted up in the bed. "I know you think I can't change, but I can."

"How many times have you told yourself that?"

Trisha hung her head.

"How many times have you told Haley and Georgie you were sorry? How many times have you told them you'd never hit them again?"

"Get the hell out of my room," Trisha yelled, her anger now turned on Maddie.

"Calm down, babe. She's only trying to help," Tony said, trying to soothe her.

Maddie slipped the strap of her purse over her shoulder. "Do what's best for your kids. That's a promise you can keep."

Before she could open the door, Trisha called, "Madison."

Maddie turned back.

"Please talk Walker into letting me see Haley and Georgie."

"That's Walker's decision."

"Bitch," Trisha shouted as Maddie walked out of the room.

AS SHE CLOSED THE DOOR, she saw Walker coming down the hall. The kids noticed him at the same time as she did. They leaped to their feet and made a dash for him. Haley reached him first, wrapping her arms around his waist. Georgie attached himself to Walker's leg.

"Hey, where'd y'all come from?" Walker squatted as both kids barreled into his chest.

"I told Maddie, Daddy. I'm sorry. I'm sorry…" Haley's brokenhearted cries were echoed by the anguish on Walker's face.

"Let's sit over here." Walker stood, both kids still clinging to him. "We need to talk."

"Haley told me some shocking news that I thought you needed to hear, but—" Maddie waved over her shoulder "—I was looking for you and had a chat with Trisha. Evidently you already know. I…I'll leave you alone…."

"Maddie."

She looked into his pain-filled eyes. "You need to talk to the kids alone."

Walking off down the hall, she didn't know if he was angry with her or not. He might not even want the kids here, and she'd taken it upon herself to bring them. At the time, she'd thought he hadn't known about Trisha hitting them. But he had. That must have caused him inexplicable pain. She wanted to be with him, to help him through this. But her presence would only be an added complication.

For now…

WALKER WATCHED HER LEAVE, his heart so tied in knots he couldn't even think straight. But one thought was very clear. What must she think of him? A man so consumed with his own life he hadn't seen the signs of abuse. He'd let his kids down. He was supposed to protect them. He…

"Daddy, I'm sorry." He had his arm around Haley and her face was buried in his side. Georgie sat on his lap.

"Sweetheart, you have nothing to be sorry about."

She raised her head. "You know, don't you?"

He nodded.

"I should have told you."

"When Ginny's baby was born and we got home, one night you tried to tell me, didn't you?"

"Yes."

"Why didn't you?"

"I was scared. I knew you'd be angry, and if Mama wasn't in jail and with Tony then…then… I didn't want you to put her in jail so I kept quiet."

"Is that why you were so angry with me?"

She nodded. "I was just so scared and I thought you didn't want us."

"Oh, sweetheart. I do, always remember that." He hugged her. "I'm so sorry you've been put through this, but please don't ever keep things from me again, no matter how painful."

"Okay. Maddie said I needed to talk to Mama."

Trust Maddie to get them to do something he couldn't. He had done it out of fear. She'd done it out of love.

"Are you ready to do that?"

"If you go with me."

Walker jostled his son. "How about you, Georgie?"

Georgie bobbed his head in agreement.

"Let's go see your mother, then." Walker knew Haley was ready. Thank God Maddie had brought them.

When they entered the room, Trisha and Tony stopped talking. Arguing was more like it.

Trisha sat up and clapped her hands. "Haley and Georgie, you're here. Oh, I've missed you. Come give your mother a hug."

Haley stepped forward, but Georgie did not. He was glued to Walker's leg. Haley took his hand and pulled him toward the bed. She had to lift her brother so he could hug Trisha, but they both hugged their mother.

"Oh, my, Haley, you're getting so pretty."

"Maddie tells me that all the time."

Trisha's face tightened and she turned her attention to Georgie. "I think you've grown a couple of inches."

"I'm big." Georgie raised his hands above his head. "I'm a cowboy. Maddie lets me ride her horse and she bought me boots and a hat."

"Well, good for Maddie," Trisha said in a sarcastic tone.

"Maddie cooks all kinds of food that I can eat," Haley told her. "I've gained four pounds."

"She gives me a bath and she even shot some doggies that were going to get me. She…"

"Shut up. Shut up. Shut up," Trisha screeched, holding her hands over her ears.

Both kids ran to Walker. Both were trembling.

"I'm sorry. I'm sorry," Trisha apologized. "Just don't talk about her, okay? Come back to Mama. I love you guys."

Neither child moved.

Then Haley said in a quiet voice, "We love you, too, but we don't want to live with you anymore. You hurt us."

Georgie nodded vigorously in agreement.

"Oh, oh, oh." Trisha began to cry and Tony reached for her hand.

"Take Georgie into the hall," Walker said to Haley. "I'll be there in a minute."

"Walker, no…"

He stepped closer to the bed, his anger on a tight leash. "As I told Tony, hire a lawyer. You're going to need one. My attorney is filing an order with the court so Baby Girl Walker will not be moved from this hospital until custody is decided."

"You can't do that."

"Watch me."

WALKER PACED, WAITING ON HIS attorney. He wanted something settled tonight. The kids were looking at the baby. He wondered where Maddie was. Why hadn't she come back? God, he needed her.

Finally, Mike stepped off the elevator. They shook hands.

"Sorry to keep you working so late."

Mike grinned. "You saved my life a time or two so I think I owe you. Now let's see if we can get Trisha to sign away her rights."

"Let me check on my kids and I'll be right with you."

Walker made sure Haley and Georgie weren't being a nuisance, and then they made their way to Trisha's room. She was sitting in a chair still in the gown, but now she had a white terry-cloth robe over it. She looked old beyond her years. Pain and sorrow filled her eyes, and it was the only thing that kept Walker from strangling the life out of her.

Tony stood between him and Trisha. Mike waited behind Walker.

"I'm sorry, Walker. I…" She began to cry again and Tony rubbed her shoulder.

"It's all right, babe."

"I love my kids," she wailed.

Tony knelt in front of her. "But you can't be a mother to them. You know that, babe."

"I can."

"No," Tony said. "You've already proved you can't. If you love your kids, you have to do what Madison told you—do what's best for them. Their father will give them a great home."

"I can't," she sobbed.

"Yes, you can," Tony persisted, and Walker was beginning to think the man was an okay guy. "It'll be just you and me, babe, against the world. I love you. Do the right thing here."

Trisha remained stubborn.

"If you don't, that's it for me. I'm gone from your life for good. Kids aren't my thing, you know that."

"You're just saying that."

"I mean it."

"What if the baby had been yours?"

"Then we'd have a problem. My mother probably would have raised it because, babe, as much as I love you, you don't need to be around kids, especially a baby."

She grabbed Tony and sobbed into his shoulder. Tony whispered something to her. After a minute, Trisha got to her feet, brushing away tears. "What do you want me to sign?"

Mike laid the papers on the eating tray and Trisha stared at them. "I want the right to see my kids."

"It's in an agreement Mike has drawn up. You can see them three times a year, but only if you're in counseling and I will always be present."

"That's fair, babe," Tony said. "Walker's a good guy."

Trisha choked back a sob and signed away her rights. Walker let out a sigh of relief.

He left feeling drained, empty and so very alone.

He had his kids, thanks to Tony. That was the most important thing.

But he didn't have Maddie.

He sank into a chair in the hall and pulled out his phone. Where was she? All he had to do was call her, hear her voice and his world would be normal again. Guilt slammed into his chest.

What must she think of him now?

His Maddie was a very understanding person, though. His Maddie… Her ring burned a hole in his pocket and he placed his hand over it. God, he had two kids and a baby. He needed her—a woman like Maddie.

But did she need him?

He sighed in torment. Closing his eyes, he could see her face. It was right there, giving him courage.

"Walker."

He opened his eyes and there she was. Beautiful as ever in a blue sweater that made her eyes brilliant. Her blond hair bounced around her perfect, sweet face.

"Walker," Maddie said again. What was wrong with him? He looked confused, worried.

She took a step toward him and he jumped to his feet. "Maddie, where did you go? I thought you left."

"I went to the chapel to pray that Trisha would do the right thing for her kids."

He ran a hand through his already tousled hair. He looked so down, so beat, and she just wanted to hold him.

"I thought you might be angry with me."

He frowned. "Why?"

"For bringing the kids and talking to Trisha."

That ghost of a smile touched his lips. "I don't think there's anything you can do that would make me angry."

She wanted to sink into his warm smile and voice, but she couldn't. Not yet. "After a lot of thought and coaxing from my sisters, I decided I wasn't going to let you go so easily. I was going to fight for our love. Then I talked to Haley and…"

"And?" The one word was barely a sound.

She swallowed. "I'm going to fight for us until you tell me not to."

He sighed heavily, as if he was expecting another answer. He slipped a hand into his jeans and pulled out her ring. "There's no way I can live with Trisha again. Will you marry me with all my faults and my problems?"

"Yes," she whispered, barely breathing. She held out her hand and saw that it was trembling. As he slipped the ring on, the trembling ceased and she threw herself into his arms.

Holding her in a bearlike grip, he cradled her head with one hand. "You came when I needed you the most. God, I love you so much it hurts."

She kissed the warmth of his neck, soaking up the scent and feel of him. "I love you, too."

His lips captured hers, and she wrapped her arms around his neck and went with the moment and everything she was feeling.

"Well, I never." A woman's voice drew them apart,

but only slightly. "This is a hospital. Some people have no decency."

"Now, Mable. I think it's kind of nice."

"Herman," the woman shrieked. "Get on this elevator and stop gawking."

Maddie spluttered with laughter and Walker drew her to a chair.

He buried his face in his hands. "I feel like such a failure. I wasn't there to protect my kids, and I thought you might want to get as far away from me as possible."

She stroked his arm. "No way, and you can't blame yourself. You had no idea what Trisha was doing, and she hid it very well by making Haley lie."

"I'm always going to feel guilty."

"I'll help you with that." She kissed his cheek. "We already have Haley and Georgie. Now we have to fight for the baby."

He smiled, a real honest-to-God smile, and gathered her into his arms. "I'm way ahead of you. Trisha signed away her rights a little while ago."

"Oh, Walker."

"Are you ready for what's about to happen—a life with three kids."

"I've never been more ready." She laughed, a happy sound that erupted from her throat.

He stood and pulled her to her feet.

"Wait." She wiped away an errant tear. "I don't want the kids to see me crying."

Walker kissed away her tears just before Haley and

Georgie came running. He held his children as if he couldn't bear to let them go. "I love you," he murmured. "And we're starting a new life with Maddie."

"Oh, boy," Georgie shouted, and leaped for Maddie.

"And with your new baby sister."

Haley leaned away. "Really?"

"Yes," Walker replied. "It's time for Maddie to meet her."

The kids darted ahead and Walker reached for her hand. The curtain was open. Haley pressed her face against the glass.

"I can't see," Georgie cried. "I can't see."

Walker lifted him and pointed to a crib on the right. "There she is." His eyes were on Maddie.

Maddie could only stare at the beautiful baby wrapped in pink. Her breath caught, and she looped an arm around Walker. All her dreams were right here just waiting for her. How lucky she was. How incredibly lucky.

She thought she would never have a family, a child of her own, but now… Her eyes filled with tears. Haley moved to her side and Maddie hugged her, feeling so much happiness she was about to burst. These were her kids. Madison's children. She may not have given birth to them, but it didn't matter. She loved them with all her heart.

She'd always thought a woman had a right to raise her own children. But not in this case.

"We have to give her a name," Walker said.

As she stared at that precious face she knew there was only one name that would fit. "Valentine," she whispered.

"We can call her Val," Haley said, her voice excited.

Walker groaned and set Georgie on his feet. "Maddie…"

He stared into her beautiful blue eyes and gave in without a protest. This day had been the worst of his life, but because of her he saw a rainbow so bright that he now believed there was a little good in everyone. Even Trisha. She had given the ultimate sacrifice for her kids' happiness. He and Maddie would protect them with their love and their lives.

EPILOGUE

Three months later.

THERE WAS SOMETHING ABOUT loving a good woman that made Walker feel good about himself. And his ex. He honestly believed she never meant to hurt the kids. She just couldn't control her temper.

That helped him sleep at night and kept the bad thoughts at bay. As Tony had promised, Trisha was now getting help. He hoped she found a measure of happiness with her biker man.

Walker put soap in the dishwasher, closed it and pushed a button. Oh, if his marine buddies could see him now. Domesticated. By the sweetest woman in the world.

Placing the dish towel across the sink, he looked out the window to the sunny April day. A scent of freshness was in the air as new leaves adorned trees and green grasses sprouted. Spring. A new beginning.

He leaned back against the counter and folded his arms across his chest. They certainly had a new beginning. Their marriage had taken place in the parlor at High Five, just as Cait and Judd's had. But theirs had been simple.

Maddie had worn a long white dress, and the top had been covered in lace. Her mother had brought it from Philadelphia. Meeting Audrey, he knew where his wife got her loving heart. He couldn't even imagine playboy Dane Belle with the prim and proper Audrey. But he supposed every good girl needed a bad boy in her life. Or else he wouldn't have his Maddie.

Audrey and her husband embraced the kids with open arms and open hearts. Haley and Georgie took to their new grandparents immediately and called them Nana and Pa. They couldn't wait until they visited Philly in May when Maddie had a checkup.

Walker would make sure Maddie never missed an appointment. She had to stay healthy. They needed her too much. *What if* wasn't in their vocabulary.

Since Maddie had segued into motherhood full-time, Sky was now running High Five. There was a lot of tension with Cooper, but Cait and Maddie insisted that he stay. The next few months should be interesting.

"Honey," his wife called. "Get the video camera. We're ready."

He dashed into the living room for the camera. Maddie came down the stairs with the baby on her shoulder, Georgie trailing behind her. The new baby was a big adjustment for his son, but Maddie handled it with love, like she did everything.

She gently laid the baby in the small crib in the living room. It had been Maddie's and Audrey thought she should have it.

Georgie peeked over the railing. "Why does she sleep so much?"

"All babies sleep. She's growing and dreaming." Maddie kissed the top of his head. "Know what she's dreaming about?"

"Uh-uh."

"She's dreaming of her big brother and how much she loves him."

"I love her, too."

Maddie hugged him and kissed his cheek. "I have to get my camera to take pictures of Haley."

"She looks dorky," Georgie said.

Maddie swung back and held a finger in front of his face. "Beautiful," she said slowly. "You don't want to hurt your sister's feelings."

"'Kay."

"Mommy," Haley called from the top of the stairs. "The bow in my hair feels loose."

Maddie darted up the stairs to fix the bow. Haley was going to a girl-boy birthday party of a classmate. Her first. Walker wasn't happy about it, but Maddie assured him it was normal.

Maddie hurried down and grabbed her camera. She glanced at him and winked. "Ready?"

He smiled. "Ready."

Haley slowly descended the stairs and he caught every second on film while Maddie snapped still shots. His daughter looked so different in a denim jumper and a pink knit top that matched the embroidery on the dress. Her blond hair was held up with a pink ribbon.

They worked hard to keep Haley's nervous stomach under control. Very seldom did she have a bad day, and it usually had something to do with school or eating the wrong food.

Haley had put on a few more pounds and he realized how beautiful she was. He didn't know if he was ready for the years ahead.

"Be sure to get a picture for Gran," Haley said. "And Nana and Pa."

"Oh, I have plenty." Maddie clicked away.

When Haley reached the bottom, Maddie lowered the camera. "Oh, sweetie, you look so pretty."

"Beau-ti-ful," Georgie corrected her.

"Oh, yes, very beautiful."

They heard a car in the driveway and Haley ran for the door. "Bye. Remember, Daddy, Cara's mom is taking us, but you have to pick us up."

"What?" He lowered the camera. "I don't even get a hug?"

"Daddy." Haley ran back and hugged him. He held her for an extra second. "Have a great time, sweetheart."

The door slammed behind her and Walker laid the

camera on the coffee table. Maddie went into his arms. She smelled of milk, soap and lavender.

"Haley will be fine," she whispered.

"I know. She's just growing up too fast."

"We have a long way to go."

"It's time for my bath." Georgie looked up at them.

"Yes, son, I believe it is." Georgie had dirt all over him from his face to his jeans. "Have you been playing in a pigpen?"

"Uh-uh. Just outside."

Maddie took Georgie's hand and they headed for the stairs.

"Can we go feed Solomon tomorrow, Mommy?"

"Yes."

"Can I play with Kira?"

"Yes."

A wail sounded from the crib. Maddie stopped.

"I'll get her," Walker said.

By the time they had Georgie tucked in and the baby fed and in her crib upstairs, they were both exhausted.

They sat on the sofa and Maddie curled into his side just as the doorbell rang.

"Damn." He got to his feet and went to the door. Nell stood there.

"Oh, Maddie." Nell walked past him as if he wasn't even standing there. "I just finished a blanket for the baby."

Maddie held up the pink-and-white knitted work. "Thank you. It's beautiful."

That made about the tenth blanket or quilt that Nell had made. How many did one baby need? But it made Nell happy so he didn't say a word. Besides, Nell was part of their family and he would never hurt her feelings.

Nell looked around. "Did I miss Haley?"

"She just left." Maddie patted Nell's hands. "I took lots of pictures, so don't worry, we have it on film."

"Good." Nell stood. "I better go. It's past my bedtime. I'll see y'all tomorrow."

Walker headed for Maddie, rubbing his hands in glee. "Now…"

The doorbell pealed.

"Dammit, if that's Nell…"

"I'll get it." Maddie hurried to the door and glanced back at him. "Be nice."

She opened the door to a man she vaguely recognized. He was her father's attorney from Austin. What was he doing here?

"Hi, Frank," she said, "please come in."

"No, thanks, Madison. I'm so sorry I missed your wedding."

"That's okay."

"No, it isn't. Dane entrusted his affairs to me and I've let him down, but I'm here to correct that." He pulled a letter from the inside of his suit jacket and handed it to her. "I was supposed to give you this at your wedding, but I had no idea you were getting married."

"It was rather sudden, so don't blame yourself."

"I wish you and Walker all the best."

"Thank you."

Walker closed the door, and Maddie sat on the sofa with the letter in her hand. She stared at it a long time. What was inside? With a trembling hand, she slipped a finger beneath the flap and opened it. One line leaped out at her in her father's bold signature.

"Now you're living, sweet angel. Love, Dad."

As she read it over and over she couldn't stop the tears that rolled from her eyes.

"Honey." Walker was immediately at her side. "What is it?" His arms went around her and he glanced at the paper. "What does that mean?"

"Dad always said if you're not willing to take a risk, you're not living. Cait and Sky were his risk-takers, but he worried about me because I was always so cautious." She brushed away another tear. "These are his last words to me and they mean so much."

"Honey." He stroked her cheek.

"I'm happy. I really am." She smiled through her tears. "I took a risk just like he wanted me to and look what I have." She curled her arms around his neck. "I have you. You're my risk, my life, my everything."

He held her for a long time and she breathed in the scent of him. Every empty, lonely part of her had been filled by his strong, compassionate love.

"Are you sure you're okay?"

"Yes." She snuggled into him, her hand slowly caressing his chest. "Are you tired?"

"Not when you're touching me."

She leaned her head back to look at his handsome face. "We have two hours, Valentine. Well, we're a little short on that now, and if the baby doesn't wake up…"

A ghost of a smile spread across his lips.

She jumped up. "I know where there's a towel." She ran for the stairs with the letter in her hand. She would keep it forever. Some risks were worth taking. Her father had taught her that.

Now she would spend the rest of her life with the man of her dreams.

Valentine Walker.

* * * * *

There's one more Belle
who needs to find her beau...
Read Skylar's story, SKYLAR'S OUTLAW
coming January 2010, only from
Harlequin Superromance®.

*Celebrate 60 years of pure reading pleasure
with Harlequin®!*

To commemorate the event, Silhouette Special
Edition invites you to Ashley O'Ballivan's bed-
and-breakfast in the small town of Stone Creek.
The beautiful innkeeper will have her hands full
caring for her old flame Jack McCall. He's on the
run and recovering from a mysterious illness, but
that won't stop him from trying to win Ashley back.

*Enjoy an exclusive glimpse of
Linda Lael Miller's
AT HOME IN STONE CREEK
Available in November 2009 from
Silhouette Special Edition®.*

The helicopter swung abruptly sideways in a dizzying arch, setting Jack McCall's fever-ravaged brain spinning.

His friend's voice sounded tinny, coming through the earphones. "You belong in a hospital," he said. "Not some backwater bed-and-breakfast."

All Jack really knew about the virus raging through his system was that it wasn't contagious, and there was no known treatment for it besides a lot of rest and quiet. "I don't like hospitals," he responded, hoping he sounded like his normal self. "They're full of sick people."

Vince Griffin chuckled but it was a dry sound, rough at the edges. "What's in Stone Creek, Arizona?" he asked. "Besides a whole lot of nothin'?"

Ashley O'Ballivan was in Stone Creek, and she was a whole lot of somethin', but Jack had neither the strength nor the inclination to explain. After the way he'd ducked out six months before, he didn't expect a welcome, knew he didn't deserve one. But Ashley, being Ashley, would take him in whatever her misgivings.

He had to get to Ashley; he'd be all right.

He closed his eyes, letting the fever swallow him.

There was no telling how much time had passed when he became aware of the chopper blades slowing overhead. Dimly, he saw the private ambulance waiting on the airfield outside of Stone Creek; it seemed that twilight had descended.

Jack sighed with relief. His clothes felt clammy against his flesh. His teeth began to chatter as two figures unloaded a gurney from the back of the ambulance and waited for the blades to stop.

"Great," Vince remarked, unsnapping his seat belt. "Those two look like volunteers, not real EMTs."

The chopper bounced sickeningly on its runners, and Vince, with a shake of his head, pushed open his door and jumped to the ground, head down.

Jack waited, wondering if he'd be able to stand on his own. After fumbling unsuccessfully with the buckle on his seat belt, he decided not.

When it was safe the EMTs approached, following Vince, who opened Jack's door.

His old friend Tanner Quinn stepped around Vince, his grin not quite reaching his eyes.

"You look like hell warmed over," he told Jack cheerfully.

"Since when are you an EMT?" Jack retorted.

Tanner reached in, wedged a shoulder under Jack's right arm and hauled him out of the chopper. His knees immediately buckled, and Vince stepped up, supporting him on the other side.

"In a place like Stone Creek," Tanner replied, "everybody helps out."

They reached the wheeled gurney, and Jack found himself on his back.

Tanner and the second man strapped him down, a process that brought back a few bad memories.

"Is there even a hospital in this place?" Vince asked irritably from somewhere in the night.

"There's a pretty good clinic over in Indian Rock," Tanner answered easily, "and it isn't far to Flagstaff." He paused to help his buddy hoist Jack and the gurney into the back of the ambulance. "You're in good hands, Jack. My wife is the best veterinarian in the state."

Jack laughed raggedly at that.

Vince muttered a curse.

Tanner climbed into the back beside him, perched on some kind of fold-down seat. The other man shut the doors.

"You in any pain?" Tanner said as his partner climbed into the driver's seat and started the engine.

"No." Jack looked up at his oldest and closest friend and wished he'd listened to Vince. Ever since he'd come down with the virus—a week after snatching a five-year-old girl back from her non-custodial parent, a small-time Colombian drug dealer—he hadn't been able to think about anyone or anything but Ashley. When he *could* think, anyway.

Now, in one of the first clearheaded moments he'd experienced since checking himself out of Bethesda the day before, he realized he might be making a major mistake. Not by facing Ashley—he owed her that much and a lot more. No, he could be putting her in danger, putting Tanner and his daughter and his pregnant wife in danger, too.

"I shouldn't have come here," he said, keeping his voice low.

Tanner shook his head, his jaw clamped down hard as though he was irritated by Jack's statement.

"This is where you belong," Tanner insisted. "If you'd had sense enough to know that six months ago, old buddy, when you bailed on Ashley without so much as a fare-thee-well, you wouldn't be in this mess."

Ashley. The name had run through his mind a million times in those six months, but hearing somebody say it out loud was like having a fist close around his insides and squeeze hard.

Jack couldn't speak.

Tanner didn't press for further conversation.

The ambulance bumped over country roads, finally hitting smooth blacktop.

"Here we are," Tanner said. "Ashley's place."

* * * * *

*Will Jack be able to patch things up with Ashley,
or will his past put the woman
he loves in harm's way?
Find out in
AT HOME IN STONE CREEK
by Linda Lael Miller.
Available November 2009 from
Silhouette Special Edition®.*

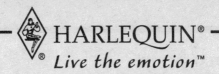

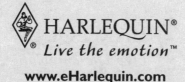

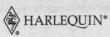

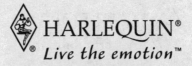

HARLEQUIN®
INTRIGUE®

BREATHTAKING ROMANTIC SUSPENSE

Shared dangers and passions lead to electrifying
romance and heart-stopping suspense!

Every month, you'll meet six new heroes
who are guaranteed to make your spine tingle
and your pulse pound. With them you'll enter
into the exciting world of Harlequin Intrigue—
where your life is on the line
and so is your heart!

THAT'S INTRIGUE—
ROMANTIC SUSPENSE
AT ITS BEST!

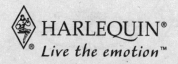

HARLEQUIN®
Live the emotion™

Harlequin® Historical
Historical Romantic Adventure!

*Imagine a time of chivalrous
knights and unconventional ladies,
roguish rakes and impetuous
heiresses, rugged cowboys
and spirited frontierswomen—
these rich and vivid tales will
capture your imagination!*

*Harlequin Historical...
they're too good to miss!*

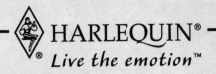